A Tale of Two Cookies

St. Martin's Paperbacks titles by
Eve Calder

AND THEN THERE WERE CRUMBS
SUGAR AND VICE
A TALE OF TWO COOKIES

A Tale of Two Cookies

Eve Calder

St. Martin's Paperbacks

First published in the United States by St. Martin's Paperbacks, an imprint of St. Martin's Publishing Group.

A TALE OF TWO COOKIES

Copyright © 2021 by Eve Calder.

For information, address St. Martin's Publishing Group, 120 Broadway, New York, NY 10271.

www.stmartins.com

ISBN: 978-1-250-31303-4

Our books may be purchased in bulk for promotional, educational, or business use. Please contact your local bookseller or the Macmillan Corporate and Premium Sales Department at 1-800-221-7945, ext. 5442, or by email at MacmillanSpecialMarkets@macmillan.com.

Printed in the United States of America

St. Martin's Paperbacks edition published 2021

10 9 8 7 6 5 4 3 2 1

To the scientists, advocates, and volunteers working together to save the oceans and this beautiful planet: This book is gratefully dedicated to you.

Chapter 1

Kate McGuire felt the spray of the salt water against her face, as the boat plowed through the choppy water. Beside her, pup Oliver peered over the railing into the teal blue sea.

Instinctively, she reached down and stroked the soft, caramel-colored hair on the back of his neck, just above his orange life vest.

"So what do you think of your first boat ride?" she asked softly. "Or *is* it your first boat ride?"

The pup's past was still something of a mystery. From what she'd been able to learn, Oliver had simply appeared in Coral Cay one chilly March day. No one knew where he'd come from, but there had been no shortage of people who wanted to give the small, fuzzy puppy a good home.

Instead, the goldendoodle (or maybe labradoodle—no one was quite sure about that, either), had the field, spending a night or three at various homes before moving on. So now Oliver was the unofficial mayor of Coral

Cay—welcomed and wanted just about everywhere in town.

But when Kate moved to the small Florida island—and into an upstairs room at the Cookie House bakery a few months ago—Oliver stopped wandering. For the most part.

"So what do you think?" Desiree yelled excitedly to Kate over the roar of the engine and the pounding of the waves against the boat.

"The island looks so different from the water," Kate shouted back.

"That's what I love about traveling by boat," Desiree said. "Complete change in perspective. Jimmy Buffet was right."

A few weeks ago, Kate had gotten a call from her old friend. Only in her mid-fifties, Desiree Goldsmith was retiring. And getting married.

The groom was, at least in certain circles, something of a celebrity: Judson Cooper. A globe-trotting marine biologist, the man made headlines with his efforts to protect the oceans and safeguard sea life around the world—from battling whaling off the coast of Japan to working to revitalize the Great Barrier Reef.

He'd also made a small fortune with a couple of inventions—one that harvested water-borne garbage and another that transformed liquid petro–chemical spills into solids, which could then be easily sifted from the water.

Kate couldn't believe it when Desiree announced just a few days ago that they were holding their intimate beach wedding on Coral Cay.

"I don't know why not," her friend had countered, laughing. "You've told me so much about this place, I feel like I know it already. And Judson wants to kick back for a few weeks and spend some time at one of his pet projects just up the coast. A marine wildlife rehab sanctuary."

"Sounds like the perfect honeymoon for a city girl," Kate had teased.

"I know, right? But the whole thing feels just . . . magical. And perfect."

And now here they were. The wedding was tomorrow evening. Sunset on the beach. To be followed by a bonfire, beach cookout, and cake—a three-tier key lime number with buttercream frosting that was currently under Sam Hepplewhite's watchful eye back at the Cookie House.

As the boat slowed, Judson Cooper emerged on deck, a boyish smile on his broad, tanned face. "Look! Someone's waving at us from the shore!" As they rounded the headland, Kate looked over and recognized the quaint cottage nestled in the cove. In its yard, two figures were each giving them full-armed waves.

"That's Iris and Sunny," Kate said, waving back.

"Woof!" Oliver barked over the din. "Woof, woof."

"See? He knows them," Kate said with a grin.

"You weren't kidding," Desiree said. "You really do know everyone in town."

"Well, to be fair, it's a very small town."

"And everyone comes into that bakery," Judson added, patting his midsection. "As I can attest."

"Do I even want to ask who's driving the boat?" Kate teased, laughing.

"Just call him 'Captain Doc Scanlon,'" Judd said, winking. "And he's not a half-bad skipper. For a land-lubber." Judd gave a mock salute and headed back up to the wheelhouse.

"I still can't believe you guys are having your wedding here," Kate said.

"Well, my first time around, I did it my mom's way.

Poofy white dress, stiff satin heels, and four bridesmaids. And the marriage lasted, what? Fifteen minutes? This time, we're doing it our way. Barefoot on the beach."

"It sounds wonderful," Kate said.

At that moment, Judd reappeared. "I forgot to mention," he called, as he approached. "I got a text from Liam this morning. He and Sarah are both flying in. They'll be here tomorrow."

"Judd, that's fantastic!" Desiree exclaimed. "What happened? How did you change their minds?"

"Search me," he said. "The boy reached out to me. Of his own volition. No arm twisting whatsoever."

"Judd's kids aren't exactly my biggest fans," Desiree explained.

"It's not you, it's any woman in my life," Judson countered.

"Well, I'm grateful," Desiree said. "Whatever the reason. Especially if it means they hate me just a little bit less."

"Oh no," Kate said. "They can't possibly hate you. Maybe they just don't want to share their dad."

"It's not me they have a problem sharing, it's my bank account," he said, shaking his head. "Or, as they've taken to calling it, their inheritance."

"Judson, that's not true," Desiree said. "Although they were definitely not in favor of our summer wanderings. Three months away from the office—crisscrossing the globe. We stayed in everything from tents and hostels to five-star hotels. What was it Liam said when you first told him? 'Over my dead body.'"

"I hate to correct you, honey, but what he actually said to me was 'over *your* dead body, Dad.' That kid of mine, he doesn't mince words." He shrugged, grinned, and ambled back to the pilothouse.

Kate tried not to look shocked. She couldn't imagine anyone disliking Desiree. Bubbly, funny, and down-to-earth, she made everyone feel at home instantly. Maybe that was why she was so good at her job—head concierge for the Manhattan flagship of a major luxury hotel group.

As Kate and Desiree carefully lurched their way to the back of the boat, Kate had to admit she'd never seen her friend happier. And it was contagious. As they settled into the cushioned bench seat, Kate glanced up and spotted Jack Scanlon looking back at them from the elevated glass wheelhouse. The vet brushed a lock of sandy brown hair off his forehead, caught her eye, and smiled.

Kate smiled back and waved.

"Hmmm, so I'm not the only one doing well in the romance department," Desiree said under her breath.

Kate shook her head. "Uh-uh. Nope. Not happening. Small island."

"Hey, I'm just relieved you ditched that other guy. Mr. Millionaire."

"You were always so nice to him," Kate said, amazed.

"Because *you* liked him. I always thought he was kind of hollow. Handsome, but he knew it."

Kate giggled. "Oh, did he ever."

"Well, you can do a lot better. And clearly, you are."

Kate risked a glance at the pilothouse: Judson at the wheel, Jack next to him looking out at the water—and Oliver happily wedged between them, all four paws planted wide for balance.

"Seriously, thanks for all the help with this," Desiree said, almost shyly.

"Are you kidding? After all the events you've arranged? You deserve this. Besides, I just happen to know the best florist in Coral Cay. Maxi may own the only flower shop on the island, but she could hold her own in Manhattan any day."

"I know. You should see the bouquet she designed. A strand of white orchids. Simple and beautiful. Which is pretty much our motto for the whole wedding."

"I love the idea of a beach wedding," Kate said. "Although, knowing this place, you may get a few uninvited guests. The folks around here love a good party. On the bright side, they seldom show up empty-handed."

"The more the merrier," Desiree said happily.

Abruptly the engine cut out. Except for the waves slapping the side of the boat, all was still.

Judson Cooper scrambled down onto the deck, adjusted his binoculars, and peered toward the shore.

"What is it?" Jack asked, leaning out the wheelhouse door.

Kate looked to Desiree, but her friend was focused on her fiancé.

"That shouldn't be here," Judson muttered. "Definitely not here."

"What?" Kate asked. "What is it?"

"That cigarette boat," Judson said quietly. "I knew I recognized it. Dammit! Not again."

"Judson, what is it?" Desiree asked as she rose from her seat and made her way haltingly toward the front of the boat. "You're scaring me."

"Nothing to worry about, sweetheart. Just business as usual, unfortunately. But we're going to have to cut this trip a little short. I need to reach out to a few people I know and have a little chat."

"Are we in some kind of danger?" Kate asked, alarmed.

"Nah, same old, same old," Judson said. "Unfortunately, it all goes with the territory. It's nothing. Really."

Despite his smile and reassuring words, Kate saw

Judson's jaw clench, as his left hand gripped the binoculars.

He rubbed Desiree's back. "And it's definitely not going to spoil our plans."

With that, he climbed back into the pilothouse, carefully shifted the throttle forward, and steered the boat farther out toward open water.

Chapter 2

"It's just flour, sugar, butter, and spices," Kate said, from the center of the Cookie House kitchen. "Honestly, anyone can do it. Only most people don't have the patience and the time."

"Easy for you to say," Maxi countered from her station across the kitchen. "The last time I made my best chocolate chip cookies at home, they came out flat and a little charred. Not that that stopped *mis niños*."

"Flat just means the butter was too warm when you mixed it in," Kate said. "And charred could be your oven."

"Nope, that one was George. That puppy had to go out, and by the time I got back, those things were smoking."

"See? Just time. You've got the skill. All of you. But hey, there's no shame in buying cookies. That's why we have a bakery."

"Well, no danger this crowd is going to put you out of business," Sunny cracked, her champagne blond bob swinging as she dislodged one oversized cookie from its baking tray.

But Kate had to admit the eighty-something yoga teacher's shortbread looked remarkably professional.

"Can I say it?" Minette pitched in from her left. "It's just nice to get out of the house for a few hours in the evening. I love it that when I do get home, my Carl is waiting for me for a change. Last week he handed me a glass of wine and wanted to taste my homework."

"Andre brewed a big pot of espresso," Rosie said with a grin. "Said it was better for dunking the cookies."

"Sounds super ro-*man*-tic," Maxi teased.

Rosie's tawny complexion turned crimson. Fifty-plus Minette just grinned.

"Speaking of romance, how's that New Yorker friend of yours?" Sunny asked. "Isn't that girl getting married soon?"

"Tomorrow evening," Kate answered. "Sunset on the beach."

"You should see the cake," Maxi bragged. "*¡Magnífico!* Right down to the bride and groom cookies for the top."

"Oooh, could we see them?" Rosie asked. "I've never seen a cookie cake topper."

"Twist her arm, if you have to—they are sooo pretty," Maxi said, winking.

"Please?" Rosie asked, scraping the last uncooperative cookie from the sheet. "Or, in my case, pretty please with burnt shortbread on it."

"Well, technically, I guess this could count as part of the class work," Kate said smiling. She walked to a far cupboard, pulled out a tin, and pried off the lid. Then she removed several sheets of wax paper and carefully lifted out two plastic freezer bags—placing them gingerly on the table.

The women gathered around, as she deftly opened one bag then the other, extracted the delicate contents, and laid the bride and groom on a large platter.

The bride's features and attire were outlined in lines of delicate shell pink icing, while the groom's were done in a soft, barely there blue.

"Ooo, now those are pretty," Minette said, brushing her brown hands against her apron. "And the icing swirls on the bride make her dress look like lace."

Kate beamed. She hated to admit it, but she was more than a little proud of how well the two cookies had turned out.

"I love the bow tie on the groom," Rosie said pointing. "And the little tuxedo. Don't see how you did that."

"I can't believe you gave the cookie bride flowers, too," Maxi said, shaking her head. "It's just like the orchid swag she'll be carrying."

"I wanted it to be personal, instead of the usual generic," Kate said, shrugging. "You know, really them. I haven't seen her dress, but I know it's short and has a bit of lace."

"Well, that cookie's gonna be better dressed than the real groom," Maxi revealed. "Judson's gonna wear a guayabera and linen pants."

"Really?" Kate asked. "Well, Desiree did say they'd both be barefoot."

Maxi nodded vigorously. "She let it slip when we were working out the details on the bouquet and the boutonniere. So what kinda cookies are we talking about here? 'Cause I wouldn't mind taste-testing a few of the rejects."

"Key lime crisps. To go with the cake. It's key lime with a rich buttercream frosting. Desiree wanted something tropical. Something specific to Coral Cay. And the decoration on the cookies is just regular royal icing.

Same as you'd use with gingerbread men. Plus a little food coloring. And I used the same cookie cutters I use for my gingerbread families."

"Oh honey, she's gonna love these," Minette said, sighing. "I just can't get over how much that little bride looks like a bride. And all with just loops of icing. I still don't see how you did it."

"Steady hands," Kate said grinning. "And at least a half-dozen sketches before I got the design right."

"Really?" Rosie asked. "It looks deceptively simple. Artistic."

Kate nodded, as she cautiously repacked the two cookies. "No one ever sees the mistakes. Just the end result."

"At my house, we eat the mistakes," Maxi said gleefully from across the kitchen as she removed the last of her cookies from the tray with a spatula.

"Speaking of houses, did you hear the news about Harper Duval's old place?" Minette announced. "There's somebody in it. Or there will be soon."

"They sold it?" Rosie asked, incredulous. "That place is so big. And worth beaucoup bucks. But after what happened, I didn't think it would ever sell."

"Rented," Minette corrected. "Just for a couple of months. To a film company."

Kate looked at Maxi, who shrugged and quickly returned to scraping her cookie tray.

"Don't tell me Coral Cay's gone Hollywood?" Sunny said, as she wadded up a paper towel and dropped it neatly into a trash can. "Can't see that one at all. This place is where all the stars come when they want to escape from that rat race. Or hide out."

"It's not for a real movie," Minette sniffed. "Carl told me it's just for one of those reality shows. One of the ones where everyone lives in the same house and they play pranks, run around all hours, and make each other's lives miserable."

"That's pretty much all of them," Sunny quipped.

"Don't I know it," Minette nodded, vigorously polishing her batter bowl with a wad of paper towels. "But they've ordered up a truckload of new fixtures and things from the hardware store. So Carl's happy. And busy, too."

Kate looked at Maxi, who met her eyes briefly, barely shook her head, and hastily went back to cleaning up her prep area.

Kate knew the entire Harper Duval situation was an emotional minefield for the florist. But she sensed something else was at play, too. Even if Maxi wasn't quite ready to discuss it. At least, not publicly.

Wedding or no wedding, Kate resolved to make a little extra time for her friend over the next few days. Just in case she needed to talk.

"OK, ladies, next week we're going to tackle sandwich cookies," Kate said, her amber-brown eyes twinkling as she brandished a roll of wax paper. "And I've got a recipe I think you're all going to love. I'll give you one hint: melted chocolate. Now, who needs some extra paper to wrap up their project?"

Chapter 3

"Oooh, I could get used to this," Maxi said, as the tuxe-doed maître d' efficiently ushered them through the light-filled restaurant. "And I love all the orchids."

"Believe me, it's all low music, happy conversation, tinkling glasses out here, but in the kitchen it's absolute chaos," Kate said. "Ask me how I know."

"Even for lunch, this is one super-expensive place," Maxi hissed. "Are you sure Desiree can afford this?"

Kate nodded. "She's one of the most practical people I know. If she's hosting us, she can afford it. And trust me, she knows restaurants. So it's not like the right hand side of the menu is going to come as a surprise, either."

The accordion wall of glass that separated the restaurant from its large stone terrace was pushed back, creating one open, airy room. On the patio, Desiree waved excitedly. Off in the distance, Kate spied yachts and super yachts cruising past.

At midday in September, it was still hot enough for short sleeves, though a briny breeze off the water—and

smart black-and-white umbrellas over every table—kept
the terrace cool. Walking through the restaurant, Kate
noticed the scent of oranges, lemons, and limes from the
bar mingled with more savory smells from the kitchen.

When she spotted the dessert cart, she nearly did a
double take. Three large sterling bowls—one of whipped
cream, one of ruby-red strawberries, and a third of rich
chocolate mousse. But right in the center, as the star of
the show, was a double-high coconut cake.

One of hers. Kate felt a spark of pride.

The maître d' pulled out their chairs in turn. "Shall I
have the champagne sent out now?"

"That would be perfect, thank you," Desiree replied.

"Desiree, this place is lovely, but you really didn't
have to do all this," Kate said, as the maître d' retreated
into the restaurant. "It's too much."

Her old friend waved her hand dismissively. "It's not
every day a girl gets married. Besides, we're counting
this as my bachelorette party—and you two are the only
people I really know on the island. Last night Judson
handed me his Black Card and said to have fun. So I've
ordered us a great bottle of champagne. And we're going
to sample the best of everything on the menu. Literally.
They've got a tasting menu, and I just ordered three of
them."

"So where is your good-looking groom?" Maxi asked.
"I haven't met the guy yet. But hearing you talk, I feel
like I already know him."

Desiree beamed. "He's on the boat. We decided to be
semi-traditional and spend our last single night apart.
So he packed a bag and camped out there last night. We
won't actually see each other again until this evening.
After that, it's back to the bungalow for a night, then
we're taking the boat up the coast for our honeymoon."

"That sounds wonderful," Maxi said dreamily, just as

the sommelier appeared with champagne, trailed by a waiter with an ice bucket and another bearing a tray with three fluted glasses.

The sommelier removed the cork with a muted *pop*, and poured a taste for Desiree.

"Beautiful," she said happily after sampling it.

Once everyone's glasses were full and the waitstaff receded, Kate raised her glass. "Ladies, I would like to propose a toast. To Desiree and Judson A beautiful, romantic wedding tonight and a long happy marriage to follow."

"*¡Salud!*" Maxi seconded. "*¡Que sean muy felices toda la vida!* May both of you be super happy for the rest of your lives!"

"OK, you girls are going to make me cry," Desiree said, fanning herself with her hand.

"Well then, take another sip of champagne, because it's delicious," Kate teased.

"*Dios mío*, is that Lola Montgomery?" Maxi said, cocking her head and staring into the restaurant. "The lady in the straw cloche hat?"

Kate and Desiree craned their necks.

"Oh wow, it really is her," Kate said. "I loved her in that rom-com—the one where they were out on the lake in a rowboat surrounded by swans."

"I know!" Maxi said. "But I really liked that TV show she did last year. She played twin sisters—one was a police detective and the other a serial killer."

"*The Same Coin*," Kate said, snapping her fingers.

"That's the one," Maxi added. "It was good. And it was, like, two weeks before I could open a closet door without thinking of that scene in the last episode."

"I wonder what she's doing here," Kate mused. "You don't think she's part of the crew filming up at Harp's old place, do you?"

"Nah, that's just a reality show," Maxi said. "For her, that would be slumming. Unless she's producing . . ."

"Judd used to date her," Desiree murmured so softly that Kate wasn't certain she'd heard her correctly. But the strain on the woman's face filled in the blanks.

"Are you OK?" Kate asked gently, setting down her glass. "Do you want to take this party somewhere else?"

Desiree took a deep breath, squared her shoulders, and seemed to reach a decision. "No. No, I don't. I'm just being silly. Idiotic, really. We each had full lives before. It's only the *after* that matters now." She raised her glass aloft. "And ladies, that wonderful man and I are going to make every minute count—both together and apart. Starting with this one. Now, who's hungry?"

Chapter 4

Barefoot bride or no, Kate still felt a little underdressed for the wedding. She'd gone through two changes of clothes before returning to her original choice: a lemon yellow sundress with a pair of matching ballet flats. Idly, as she finished off the outfit with small diamond stud earrings, she wondered what Jack would be wearing. Or, with a busy practice in full swing, if he'd even manage to make the ceremony.

Since autumn evenings on the beach could get chilly, Kate opened one of the drawers under her bed and gently lifted out the coral pashmina she'd picked up at a Manhattan thrift store last winter. She snatched her small purse from the bed and stepped lightly down the stairs, just as she heard Maxi knocking on the front door of the Cookie House.

"Hey, Cookie Lady, your fancy ride is here!"

Kate opened the door and Maxi floated into the bakery, stopped just short of the counter, and gave a little twirl. The florist had opted for a fuchsia silk blouse and a soft, tan batik skirt with leather sandals.

"You look great!" Kate said.

"Ooo, you too," her friend said. "*Muy elegante*. And super-pretty earrings. I might have to borrow those."

"Any time. Got the flowers?"

"All packed in the Jeep. Along with a folding table, a linen tablecloth and plenty of room left over for a small cake. I figure if it's in a box and we put it in the front seat with a three-point seatbelt, it should ride just fine. That is, if you don't mind sitting in the back?"

"That's a brilliant idea," Kate said.

"Hey, it works for big flower arrangements, too. And, in honor of the occasion, Peter is meeting us there. But between you and me, I think *mi amor* is hoping to miss the ceremony and just show up for cake."

"Smart man." Kate waved a hand toward the counter, where she'd piled a collection of diverse boxes and bags. "I've got the cake, plus a hamper with paper napkins, paper plates, a cake knife, and trash bags for cleanup. And that carton holds enough champagne glasses for an army. Just in case."

"What about the champagne?" Maxi asked.

"The groom's bringing that. And the ice."

"Before a wedding? He'll be lucky to remember to bring himself. I can tell you what that day was like for Peter and me. ¡*Loco!*"

"From what Desiree's said, Judd *is* a little bit of an absentminded professor type," Kate admitted.

"OK, I think I have some prosecco in the storeroom," Maxi said. "Sometimes clients like to send a bottle of something bubbly with flowers to celebrate stuff like promotions and engagements. I'll grab a few bottles."

"I'll get Sam's cooler and empty out the ice maker in

the kitchen. When it's time to set up we can just put the bottles on ice in the cooler box. It is a beach wedding."

"*Perfecto*," Maxi agreed as she breezed back out the front door.

Fifteen minutes later, as Kate snapped the seatbelt in place across the tall cake box and gave the strap a tug, she felt pleased with their plan. No matter what happened, Desiree and Judson would have a little cake and bubbly to toast their sweet, new life.

Chapter 5

"Shouldn't that groom of hers be here by now?" Maxi asked, not for the first time.

The reception table, anchored in the dry sand and cloaked in white linen, looked like something out of an island travel brochure. The cake, with its cookie bride and groom, took center stage. Pink roses and fragrant white jasmine spilled out of two low glass cylinders flanking the cake. Nestled in the sand, Sam's battered white cooler—scrubbed clean and filled to the brim with ice—sported six chilled bottles of prosecco. Nearby, the case of champagne flutes and hamper of picnic-ware stood ready for action.

Kate was just relieved that it was cool enough outside to accommodate the buttercream frosting. And the pashmina would definitely come in handy later.

True to his word, Maxi's husband had arrived at the beach first and helped them set the scene. Not that they'd be able to improve on a South Florida sunset.

For all Desiree's protestations of not knowing anyone

on the island, Kate was not at all surprised to see a sprinkling of local faces.

Andre Armand chatted amiably with Peter and Jack— who had made it after all, Kate was glad to see. Clad casually in a faded pair of jeans and a pressed blue dress shirt with the sleeves neatly rolled up, the veterinarian did a double take when he saw the cake table and grinned.

"Judd invited me to a beach party," Jack said. "He never said anything about a wedding."

"Usually that means you're the groom," Maxi quipped. "But in this case, the job's already taken."

"Desiree was in the shop first thing this morning," Rosie explained in a hushed voice. "Let's just say we took care of something old and something blue."

"*Ay*, this I've got to hear," Maxi said. "Spill."

"You're going to love them," the store owner said. "They're these really beautiful antique sapphire and diamond earrings. It's like they were made for her. Anyway, before she left, she invited us to her wedding."

"I'm a little worried that the justice of the peace isn't here yet," Kate said. "But I don't know if the resort arranged that or if it was Judson, so I'm not even sure who to call."

"Well, Desiree booked the photographer," Maxi said quietly, surreptitiously pointing to a thirty-something in a khaki travel vest and backward baseball cap taking snaps of the cake table with a substantial-looking camera. "And the guy keeps clumping around mumbling about 'losing the light.'"

"He's right about that," Kate said. "If they want a sunset wedding, they're both going to have to get here pretty soon." She looked up just in time to see Claire and Gabe hiking down the beach toward them.

"We were visiting friends nearby and just wanted to deliver some champers to the happy couple," British-born Claire announced in her clipped accent, as Gabe handed off the champagne bottle to Maxi. "I've only met the groom to say hello, but he is rather a hero of mine. And his fiancée is absolutely lovely. I chatted with her earlier this week when she came in to reserve bikes for their stay."

"You guys should stick around," Maxi said brightly. "Their whole attitude is 'the more the merrier.'"

"Maxi's right," Kate said. "Plus we've got cake."

"As the man said, 'To love or have loved, that is enough—ask nothing more,'" Gabe quoted. "But a glass of this stuff wouldn't be bad, either."

The bike-shop owner wrapped her hands protectively around his burly arm and smiled. "Well, turning down cake just seems rude."

The mechanic's eyebrows went up, and he looked at Claire. "Beach wedding would be cool," he said, nodding as he surveyed the landscape.

Claire smiled, her eyes twinkling. And Kate caught the look that passed between them.

"OK, that looks like one of the resort limos, so this must be at least one of them," Maxi said.

A black Lincoln Town Car pulled up and the driver hopped out, ran around to the back passenger door, opened it, and offered a hand to someone within.

A beaming Desiree emerged. Her dress was cream silk that fell just to the knees. As promised, the short-sleeved sheath was covered in a layer of matching lace.

Maxi grabbed the carryall with the flowers and hustled up the beach to meet her, with Kate just a few steps behind.

"*Ay*, how are we going to tell her that the groom and justice of the peace are missing?"

"Maybe they're riding over together and got delayed?" Kate ventured.

"It's a small island, and there's no traffic—not this time of year," the florist countered.

Desiree paused and bent down to remove one low-heeled sandal, then the other. Straightening, she squared her shoulders and strolled out onto the sand.

"I'm just so relieved I made it," she said breathlessly, dangling her strappy shoes in one hand. "I didn't think I was going to get here in time. That man of mine swore he ordered a limo to pick me up. But the resort never sent it. Once they realized the mistake, we had to start from scratch. And the cell service on this island! I kept calling Judd, and it kept going straight to voice mail. At one point, I considered just putting on my track shoes and running down the beach."

Desiree took a deep breath and hiccuped. "Well," she said with a giggle, "time to get this show on the road!"

Kate and Maxi exchanged glances.

"What?" Desiree asked. "What is it?"

"Judd and the officiant aren't here yet," Kate said.

"What?" The bride's face crumpled. "No. That's not possible. Where are they?"

For a moment, Kate was afraid she was going to cry.

"We're not sure," Kate said softly. "We were kind of hoping you might have heard something. But it sounds like some wires must have gotten crossed. Maybe I should call the resort and ask. Could they have gone to a different beach?"

"No, no, he wouldn't do that," Desiree replied, shaking her head. "Judd knows this beach. He chose this spot. He's the one who showed it to me. He wouldn't get lost. What if he's hurt? What if there's been an accident?"

"OK, deep breaths," Kate said, patting her friend's

shoulder. "Could he have gone back to your bungalow at the resort? To pick up something he forgot?"

Desiree shook her head. "I just came from there. I was there the entire time I was waiting for the car."

"Maxi," Kate said over her shoulder. "Did Peter bring his cell?"

"I'm on it. We'll call Ben," the florist said, trotting down the beach toward the cluster of guests.

"Excuse me," Kate called to the limo driver. "Do you have a two-way radio?"

He nodded. "Doesn't work everywhere on the island though. Why? What's up?"

The driver looked to be in his late teens or early twenties, and Kate noticed that while his white dress shirt fit, the vest and pants of his uniform were at least a size too big. A college student picking up extra cash on the weekend?

Kate forced herself to smile. "Well, we've got our bride, but we're missing a groom and a justice of the peace. Can you check with the resort and see if any other cars are coming?"

"Sure," he said, smoothing his dark hair. "Would they have originated at the same place? Palm Isle?"

"Was the justice of the peace booked through the resort?" Kate asked Desiree softly.

The bride nodded vigorously.

"The justice of the peace would," Kate called over the breeze. "The groom would have been picked up at his boat. He's docked at—"

"Sullivan Harbor," Desiree interjected.

"I'll check—no problem," the driver said, grinning. "Can't have a runaway groom. Um, I mean, let me see what's going on," he added quickly.

Kate saw flashes behind her, accompanied by a

whirring sound. She turned and saw the photographer clicking shots of her and Desiree.

"Just act like I'm not here," the man said, following Desiree as she walked back to the car. "'Candid' is the name of the game."

Kate stepped in front of the photographer and blocked his shot. "Look, we might have a small problem here," she said quietly. "Maybe you can photograph the guests and the setting and do shots of the bride later?"

"Are you the maid of honor? Anyone ever tell you you have great bone structure?" he said, still clicking off frames.

"Please stop!" Kate hissed. "We can't do pictures right now."

"I'm Alan—Alan Tremaine," he said, finally lowering his camera. "And it's now or never because we're losing the light."

"Well, we might have lost the groom and the officiant, so we've got bigger problems."

"For real?"

Kate nodded.

"Ouch, that stings," Alan said, reaching into one of the many pockets of his vest. "OK, guests and venue it is. By the by, here's my card. You know, in case you want to reschedule. Or maybe grab a coffee sometime."

And with that he sauntered down the beach toward the crowd.

The limo driver got out of the car frowning. Kate braced herself.

"Sorry, ladies. My dispatcher says no more cars to this beach today. And no grooms or other weddings period. They didn't even have this trip on the books, which is why we had to scramble at the last minute. Maybe your guy got a cab or a rideshare? Or one of his friends gave him a lift?"

Desiree dropped her shoes onto the road with a clatter and flattened both palms against the side of the car, steadying herself.

"He's OK," Kate said, putting a hand on her friend's shoulder. "He's on his way. We'll find him."

Maxi appeared behind them in the sand, a phone at her ear, with Rosie and Claire trailing behind her.

"The good news is, no accidents on the island all day," the florist announced. "A minor miracle, believe you me. And Kyle Hardy's volunteering to go out to the boat and see what's up, if we tell him where it's parked."

"He's docked at Sullivan Harbor, slip thirty-two," Desiree said turning. "The *Starfish*."

"You got that?" Maxi said into the phone. "OK, *gracias*."

"Kyle's gonna phone back from the boat, if he can get a signal," she added, clicking off.

Desiree looked up—her eyes wide and unfocused, her pale face full of dread. "Where *is* he?" she said to no one in particular. "Where on earth is Judson?"

Chapter 6

"Maybe we should take you back to the resort," Kate suggested, as the sky transformed from a blanket of blue to horizontal slashes of orange and scarlet.

"No!" Desiree declared decisively. "He's coming. I know he's coming. Unless he's hurt. What if he's *hurt*?"

The electronic buzz of Peter's cell phone cut through the murmur of the waves. He slipped it smoothly from his pocket.

"Peter Buchanan," he said automatically, then paused.

Kate tried to read his face, but got nothing from his expression.

"Are you sure? When? OK. Thanks, Kyle."

"What happened?" Desiree asked, her face tight. "Did they find Judd? Where is he?"

"No sign of him, but the boat left the harbor last night."

The bride shook her head in disbelief. "That's not possible. We're not sailing out until tomorrow. Where did it go? Who took it? And where is Judd?"

"They don't know yet," Peter said patiently. "Kyle's checking a few things. And Ben's on his way over from the station. He's a detective—a good detective—and he'll get to the bottom of this."

"This is not happening," Desiree whispered, sinking to her knees in the sand.

"We're going to find him," Kate said, kneeling to wrap the pashmina protectively around her friend.

"Here," Gabe said, pressing a hot to-go cup into Desiree's numb hands. "Coffee joint just up the beach," he added, by way of explanation.

Kate looked over and saw two cardboard trays of coffee on the table next to the cake. Claire held a third one and was passing them out to the group.

In the twilight, she could see a familiar figure ambling down the sandbank from the roadway: Ben.

The police detective had compromised exactly nothing in his attire to the surroundings. As usual, he wore a blazer (navy) suit pants with razor creases (gray), a starched dress shirt (spotless white), and a tie (gray with burgundy stripes). Kate knew before she looked that his wingtips would be polished to a mirror shine. And he topped it all off with a straw fedora, which he tipped when he spotted Kate walking toward him.

"I understand the bride is a friend of yours? How's she holding up?" he asked, dispensing with the preamble.

"Longtime friend. From Manhattan. And not well. Her groom's missing, and we just heard from Kyle that his boat's gone, too. She's terrified."

"Problem is, at this point, we know precious little. Kyle's trying to get a lead on what happened to the boat and any witnesses at the marina. And I've got another guy talking to the folks at Palm Isle, where they were staying. Between you and me, any chance this guy could have done a runner?"

"None," Kate said. "You should see them together. They have so much fun. This wedding is the perfect example. They both love the beach. They wanted to get married. And they were in Coral Cay. So they just decided to do it here. And keep it carefree and simple. A little cake, some champagne, a few flowers. Judson even picked this spot. I've never seen two people more in love. Or more suited to each other."

Even in the twilight, she could see Ben smile. "OK, that's good enough for me," he said lightly. "I need to chat with her, but it's getting dark. Any chance we could move this party indoors?"

"We've tried. Every time someone mentions leaving the beach, Desiree gets upset. She's convinced he's still coming. She wants to be here just in case."

"Oh geez," he said.

Kate sighed.

"How are *you* doing?" Ben asked. "I know this isn't easy."

"I'm fine. I just . . . I want to help, and I don't even know what to do."

"You're here," he said. "Right now, that's about all you can do. I'm going to take her back to the resort. She'll be more comfortable there, and I might get more out of her. Also, since it's where they've been living for the past week, she's more likely to remember something that might help. You're welcome to come along, if you like."

"Definitely. I rode over with Maxi. She and Peter took separate cars. Let me just tell her."

As Ben Abrams introduced himself to Desiree, Kate pulled Maxi aside and told her Ben's plan.

"If I come along, I can drop you back home after," the florist said.

"That would be great. But what do we do about the cake and everything?"

"Peter, Jack, and Gabe said they'd box everything up once you-know-who is gone," Maxi whispered. "They can pack it into Peter's car, and he'll drop it all off at the flower shop. That way, you can collect your gear tomorrow. Except for the cake. I'm gonna buy it for *mi mami*. As a thank you for watching our three little gremlins. She loves key lime."

"Consider it my gift," Kate said quietly, relieved that Desiree wouldn't have to watch them disassembling the remains of the wedding that never was. "I'm just glad someone will get to enjoy it."

Chapter 7

"Was there anything unusual you remember from the last twenty-four hours?" Ben asked, sitting forward with a gold pen in one hand and a small notebook in the other palm. "Anything that was out of the ordinary for Dr. Cooper?"

Sitting barefoot at one end of a small settee, still clad in her lace dress, Desiree's face was blank. She shook her head. "I hadn't seen him since Friday night. We wanted to spend our last night apart. He slept on the boat. That seems so stupid now! Why did we do that?"

"Desiree, this isn't on you," Kate said, setting a tray of coffee cups on the low table. "Sorry guys, this instant is all they had in the kitchenette. It's hot and it's caffeinated, but no promises on the taste."

"Do you want us to order you up some soup or something from room service?" Maxi asked, reaching for a cup from the tray. "I'm pretty sure you haven't eaten since lunch. You gotta stay strong. For you and your guy."

Desiree shook her head. "This is fine," she said, smiling grimly. "More than. It's about all I'm up to right now."

"What about the boat?" Kate asked suddenly. "Remember that cigarette boat?"

"You're right!" Desiree said, her face lighting up. "I'd forgotten all about that."

"What cigarette boat?" Ben asked, sitting forward in the overstuffed floral chair.

"We took the boat out yesterday afternoon," Desiree said. "Judd's boat. The *Starfish*. To do a spin around the island."

"Who is 'we'?" the detective asked.

"Judd and me and Kate and Oliver and Jack Scanlon."

"Got it. What time was this?"

"Well, it was supposed to be noon sharp. But Judd was running late. He'd gotten a call from a sea-watch group in California. So it was, what, about ten after or so before we set out?"

Kate nodded.

"And we'd been on the water about thirty or forty minutes. It was so beautiful, and we had just passed your friend's house . . ."

"Iris's place," Kate explained.

"Yes," Desiree agreed. "And then we saw the nature preserve. And that's when he spotted it. In one of the coves there. The boat."

"What did it look like?"

"All I could see was a cigarette boat," she said. "Judd had binoculars, so he got a better look."

"It was black," Kate said. "With a red stripe down the side."

"What did he say about it?" Ben asked.

"Nothing, really," Desiree continued. "But it upset

him. He recognized whoever it was. He'd obviously run into them before. And he was not happy to see them again."

"Are we talking smugglers or poachers or what exactly?" the detective asked, shifting in the chair.

Desiree shook her head. "He didn't say. Whoever it was, I think it must have been from before we met, because I'd never seen the boat before."

Ben looked at Kate. "What do you remember about the incident?"

"It's just like Desiree said. That's when Judd cut our trip short. He said he was going to talk to someone about it—that boat. But he didn't say who."

Ben looked back at Desiree. "Any idea who he'd go to with a problem like that? Harbor master? Coast Guard? Green groups?"

"I was an idiot," Desiree said glumly. "Looking back, I think Judd was being purposefully vague. He didn't want to upset us. Upset *me*, more like. I should have pressed him on it. And I didn't."

"Hey, this whole angle could be completely unrelated," Ben said evenly. "It's just best to throw everything out on the table at the very beginning. That way, we can investigate and eliminate. And trust me, most of this we'll rule out pretty quickly."

Desiree clutched her coffee with both hands. But Kate noticed she hadn't taken so much as a sip.

"So when did you see him next after that?" Ben asked smoothly.

"That evening," Desiree said. "We went out for dinner, then after it stopped raining, we took a walk on the beach. At the resort. We stopped at one of the cafés for a nightcap. Then we came back to the bungalow."

"How was his mood?"

"Happy. Goofy. We were getting married the next day. I think we were both a little giddy. He'd packed his bag earlier, so he just took off for the boat."

"When he left for the boat, did you give him a lift to the harbor?"

"The hotel did. In one of the golf carts." She hesitated. "I waved goodbye just out front," she added, her voice breaking.

"Did you talk to him after that?"

Desiree shook her head. "We promised we wouldn't. But I missed him. So I called a few hours later. It went straight to voice mail. I just thought he was asleep."

"This wedding. Who was supposed to be there?" Ben asked.

"It was kind of spur-of-the-moment, so it was just a small gathering," Desiree said. "Kate was there, and Maxi and her husband."

At the other end of the sofa, the florist nodded and gave an encouraging smile.

"I invited a couple I met in town," Desiree added. "Rosie and Andre. And Judd invited his children, his business partner Zoey West, and Jack. He met Jack a few years ago doing wildlife rescue work after one of the big hurricanes."

"Was that everybody?"

"Claire and Gabe stopped by with a bottle of champagne," Kate said. "They ended up staying."

"Sounds like a Coral Cay party," Ben said, smiling.

"Everyone's been so warm," said Desiree.

"That's because we like you guys," Maxi said, cradling her coffee cup.

Ben flipped through his notebook. "I don't see Dr. Cooper's children or his business partner on the list of people who were at the beach tonight."

"No," Desiree said. "They didn't come."

"Do you know why?"

"Zoey said she was coming. And with everything that's happened, I didn't even realize she wasn't there until now. Judd's children, well." Desiree sighed. "The truth is they hate me."

"I'm sure that's not true," Kate said. "They just don't know you yet."

"It doesn't matter," Desiree said quickly. "Judd's kids love their dad. They'd never hurt him."

"What about the business partner? Any tension there?"

"Zoey? No, she's wonderful. Judd's the scientist and the public face. But she takes care of the day-to-day administration for both the nonprofit group and for their business. And she's always been fine with whatever Judd wants. Including extending our trip to allow for a wedding and a honeymoon."

"OK, I'm hitting the ground running on this," Ben said.

As Desiree set the cup on the table and released her grip, Kate watched the circulation flow back into her friend's white knuckles.

"This is my number," the detective said, handing her a business card. "If you think of anything, no matter how trivial it might seem, give me a buzz. Let me sort it out."

Desiree nodded gratefully, clasping the card carefully in both hands.

"One other thing, and I hate to bring this up. But Dr. Cooper's a bit of a public figure. Which means you could get some press interest at some point. If that happens, my advice is to ignore it and let us field it. We want people keeping an eye out for him, but we don't want a frenzy. And that can be a fine line to walk."

Desiree sat up straight, clutching Ben's card like a talisman. She started to open her mouth, then clamped it shut.

"Now, if you ladies will excuse me," he said, plucking the straw fedora from a side table and dropping it on his head. "I have a couple of avenues I want to explore tonight."

"Detective," Desiree started, "if you hear anything . . . no matter what time . . ."

"Ma'am, I promise," Ben said, tipping his hat, "you'll be the first person I call."

Chapter 8

Kate pushed a rolling rack of lemon drop cookies into the bakery's oven. She flipped the door latch and glanced at Oliver, sacked out under the kitchen table. While he'd spent the evening at Maxi's house—with her mom, three kids, and their new Parson Russell Terrier puppy, George—he'd been waiting politely in the kitchen when Maxi dropped off Kate at the bakery. With his purple Frisbee in his mouth.

And it turned out that an extended session of backyard catch was just the stress-reliever Kate needed. Even if her mind did keep creeping back to the wedding that never was.

The phone rang and Oliver stirred, opening a drowsy eye.

"So who's calling us at this hour?" she asked him.

She checked the clock as she reached for the wall phone. At 10:25 p.m., it was either a bakery emergency—or just an emergency. Her mind went to Judson and Desiree, and her stomach tightened.

"The Cookie House, this is Kate," she said.

"Kate, it's Ben."

Her heart started to race. Had they found Judson? Was it bad news?

"Have you got a minute?" the detective asked. "I'd have stopped by, but we're still finishing up at the resort. And I wasn't sure if you'd be in the bakery tonight."

"I have a big cookie order for one of the resorts tomorrow. To be honest, I wanted to keep Desiree company, but she needed to catch a shower and try to get some rest. She wants to help out with the search first thing tomorrow morning. Is this about Judson? Did you find him?"

"No, sorry, I should have led with that right off." He paused and sighed. "This is more in the way of background. I'm hoping you might be able to help me fill in a few blanks."

"Of course, but I only met Judson this week. I don't really know him all that well."

"That's OK, I'm just interested in what you've observed this week," Ben said. "How were things between him and Desiree?"

In spite of the situation, Kate felt herself smile. "Wonderful. Those two are made for each other." Leaning against the counter, she saw that Oliver was now fully stretched out under the table with his eyes closed. Not quite fully grown, he looked like a small, shaggy bear.

"So no arguments? No tension?" Ben prompted.

"Not a bit. He seems to live to make her happy. And she's the same way with him."

"Any disagreements over the wedding arrangements?" the detective asked.

"No, but to be honest Desiree handled most of that," Kate said. "She'd done events planning in her job. And she's the kind of person who can pull off a complicated event and make it look easy."

"How long have you known her?"

"At least seven years. One of my first professional jobs was in the kitchen of The Cascadian Hotel. Desiree was the concierge."

"High-pressure job?"

"Definitely. Guests were spending tons of money, and they expected perfection. But no matter what happened, Desiree never got ruffled. What she did every day? Last-minute tickets to sold-out shows, securing impossible-to-get dinner reservations, arranging impromptu events? She made it look like magic. But what meant the most to me was the way she looked out for the new employees. She didn't have to. It wasn't even part of her job. It's just who she is. Kind. Trust me, if she'd asked, there are probably at least a hundred people like me who would have happily traveled across the planet just to stand on that beach tonight."

"Understood," Ben said. "She left the job though?"

"She took early retirement."

"Burned out?" Ben asked.

Kate stopped and considered how to put her thoughts into words. "More like ready to start a new chapter. She'd been considering it for a while. I think she was ready for a change. And maybe a change of scene."

Kate recalled her own, almost split-second decision to leave Manhattan four months ago and take a chance on a place she'd always dreamt of seeing: Coral Cay, Florida. Less methodical than Desiree's more measured decision, Kate's *carpe diem* moment was prompted by a single day's trifecta of job loss, apartment gone condo, and the discovery that her then-fiancé was cheating.

"When's the last time you saw her?" Ben asked. "Before this week, I mean."

"This past Christmas. She threw a big holiday party. I went with Evan."

"How was she?"

"Happy. Buoyant. She was talking about maybe taking early retirement then. But she was still exploring the idea."

"Had she met him yet? Judson Cooper?"

"No, that was kind of a whirlwind thing. This past spring. One of the ocean conservation groups was holding a fundraiser at the hotel. She was helping out, and she and Judson hit it off. The day after the event, he marched in with flowers and asked her to lunch. He had reservations at this five-star French place he'd heard about. Desiree insisted on hot dogs in the park. A real New York experience. And that was it. They've been together ever since."

"Sounds like they're a good pair," Ben said.

"When they're together, they're like a couple of naughty kids cutting school. The past few months, they've been all over the world and they've had a blast."

"But she doesn't get along with his family?"

"Apparently not. Which floored me. Desiree thinks his kids don't like her. But Judd said they just didn't like him dating, period. He said they didn't want him squandering their inheritance. But he was convinced they were coming around. On the boat trip yesterday, he told us they'd be in Coral Cay today. He and Desiree were thrilled."

"But his kids weren't at the wedding?"

"No, you're right. With all the excitement, I didn't even realize that until you mentioned it earlier this evening."

"Anything else about the wedding that was off?"

"Well, the justice of the peace never showed, which was weird. And there was some kind of mix-up with Desiree's limo. So she was late."

"Who booked the limo and the justice of the peace—do you know?"

"Judson handled both of them."

"So Desiree was late. What happened when she arrived?"

"That's when we realized that Judson was actually missing. Should we call his children? To let them know what happened?"

"Already done. They're on their way to Coral Cay."

"Now? You mean they weren't already here?"

"No, they definitely were not," Ben said matter-of-factly. "Did you ever talk with Judson about the wedding itself? About the location, maybe? What he was going to wear? The cake?"

"We've been talking about it all week," Kate said, puzzled.

"What, specifically, did he say? Not her, but him."

"Come to think of it, I don't think he and I ever discussed the wedding, exactly. Desiree and I did, though. Judson and I chatted about his foundation, and the bakery, and a couple of spots he wanted to visit while they were here in Coral Cay. Oh, and we talked about how to get more volunteers for that wildlife rehab facility he's involved in on the mainland. The one up the coast. And at one point he even asked me about Harper Duval's house. Why?"

"Well, I've talked to his kids—Liam and Sarah. And they said they'd been in touch with their dad fairly regularly over the past couple of weeks. Mostly by text. And while he never mentioned getting married, he did want to spend some family time together—just the three of them. That's why they were already on their way to Coral Cay when I called."

"Why didn't he tell them about marrying Desiree?" Kate asked, incredulous.

"Oh, it gets better," Ben said, exhaling, as Kate could hear the exhaustion in his voice. "The problem is, out of all the people I spoke with who've crossed paths with Judson Cooper this past week—including the folks at the resort—not one of them recalls him ever saying anything about a wedding."

Chapter 9

"*Corazón*, that's just *loco*," Maxi said, sliding a tray onto the low table on the front porch of Flowers Maximus.

Kate placed a box of freshly baked cinnamon rolls on the table and popped it open, as Maxi poured two steaming cups of dark Café Cubano.

Still in the cool of the morning, the grass was wet with dew. Out on the lawn, Oliver gave himself a thorough shake and bounded up the steps toward the cheery orange water bowl in the corner.

"I know," Kate said, ladling coconut cream into her coffee. "I keep trying to remember something—anything—Judson might have said specifically about their wedding. The problem is, I can't recall a blasted thing. But even if Ben's right about that, he's definitely drawing the wrong conclusion."

"Did you tell him that?" Maxi said, placing a warm cinnamon roll on her plate. "And did you bring anything for you-know-who?"

Oliver stretched into a downward dog, rolled over a few times, and ended up at Kate's feet. He looked up hopefully.

She nodded. "Yes to both questions," she added, opening a wax bag and removing what looked like a large flat roll with a thick swirl of filling. "My latest experiment—sausage swirl biscuits. A little extra protein for our rapidly growing boy," she explained, presenting it to the pup.

Oliver took the edible disc gently from her hand, settled himself by the table, and devoured his snack.

"That's only his second breakfast," Kate said, a sparkle of amusement in her amber eyes.

"Well, no wonder the poor boy's starving," Maxi said. "Someday, I'm gonna actually follow him around town and see just how many breakfasts that puppy eats."

Kate finished a bite of cinnamon roll. "I told Ben that Desiree is about as levelheaded and rational as they come. And I know he and his team are still searching for Judson, just to make sure he's OK. Although I can't help but feel Ben's looking at Desiree a little differently now."

"Like a suspect?" Maxi asked, spooning fluffy coconut cream into her cup.

"More like the reason Judson left Coral Cay. Ben's too much of a gentleman to say it, but I'm afraid he thinks the ceremony was all Desiree's doing. And that when Judson found out about it, he dumped her and left town."

"*Ay*, this is beginning to sound like one of *mi mami*'s telenovelas. So what do we do?"

"Well, Ben and his team are definitely looking for Judson. He was crystal clear on that point."

"But . . ." Maxi interjected.

"But I don't know how much information they're

going to share with Desiree. Or how seriously they're taking her. And there's something that bothers me."

"Does it have something to do with that weird boat you guys saw at the preserve?"

"No, but that's a good point. And I think that bothered Ben, too."

"Yeah, trust me he's already looking into that," Maxi said. "Smugglers have been a problem here before. It kinda comes with the territory when you live in a place that was founded by pirates. So what's the part that's bugging you?"

"When we were on the boat, Judson went out of his way to tell us that his kids were coming to Coral Cay on Saturday. The implication was they were coming to the wedding, and he and Desiree were over the moon. But when Ben called them last night, Liam and Sarah said they were just getting ready to leave. They weren't even here yet."

"That is weird," Maxi agreed. "So was Judson fibbing to his lady, or were the kids lying to Daddy?"

"No idea. If they checked in to a different resort under another name, we'd never know."

"Or if they have their own boat," Maxi interjected.

"Exactly! Oh geez, what about Lola Montgomery?"

"You think Desiree's groom rekindled the old flame?"

"I don't think so," Kate said slowly, setting down her cup. "Besides, we saw Lola at the restaurant after Ben thinks Judd left Coral Cay. But it would be nice to know if she's here now."

"Or if she sailed off into the sunset?"

"I really hope not," Kate said, sighing. "That would kill Desiree."

"So maybe we nose around without telling her," Maxi said, setting her cup on the table. "Or Ben."

"I hate to do that," Kate said, glancing down to see that Oliver, suddenly silent, had fallen asleep right where he'd dropped next to the table. "But I think you're right. Desiree came here in part because of me. Because of what I told her about Coral Cay. Now Judson's missing, the wedding's off, and the police are doubting if there was even going to be a wedding in the first place. I owe it to her to try and figure out what's going on."

"Uh-oh, you got that look in your eye," Maxi said, re-filling Kate's cup and then topping off her own. "The one you get when you have an idea."

"If I disappeared tomorrow, who would you talk to first?"

"Besides that cute UPS guy? Sam. *Mi padrino* may not talk much, but he knows stuff."

"Exactly. Because even if you're looking to exit a re-lationship, you're not going to leave your business part-ner in the dark."

"So Miss Zoey West is first on our list. Let's see what Judson told her about his travel plans for this week."

Kate nodded. "If we're really lucky, maybe she'll also know something about that cigarette boat."

Chapter 10

As the sun climbed into the sky, Kate glanced at the big industrial clock on the wall: 11:22. The lemon drop cookies for the resort order were out of the ovens and cooling. They'd get a light dusting of powdered sugar and be ready to go. She and Maxi were making that delivery right after lunch. And checking on Desiree, if they hadn't heard from her before then.

Later this afternoon, she planned to fire up the ovens and get the store restocked for Monday morning. But this was a good time for a break. And, fortified with a cup of coffee, maybe a good time to reach Zoey West.

Sam Hepplewhite was taking a rare day off. Which is why she was surprised when the senior partner of the Cookie House ambled in the back door.

But his outfit was the real revelation. The man normally favored a small, high-mileage collection of clean, serviceable jeans and T-shirts with a battered pair of running shoes. This morning, he was sporting a brand-new navy and white rugby jersey, pressed khakis, and boat shoes that looked like they'd never been out of the box. Along with a jaunty white captain's cap.

"Needed the cooler," he explained, as he hoisted it onto a kitchen chair. Then he buried his face in the refrigerator, whistling as he gathered supplies.

"Those friends of yours have a nice wedding?"

"There were a few hiccups. The groom didn't show."

Sam shook his head. "Nothing puts a crimp in a wedding like a case of cold feet."

As happy as he was, Kate didn't want to dampen his mood with the full story of Desiree and Judd—and Judd's possible abduction.

She watched as Sam carefully assembled four sandwiches with mayonnaise, Gouda, fresh tomatoes, and a healthy dash of salt on thick slices of his famous crusty sourdough—expertly wrapping each in wax paper. Whistling, he packed a couple of tumblers and a thermos of iced tea into the cooler, gently placed the sandwiches on top, added a few small zipper bags of ice, and sealed the lid. But the real tell was when he went to the cooling rack and loaded up a large bakery box with a dozen peanut butter chocolate chip cookies.

"Don't stay too long," Sam cautioned, as he headed out the back door. "Comin' in early tomorrow. We'll catch up then."

And with that, he was gone.

Usually, when Sam strolled the beach on Sundays, he took a metal detector. This time, Kate suspected, he was taking a date. Effie the librarian?

She suppressed a smile.

Finishing the last of her coffee in one swallow, she slid open the counter drawer by the phone, carefully removing a sheet of paper. After she and Maxi met this morning at the flower shop, she'd used her friend's computer to visit Judson Cooper's website and copy down the contact numbers for him and Zoey.

Someday, Kate was sure, Coral Cay would have cell phone service blanketing downtown, and locals wouldn't be limited to landlines and desktops. But she was willing to bet two dozen of her best chocolate chip cookies that wouldn't be anytime soon.

After being tied to her cell for eight years in Manhattan, she wouldn't have it any other way.

Kate dialed Judson's phone number and crossed her fingers. If he'd been avoiding Desiree, maybe he'd answer a call from someone else. Instead, it went straight to voice mail. She hung up.

Next she tried Zoey's office number. Like Judson's phone, it didn't even ring before voice mail clicked in. She tried the cell.

"This is Zoey. Leave a message, I'll call you back." Friendly, but no-nonsense.

For a split second, Kate hesitated. "Hi, Zoey, this is Kate McGuire on Coral Cay. I'm a friend of Desiree's. When you get this, just give me a quick call." She recited the bakery number twice.

Kate replaced the old handset into its wall cradle, as her thoughts gathered steam. Judd was last seen boarding his boat Friday night. Then he'd vanished. Almost two days later, they were getting nowhere fast.

Chapter 11

As Maxi's red Jeep hugged the sharp curve, Kate looked out at the beach—and the glassy blue water beyond—through her open window. Just after noon, the sun was bright and hot.

She could see small children chasing one another across the sand—their squeals mingling with the screech of seagulls overhead. On the breeze, the late-summer heat released the scent of jasmine, which grew wild all over the island.

Her friend Rosie Armand had blithely dubbed it "a typical Coral Cay September." For Kate—who'd only arrived on the island a few months ago—it was glorious.

Eleven large white boxes of lemon drop cookies were carefully strapped into the back seat. And two very large, very ornate arrangements of bright yellow roses and orange lilies were tightly secured in the Jeep's cargo hold.

"So you didn't hear anything from Desiree at all this morning?" Maxi asked incredulously.

"Not a peep. I called a couple of times. And even left

a message once. But nothing. I don't want to crowd her. But after last night, I'm worried."

"So we swing by and say *hola*. Maybe take her for lunch to make sure she's remembering to eat. And we can stay to help her make phone calls or whatever. Then we bundle her off to my place for a good dinner."

Kate smiled. "One of the boxes in the back seat is for Desiree. I know her. When she gets focused on a project, she forgets everything else. Including food. But a cookie . . ."

"Ay, you can always nibble on a cookie," her friend finished. "No matter what you're doing."

"Exactly." Kate nodded. "Such a beautiful day. In such a beautiful place. It's hard to believe that something so awful happened here."

"Well, to be fair, we don't know that it did," Maxi countered, turning the wheel slowly into the entrance of the Tradewinds resort. "Maybe ol' Judson is just holed up somewhere feeling like a sorrowful slug and trying to figure out how to crawl back and make amends."

"Let me guess, you'd suggest flowers."

"With a giant side of jewelry. Big sparkly diamonds."

"Because they symbolize love?"

"Because they hold their resale value. I'd tell your friend Desiree to take the loot and kick Boyfriend to the curb. No call, no note? Not even a text saying 'It's over—buh-bye'? That's just thoughtless. And you don't want to marry thoughtless."

Kate couldn't help grinning. "And Peter's never done anything thoughtless?"

"Absentminded, plenty. Ask me how long it took him to get around to cleaning out our garage this summer. But thoughtless?" She shook her glossy black pageboy. "Nope."

As they pulled up to the service entrance behind the

kitchen of the Tradewinds, Kate recognized one of the sous-chefs taking a smoke break and waved.

He raised a hand in greeting as he flicked ashes into a paper cup.

"Don't worry, *Corazón*. We'll do our delivery super quick, then we can go check on Desiree."

"Sounds like a plan," Kate said, unbuckling her seatbelt as Maxi shifted into park. "And hopefully, with the three of us pitching in, we can help Ben find Judson Cooper."

* * *

Cradling the box of cookies in one arm, Kate knocked on the door of Desiree's bungalow. From within, she was relieved to hear her friend's voice. She sounded animated, almost upbeat.

The door opened, and Desiree's face lit up. A cell phone in one hand, she ushered them in, never pausing her conversation.

"Exactly!" she said into the phone. "That's exactly what I mean. So just give me a jingle if you hear anything, Julio."

Desiree clicked off the call and placed the phone carefully on the coffee table.

"Any news yet?" Kate asked, as she put the bakery box next to it.

Her friend shook her head and sank onto the small floral sofa. "Not a blasted thing. "That cop friend of yours—the detective? He won't tell me anything."

"Ben? That's probably because he doesn't know anything yet. When he does, he'll share what he's found. Ben's a good guy."

"Well, he may be a good guy, but he thinks I'm a crazy woman. If Judd had disappeared on his way to his office or the bank, they'd take it seriously. But because he vanished the night before our wedding, it's like 'Oh, it's just cold feet.' Or, 'Tee-hee, a runaway groom!' Kate, he's missing! Believe me, if that man had wanted to call off our wedding, he'd have done it. He wouldn't just take off."

Kate smiled. "I've seen the two of you together—I know that. And I promise you, no one on this island is laughing about anything. Least of all Ben. I talked with him right after this happened. He's taking it very seriously."

Even if he's wrong about why Judd's gone, Kate thought.

"Well, I'm not helpless either," Desiree said brightly. "I've phoned everyone I can think of who might know anything. That's what this is," she said, hefting a heavy spiral notebook. "Everyone he might have called recently. Anyone he might have reached out to while we were here—or planned to contact over the next few weeks."

"You're calling them all?" Kate asked, astonished.

"I've *called* them all," Desiree corrected. "Some of them twice. It's the weekend, and I don't have cell numbers for everyone, so some I've heard back from and others I haven't."

An image of Lola Montgomery's face flashed through Kate's mind. She was pretty sure that was one number Desiree hadn't dialed.

"But I'm keeping after them," her friend continued. "Any little bit of information will help. Anything. Even if all we get is a few tidbits, we can string them together. That's what that is."

She gestured to a large corkboard on the wall that Maxi was studying. With photos, bits of notes, a postcard from the resort, pieces of maps. Including—thumbtacked off to one side—a line drawing of a cigarette boat.

At the very top, Desiree had thumbtacked separate

photos of herself and Judd, connecting the two pushpins with a piece of orange yarn.

"What is this?" Kate asked, fascinated.

"That's everything we know right now. Every single thing I can think of that happened in the days before Judd disappeared. Where we were, what we were doing, what we saw, what we were planning. If we find connections, we connect them on the board with yarn. I know I don't have much right now, but . . ."

Kate and Maxi exchanged a quick, worried look.

Kate joined her friend on the sofa. "Desiree, maybe it would do you some good to get out of here for a few minutes. We could walk down the beach and get a sandwich. Or even bring it back here."

"I can't leave," she said, looking distraught. "What if they call?"

"They?"

"The people who took Judd. He's quite wealthy, thanks to those inventions of his. So it's got to be a kidnapping. Sooner or later, there's going to be a ransom demand."

"I can stay here," Maxi volunteered. "I'll answer the phone and take messages."

Desiree shook her head resolutely. "No. No. Absolutely not. Judd would never desert me, and I won't abandon him. Besides, if they call here, they'll expect to talk to me. I'm not going to blow any chance of getting him back because I'm skipping down the beach."

"When's the last time you slept?" Kate asked, concerned.

"I caught a few hours last night," her friend said defensively.

"Have you eaten?" Maxi asked.

"They have great room service here," Desiree replied.

"And you ordered what?" Kate pressed.

Desiree waved her arm toward the kitchenette, where a teapot, crumpled cloth napkin, and half-filled china cup rested on a room service tray.

"Did you ever get that shower you wanted last night?"

Desiree shook her head sadly. "Kate, he's missing," she said softly. "Not run out. Not run away. Missing."

"I know," Kate said, wrapping her arm around Desiree's shoulders. "You are doing everything you can to find him. And we're here to help. But you also have to take care of yourself, so you can keep going and keep searching for him. Now why don't you duck in and take that shower and maybe catch a little nap. We'll man the phones. And if it's important, we'll come get you. After that, we can order up some of that room service and strategize about what to do next. And that includes having a little chat with our friend Ben."

"It's kinda like the chalkboard thing Harp dragged in when we were trying to figure out who killed Stewart Lord," Maxi said, running her finger across the lone piece of orange yarn.

"Yes, that's what I thought," Kate said, as they heard the shower start up in the bungalow bathroom. "But there are a couple of people and places missing."

"Lola Montgomery," Maxi said quietly.

"And Judson's kids, Sarah and Liam. Ben said they'd been in touch fairly regularly lately, mostly by text."

"Do we add to this?" Maxi asked, pointing a thumb at the board.

"I think we have to. This is how Desiree wants to attack it. So I think she'll appreciate it."

Maxi wrinkled her nose. "The kids, maybe. But I don't think she's gonna welcome seeing his ex on the board."

"Right now, she just wants to find him. I don't think she cares where he is or who he's with. And if we genuinely want to help, we have to be honest and share everything. It's not like she didn't see Lola Montgomery at that restaurant, too."

Maxi wrote neatly for a minute on a small pad she'd pulled from her purse. Then she grabbed a couple of pushpins from the table and added two more small bits of paper: one with LIAM & SARAH, the other with LOLA MONTGOMERY.

"That cigarette boat reminds me, I want to talk to Sunny," Kate said, snapping her fingers.

"That's a great idea! If someone was sneaking something in or out of that cove, she or Iris might have noticed something."

Maxi penned SUNNY & IRIS on a small scrap of paper and tacked it just below the cigarette boat. "While we're at it, I was wondering about the guy who drove Judson out to his boat Friday night."

"What do you mean?" Kate asked.

"Well, when he travels for work, *mi amor* is always taking ride-shares or shuttles. And half the time, by the end of the ride, he knows the driver's life story. The thing is, if you put two guys together in a tiny space for five minutes, they're gonna talk. Maybe just about sports or cars. But they'll talk about something. So what did this guy talk about with Judson Cooper? 'Cause they woulda been on that golf cart for at least fifteen minutes. And that driver had to be one of the last people to see our groom before he disappeared."

"Maxi, that's brilliant."

Maxi doodled a quick line drawing of a golf cart and stuck it to the board.

"Since the guy works for the resort, we might even be able to talk with him today, if he's working," Kate added, excitedly.

"Good, 'cause I'd like to see a little more yarn on that

board. Right now, we've got a lot of little stuff, but no connections."

A hard rap on the door startled them both.

"You don't think Desiree ordered room service and forgot, do you?" Maxi whispered.

"I don't think so," Kate said softly, peeking out the peephole. "It's a girl."

"Maybe she's lost," Maxi hissed. "All these little bungalows look alike."

Kate opened the door. Without the distortion of the peephole lens, she realized their visitor wasn't a teenager, but an adult woman—probably a few years older than herself.

"You're not Desiree," the woman said, smiling.

"I'm a friend—Kate McGuire."

"Ah, you left a message on my cell. Nice to meet you. I'm Zoey. Zoey West."

"Would you like to come in? Desiree's been up pretty much since it happened, so she's catching a little break."

"I can imagine. Hurricane Judson strikes again," Zoey said, stepping inside and scanning the room. Pale, slim, and barely five feet tall, she was clad in a worn tan skirt with a simple white tee. Thick tawny curls were pulled back into a messy bun, set off with cat-eye framed glasses in emerald green. No trace of makeup, just a sprinkle of freckles across her fair-skinned nose.

If she hadn't known better, Kate would have taken her for a struggling grad student. Not the CFO of an uber-successful eco-tech company.

"I'll make us some coffee," Maxi said, quickly grabbing the corkboard and spiriting it off to the kitchenette.

"Did Desiree know you were coming?" Kate asked lightly.

"No. I thought she might need a little support. This

part's never easy. And I really like Desiree. She's cool. Not like some of the others. But if anyone asks, I'm really here to check in with the marine rehab facility up the coast," she said.

Kate neatened up the coffee table, and snagged Desiree's notebook, tucking it carefully into a credenza out of sight. She popped open the bakery box and moved it closer to Zoey.

"Lemon drop cookies. Fresh from the bakery this afternoon."

"I'm starved," Zoey confessed. "I drove straight over from Miami when I heard. After the police called." She carefully scooped a cookie out of the box, took a bite, and smiled. "Hey, these are really good. Lemony. Sweet. And buttery. I might have to hit that bakery before I blow town."

"It's the Cookie House. Just at the end of Main Street. Come by anytime."

"Your place?"

"Partly mine. Sam Hepplewhite is the founder and senior partner."

"Like me and Judd. Well, if you made these, you've got skills." She lifted two more cookies from the box. "When you said lemon drop, I was thinking of those little hard candies."

"They're drop cookies. Meaning you don't roll out the dough and use a cookie cutter. You just push the dough off of a spoon onto the cookie sheet."

"Sink or swim, baby," Zoey said, smiling.

"Pretty much. Although, with a little practice, they all come out roughly the same size and shape."

"Man, *mine* wouldn't. Can't cook or bake to save my life. I'm living on takeout."

"Baker's secret: That's what the powdered sugar is for. Adds sweetness and covers a multitude of sins."

Zoey beamed. "You're OK, Cookie Lady. And these things," she said, waving a lemon drop cookie, "are amazing."

"*Sí*, but they taste even better with a little coffee," Maxi said, appearing as if by magic with a tray of cups and saucers. "Nice and strong," she said, setting it on the table.

"This is Maxi Más-Buchanan," Kate said.

Maxi smiled and placed a cup of hot, dark coffee in front of Zoey, along with a little pitcher of creamer and a box of sugar packets. Kate took the remaining two cups and put them in front of Maxi and herself.

"Another friend of Desiree's?" Zoey asked.

Maxi nodded.

Zoey grinned. "I didn't know she had so many friends here," she said, shrugging. "If I had, I probably could have saved myself the trip. I just wanted her to know she wasn't alone. She's not the first. And she probably won't be the last."

"What do you mean?" Maxi asked, snagging a cookie.

"Don't get me wrong," Zoey said. "I love Judd. He's a great guy. And super bright—like, genius-level bright. But when it comes to women, let's just say he has the emotional maturity of a sixteen-year-old boy."

"How so?" Kate asked.

"Well, it's pretty much the same script every time. Honestly, when it comes to that man's love life, I feel like I'm watching the same movie over and over again. He meets someone. He decides he really likes her, and goes all out. Whirlwind courtship—no brakes. Flowers. Notes. Dinners at the best places. Cool vacations. Plans for the future—*their* future. His whole and undivided attention, like a spotlight. And it's not fake. I think he's genuinely convinced that each one is, like, The One. Then, just as suddenly, he's bored and he's done. Never looks back. In anyone else, I'd say it was cruel, but Judd doesn't have a cruel bone in his body. He honestly believes what he's saying to these women when he says it. He just, I don't know, changes his mind."

"What happens then?" Kate asked, dreading the answer.

"Nothing, really. He stops taking their calls. A lot of times, he disappears for a while. Or the breakup coincides with a long overseas trip for work. South China Sea. Great Barrier Reef. Arctic Circle. Whatever. Meanwhile, I'm in the Miami office getting frantic phone calls from the latest broken heart. 'Where is he? Why isn't he calling? When's he coming back? Should she book their tickets to Bora Bora?'" Zoey shook her head. "It's brutal."

Kate and Maxi exchanged worried glances.

"Any idea where he is now?" Kate asked quietly.

Zoey shook her head. "All I know is he said he needed a break. I got the impression he was taking the boat—the *Starfish*. But I don't know if he actually said that, or if I was just kinda filling in the blanks. This time, I think he knew better than to tell me where he was headed. 'Cause I'd have told Desiree in a minute. And booked her travel arrangements."

"So he's not scheduled to be anywhere for work right now? No big overseas projects?"

"Not that I know of. I mean, there are always last-minute emergencies. That's a big part of the job. Disaster mitigation. Accident cleanup. But we always discuss those projects first. There's a ton of planning that goes into it, even with a last-minute job. And there's absolutely nothing like that on the books right now. Why?"

Kate stopped, weighing her words. She looked at Maxi, who nodded encouragingly.

"Did you know that Judd and Desiree were getting married Saturday?" Kate asked finally.

Zoey burst out laughing.

She noticed Kate and Maxi's stunned looks and quickly stopped. "OMG, you're serious!" she said. "No way. I guarantee you that man is allergic to commitment. He may be great at planning a 'someday life' together," she said, using air quotes. "But there's no way he'd actually do something as real as booking a wedding. Uh-uh."

"This time, he did," Kate said softly.

"What happened?" Zoey asked, eyes wide.

"He didn't show up," Maxi said.

"Man, that's a new low, even for him. When the cops mentioned something about a wedding, I just thought they got their wires crossed. So Desiree thought he was going to marry her? That poor lady. No wonder she's so upset."

Zoey stopped suddenly, eyes glued to a spot on the bamboo floor. She shifted in her seat, adjusting her skirt. Then shifted again. Her mouth clamped shut, she looked quickly at Kate and Maxi, then down at her coffee cup.

"What's wrong?" Maxi asked.

"What makes you think something's wrong?" Zoey asked.

"*Mis niños* do the same thing when there's something they need to tell me. So what is it?"

"Don't get me wrong, I know how exasperating Judd is. I've seen what that behavior can do to accomplished, confident women. But he's never actually promised marriage. Or anything as concrete as a wedding. Could she have, I don't know, misunderstood?"

Zoey looked up and Kate could see the turmoil on her face.

Behind them, a door opened and Desiree appeared.

She was clad in a turquoise tunic and jeans, her short sandy hair still damp from the shower. But her face looked less drawn, more tranquil.

"Zoey! Oh honey, it's so good to see you! How are you?" she said, folding her unexpected visitor in a hug.

"I'm fine," Zoey said, almost embarrassed. "I'm on my way up to the wildlife rehab center. But I wanted to stop off and see how you were doing. See if you needed anything."

"I'm really glad you're here," Desiree said, sinking into the sofa beside her. "I guess you've heard the news. Judd's been kidnapped."

Kate saw Zoey flinch. When Desiree first walked in, she'd been worried that her friend might have heard Zoey's theory on Judson Cooper's disappearance. Now it was obvious she hadn't.

"If you can take a couple of minutes to talk with the local detectives while you're here, that would really help," Desiree continued, almost without taking a breath.

Zoey looked first at Kate, then at Maxi. The proverbial deer caught in the headlights, Kate thought.

"Well, I, of course," Zoey said finally, standing up. "I'll do anything I can. You know I will. I, um, have to make some calls. For the company. But I booked in here. In fact, I'm just down the beach in number forty-eight. Maybe we could grab a bite later and compare notes?"

Kate could tell that Zoey West was mentally calculating the distance to the door in her mind—and couldn't get there fast enough. It was one thing to field frantic phone calls from Judson's heartbroken exes. From the miserable look on Zoey's face, Kate surmised it was quite another to witness the wreckage first hand. Especially if that girlfriend was still in the dark.

Desiree stood and gave her another hug. "I was so

sorry you couldn't make it to the wedding. But I can't tell you how much it means to have you here now. And Judd will be so grateful. All the people who care for him are working to bring him home."

Chapter 12

Just as the last of the customers trundled out of the Cookie House, Kate ducked into the kitchen to refill some very empty bakery cases. A lot of the locals visited on Monday. Between weekend cookouts, beach picnics, and Sunday evening suppers, a lot of homes were out of baked goods by Monday morning. Plus everyone was packing sandwiches and cookies into school lunches.

Good to his word, Sam had come in at four a.m., and between the two of them, they had restocked the cases by the time the store opened at eight.

Still, her mind kept wandering back to Desiree and Judson. She, Maxi, and Desiree spent all of Sunday afternoon and most of the evening sharing every detail they could think of and adding it to Desiree's corkboard. A lot of tantalizing bits of information. But, as Maxi summarized, "No yarn yet."

Now they were running down those leads.

Maxi was taking Sunny's early morning yoga class

on the beach—dubbed "stretch and starch" by the locals
for the spread of fresh rolls, hot tea, and local jams she
provided after the workout. Along with dropping off a
batch of rolls from the Cookie House, Maxi was also
planning to chat with Sunny about what—if anything—
she or her mom might have noticed lately in the coves
on that side of the island.

The golf-cart driver turned out to be a local high
schooler—Mike Case—who worked at the resort a few
afternoons a week and sometimes on weekends. He
wouldn't be back at Palm Isle again until Wednesday.
But Kate had managed to get his cell number from one
of her contacts in guest services. She just hoped the teen
might be able to shed some light on what was going
through Judson Cooper's mind in the hours before his
wedding.

She called Jack Scanlon's office, and a crisp recep-
tionist relayed the news that the clinic was closed to pa-
tients until Wednesday morning. The vet was attending
a symposium in Miami.

Earlier, she'd also left a message for Ben. But the detective had been strangely silent.

Just busy, Kate reasoned. Besides, with zero evidence
of foul play, he couldn't exactly make the case a high
priority—celebrity or not. Ben had promised he'd touch
base with Judson Cooper, and Kate knew the detective
was a man of his word.

But what if Judson Cooper wasn't? What if the eco-
warrior with a heart of gold was also as big a jerk as Zoey
had indicated?

Could practical, levelheaded Desiree have fallen for
him anyway? She certainly wouldn't be the first woman
to make that mistake, Kate thought, absentmindedly
chewing on an orange madeleine.

It was something Kate had almost done herself. Up

until four months ago, she'd been set to marry Evan Thorpe, scion of the Thorpe family and—it turned out—a pretty big louse in his own right. But he'd also been smart, charming, fun, and devilishly good-looking. She'd fallen hard. Luckily, she'd realized the truth in time—exactly one month before their wedding. But maybe Desiree hadn't been so lucky.

Suddenly, she heard heavy footsteps and a clatter on the front porch. Customers.

Kate brushed a few scant cookie crumbs from her pristine navy-and-white-striped apron, just as a man's voice called, "Just leave it on the bench—it'll be fine. It's not like anyone around here even knows what to do with it."

The bakery door banged open just as she heard another loud clatter. She looked up to see two men. The first, in perfectly pressed linen slacks, short-sleeved aqua dress shirt, and aviator sunglasses, carried a clipboard. The second, sweaty and pale, had gone for a rumpled olive green T-shirt and wrinkled tan cargo shorts. Clearly worried, he kept glancing back at the porch.

The first man pushed the sunglasses onto his forehead as he swiveled to take in every detail of the immaculate shop. "If you built this place on a set, no one would believe it. It's like the eighteen-nineties meets Disney World."

"Yeah, well, Florida or not, I still say it's not supposed to be this hot in September," said his companion, who sported a beat-up Mets cap. "Got to be global warming. I don't ever remember it being like this before." He cast another quick look to the porch. "You sure the equipment's gonna be OK out there? If I lose anything, it comes outta my pay."

"Don't worry, we'll be fine," his friend assured him.

"I just wanna get something to hold me over until lunch. What do you want? My treat."

"How about some cold lemonade while you're waiting?" Kate asked. "On the house."

"Oh yeah," said Mets cap in a broad Brooklyn accent. "You got ice? I'd kill for some ice."

"I'm on it," Kate said as she ducked into the kitchen.

She returned with two tall paper cups full to the brim with lemonade and ice, wrapped a paper napkin around each, and passed them across the counter.

The man in the ball cap chugged half of his without pausing. "Lady, you saved my life," he said when he finally came up for air.

The other man sipped his more slowly. As his eyes roamed the store, she had the impression that he was a human perpetual-motion machine. She also noticed that he seemed to be taking mental inventory of the bakery. And her. But she also couldn't get over the feeling that he looked vaguely familiar. She searched her brain. Her past restaurant career? Culinary school? Friend of a friend in New York?

"What part of Brooklyn are you from?" she asked the man in the Mets cap.

"Bushwick," he said, removing his hat and wiping his red face with the napkin. "Born and raised. And that was before it was all hipsters and handmade pickles. Just your average working-class neighborhood. You from the city?"

"Manhattan," she said, returning his broad smile. "Just landed here this summer. One trick I learned from the locals—when it's this hot, you only go out in the mornings and the evenings. At least, as much as you can. And I'm Kate McGuire, by the way."

"Howard Nichols," he replied. "Howie. And this is Ken, obviously. I really wish we could stick to mornings and evenings," he added, pausing to polish off the last of his drink and pop the empty cup on the counter. "But we're scouting locations. And we don't have a lot of time as it is."

He stole another glance at the porch.

Kate concentrated for a moment, then reached into the bakery case with a piece of wax paper and retrieved a chocolate crinkle cookie, freshly dusted with powdered sugar and still slightly warm from the oven. She presented it to Howie.

She then studied Ken, who was staring intently into the bakery case, like a hummingbird paused in mid-flight. She plucked a sugar cookie out of its tray and handed it across the counter.

"Oh geez, this is the best thing I've had since I've been here," Howie said, making short work of the cookie. "My mom used to make these things. How did you know?"

She shrugged. "You bake enough cookies, you get a feeling for what people like."

His friend took a nibble. Then a bigger bite. Closing his eyes to savor the cookie, he'd gone silent—and Kate got the impression that might be a very rare occurrence.

"I've never had a sugar cookie this light before," Ken said. "Buttery, too. My aunt Kay used to bake them for me special. And hers were good. Really good. But nothing like this. Let's just say you needed a lot of milk to get hers down."

"I'm a pastry chef," Kate explained, smiling. "I took a degree in pastry arts at the CIA. Then spent the last eight years working in restaurants and hotels all over New York. Most recently at Soleil."

"Oh man, I loved that place," Ken said, as he brushed a hand through his sun-streaked hair. "I used to eat there all the time when I was in town. Once a week at least. Came back from shooting in Curaçao, and it was closed.

Just gone. What happened? Because the food was spectacular, and the place was always packed."

"The owner was embezzling," Kate said, shaking her head. Could that be where she'd seen Ken before? At Soleil? "Looted the place and left town. Owed everyone—including the staff."

Ken pointed to a sign on the wall. "Ask about our cookie classes," he said. "What's that all about?"

"Something new we've started. Evening classes in the basics of cookie baking. It can be a series of classes, where we cover a different cookie in each class—along with some of the techniques and tools. Or a one-off, where we bake up a couple of different kinds, and I share some of the secrets. It's a lot of fun. Plus, you get to eat your homework."

"The classes, I guess they're here?" he asked.

"Most of the time. Although I've held a couple at the resorts. And, if the kitchen can accommodate it, I've done a few in people's homes, too. Mostly birthday parties, baby showers, bachelorette parties, that kind of thing."

The two men exchanged glances, and Ken snapped his fingers. "This would be perfect, Howie. Perfect! We could do it at the house. That kitchen is huge. And if the segment catches fire, we could make it a regular thing."

But Kate had disappeared into the back room. She returned half a minute later, with a large pitcher of lemonade and refilled their cups.

"You both want to take a cookie class?" she asked.

"Not us, our house guests," Ken explained. He pulled out his wallet, extracted a business card, and handed it across the counter. "I'm Ken Salazar. I produce *Last Resort*. We're shooting on the island. And our guests like to frequent local businesses, volunteer with nearby charities, take part in the neighborhood activities. You know, become part of the community while they're here."

Ken Salazar! *That's* where she knew him. Salazar hosted and produced a string of super-popular reality shows. While she'd never actually seen any of them, the man was a fixture on the talk-show circuit. No matter the time of day, Salazar—armed with juicy tidbits and quotable quips—chatted amiably with hosts, telling stories and relentlessly promoting whichever one of his top-rated offerings was currently on the air.

Kate may not have been a fan of his programs, but she had to admire his work ethic. And the skill with which he marketed his product.

"The reality show? You guys are renting Harper Duval's old place."

"Big house on the bluff overlooking the ocean? Yeah, nice digs. But I hate the term 'reality show.' Or 'reality TV.' It sounds contrived. Like it's all about stunts and ratings. This series shows off the beauty of some of the world's best, most exclusive resort communities. All through the eyes of a handful of newcomers who are sharing a house for the season. More of a documentary travelogue with a big helping of sociology."

Was it Kate's imagination or did Howie roll his eyes?

"Sociology?" she asked.

"Well, yes," Ken enthused. "Along with vicariously traveling to some of the most beautiful vacation destinations, viewers also get an unvarnished, unscripted look at the interpersonal relationships of the people who are sharing the home."

Definitely reality TV, Kate concluded.

"And what we'd like to do—as sort of a test run—is arrange for you to come out and give one of your cookie classes for our house guests. We have twelve this year. And depending on how it goes, it could become a regular feature. We'd pay you, plus it would be great exposure for your bakery. Trust me, you can't buy publicity like this. And if you could, in our time slot it would cost a fortune."

"I'd have to talk it over with my partner. Sam Hepplewhite and I run the bakery together."

"Well, of course. Definitely talk it over. And let me know if either one of you has any questions. Do you both teach? Because we'd want you leading the classes. These cookies are phenomenal. And something tells me you'd get on great with our guests this season. They're a fun bunch. What do you want, Howie, a half dozen of each of the sugar cookies and the chocolate? And give us five dozen mixed—whatever you've got in the case—to take back to the house. Wait 'til they try these. Anyway, that card has my cell number. It's always on me, and it's always on."

"Ain't that the truth," Howie said ruefully.

"I know, right?" Ken returned. "Weird thing is, it hasn't rung all morning."

Chapter 13

"So are you going all Hollywood on us?" Maxi teased, as she centered a blue glass vase on a pedestal.

"I don't know," Kate admitted. "It's actually not a bad idea, publicity-wise. But I'm not wild about the idea of teaching on camera. Plus Sam's not exactly in favor of the Cookie House being featured on a reality show. And trust me, that's putting it mildly."

Kate reached down and gave Oliver a two-handed double-ear scratch. The pup stretched upward, closed his eyes, and she could have sworn he smiled.

"Yeah, I don't see *mi padrino* as a big reality TV fan. But I figured maybe it was the idea of going out to Harp's place that would bug you. You know, after everything that happened."

Kate remembered Maxi's reticence when the subject of Harper Duval's house came up at the last cookie class. She paused, weighing her words as she watched Oliver trot to the bright yellow water bowl in front of the French doors. The pup stopped, staring out into the backyard.

Kate wondered if he was thinking about what he had discovered there earlier this summer. She cast a quick glance in the same direction. "If you were in my place, what would you do?" she finally asked her friend.

"If they asked me to teach, I'd give those people a flower class like they'd never seen before. And I'd end every other sentence by saying 'like we do at my award-winning shop, Flowers Maximus, conveniently located off Main Street in Coral Cay.'"

Kate smiled, relieved. "You wouldn't feel weird about going out there?"

Maxi shook her head enthusiastically. "I've been out there. Every day for more than two weeks."

Kate's eyes went wide. For a split second, her mouth dropped open. Then she caught herself.

"When that reality TV bunch was getting that house ready for filming, Carl wasn't the only one they called," Maxi explained. "The yard was bad. A real mess. It took me more than two weeks with a crew of teenagers to whip it into shape. But now it looks really good. And your friend Ken has some big budget. He needed it done in a hurry, so he wrote me a pretty hefty check."

Kate shook her head. "That's why you got so quiet when Minette mentioned Harp's house the other night. I was afraid it was the subject that was bothering you. Harper Duval. Because he was a friend, and he was looking out for you. And because you knew Caroline."

"In the beginning, there was some of that," Maxi admitted. "When I took the job, I didn't tell anybody, except Peter. I didn't know if I could go through with it. Even that first day, I thought, if I can't do this, I'll just give back the money. No one will know. Ken can hire someone else. But when I got there, I saw what had been a super-pretty yard. And it just looked so sad. *Muy malo.* It needed me. And working out there? It helped."

"Putting old ghosts to rest?" Kate said quietly.

Maxi nodded. "I didn't know how anyone else would feel, either. So I didn't say anything."

Oliver trotted back, turned around several times and settled in at her feet.

"I totally get it," Kate said, reaching down and ruffling his fluffy curly back. "So your advice is to do the show?"

"Oh yeah. Look at it this way—it's a new client and another cookie class. You've done tons of them. And if it gets on TV and you guys get more customers, that's just the icing on a pretty sweet cake."

"So exactly how hefty was this hefty check?" Kate asked smiling.

"Let's just say I'm already planning a very nice weekend getaway with *mi amor*."

"Miami? Or New York?"

"Nope. I want one of those little bungalows on the beach with the champagne and the room service. But as far as anybody knows, we'll be a thousand miles away."

"That sounds absolutely perfect," Kate said, giving Oliver a gentle pat on the back.

"*Sí*, that's kinda what I thought. But first we help Desiree find Judson Cooper."

Maxi snipped a rose stem decisively and slipped it carefully into the large blue glass vase. She stepped back, studied it, turned the pedestal slightly, and reached for another flower.

"The weird thing is, Iris did notice something in the next cove," the florist said. "She saw a bunch of footprints leading from the water into the undergrowth and back again when she was walking on the beach Saturday."

"Did she tell Ben?"

"Nah, she didn't think anything of it. It was the weekend. And hikers and teenagers use that area a lot. For campouts and cookouts. As long as they clean up after, she doesn't care. And she didn't find anything but footprints and drag marks."

"Drag marks?" Kate tensed.

"She thought maybe they brought a cooler."

"When was it?" Kate asked, her jaw clenched. "Did she remember?"

"That's what was so strange," Maxi said, plucking another rose from the pile at her elbow before giving the end of the stem a quick snip. "It was Saturday morning. Super early. Like right after sunup. Iris likes to get up early and take a long walk along the beach while it's cool."

"It rained pretty hard late Friday afternoon," Kate said. "I remember it started not long after I got back to the bakery. So the prints couldn't have been from any earlier than, what, late that afternoon or early Saturday morning?"

"And Judson sailed off into the sunset Friday night," Maxi added.

"I know. The question is, where did he go? We don't know that yet. But we do know there was someone or something in the cove that was worrying him. So it would make sense for him to at least swing by there. I think we need to tell Ben."

"Speaking of telling Ben, what's Desiree heard from him?"

"Nothing," Kate replied. "And it's driving her crazy. She still doesn't want to leave the bungalow, in case someone calls. And at the same time, she wants to mount a search party. She's going out of her mind with worry. She's talking about offering a reward for information."

"*Ay*, Ben will hate that idea. It'll bring out every cuckoo between here and St. Augustine. Anybody who wants to make some easy money. Like those treasure hunters who were convinced I had pirate gold buried behind my shop. So maybe we phone him with Iris's tip," she said, clipping another stem. "It's not much, but it gives us an excuse to call him. And see if he might have something he can tell us. Like a trade."

"I'm thinking we do this in person," Kate reasoned.

"You mean because it's easier for him to dodge a phone call?"

"I was thinking that a goodwill offering of some cookies might smooth the path a little. Kyle was in the bakery right after lunch . . ."

"Let me guess, the peanut butter cookies?"

"Uh, yes."

Maxi grinned, shaking her head. "That boy's seriously hooked."

"Well, he also happened to mention that Ben's got the late shift tonight, and . . ."

"Right, and he just happened to drop that into the conversation?" Maxi prodded, grinning.

"OK, so I might have fished around a little," Kate admitted. "Anyway, I was thinking of stopping by the station after dinner with some cookies."

"Ooo, that's sneaky. I like it. It sounds like something *mi mami* would do. You want some company? After, we could go over and check on Desiree. If she won't leave for a home-cooked meal, maybe a home-cooked meal should come to her."

"You'd do that? Maxi, that would be wonderful."

"Hey, I might not be able to take her to a super-expensive resort restaurant. But tonight at my house we're having *picadillo*, fried plantains, and fluffy rice. Cuban comfort food. And I don't think even those fancy-schmancy resort chefs can top that."

Chapter 14

Kate was pushing the last rolling rack into the oven when she heard the phone. She flipped the latch and looked over to see Sam's head above the swinging kitchen doors.

"Young man calling. Name's Mike Case. Says he's returning your call."

Mentally, Kate slapped herself. "With everything else going on, I almost forgot," she said. "He drives the golf-cart shuttle at one of the resorts. He took Judson Cooper out to his boat the night before the wedding."

"Got the shop for now," Sam said. "Bit of a lull, anyway. Talk in the kitchen. Least you'll have some privacy."

Kate took a deep breath and lifted the yellow receiver from the old wall-mounted landline beside the sink. "Mike, this is Kate McGuire. Thanks for calling."

"Well, sure. I got your message this morning. Right before trig. But we're not supposed to have phones in class, so I couldn't really call you back 'til now. You run the Cookie House, right?"

"Exactly. And you drove a friend of mine at the resort Friday night. Judson Cooper? You took him to his boat."

"Oh yeah, the ocean guy. He was cool. Nice boat, too. Wouldn't mind having one like that someday."

"While you were driving out there—to the harbor—do you remember what the two of you talked about?"

"Well, let's see. Uh, he asked me if I lived on the island. And I told him yeah, my whole life, pretty much. 'Cause we moved here when I was, like, two. But my dad's from here. So I'm pretty much a native. And he asked how I liked it. And then we talked about the beach. Oh, and he asked me about the old Duval place."

"Harper Duval's house? The big mansion on the bluff?"

"Yeah. He knew all about it. Did you know they're filming a show out there?"

"Did Judson mention that? The show?"

"Nope. I told him. He just said that he was interested in it. 'Curious' was the word he used. Wanted to hear more about it, and what did I know?"

"What did you tell him?"

"Well, Keith told me they were filming out there. *Last Resort*. Keith's my lab partner in AP bio, so that's solid intel. Dr. Cooper hadn't seen the show, so I told him a little about it. Last season was pretty hot. Can't wait to see what they're going to do this year. And it'll be pretty cool to see Coral Cay on TV. Oh, and I told him about the Duvals. You know," he said, lowering his voice to a whisper, "what happened this summer."

"What did Dr. Cooper say?"

"He was real interested in the filming stuff. And I think he said he knew the guy who hosts it. You know, Ken Salazar."

"He knows Ken Salazar?" Kate said hopefully. It was the closest thing to a lead they'd uncovered.

"Or maybe he said he knew *of* him. But he'd definitely heard of him, I remember that. 'Cause I was kinda surprised. I mean, Dr. Cooper's older than my dad."

"So he wanted to learn more about the Duval place. He was curious about it. Did he mention why?"

"Nope. Well, he said it was important. Or could be important. In the future. And it was sensitive."

"Sensitive?"

"Yeah. I guess he meant the beach. Or the bluff or whatever. Then we talked about the turtles."

Following Mike's account of the conversation was beginning to make Kate dizzy. How did Ben Abrams do this day after day? Or maybe his witnesses were a little more organized than Mike Case?

"Turtles?" she asked.

"Yeah, there are these giant turtles—loggerheads. They swim all over the world then come back to the beaches where they're born to lay their eggs. And the babies hatch, and crawl out to sea, and the cycle starts all over again. I told him my dad must be part loggerhead. 'Cause when he and mom wanted to buy a house, they came back here to the same island where he was born."

"What did he say to that?"

"He laughed. And he said that would make him a pretty smart loggerhead. 'Cause this was a pretty nice island to come home to."

"Did he talk about where he was going next?"

"Oh yeah. His boat. The *Starfish*. Did you know he rehabbed it himself? Bought it for scrap at a salvage yard and completely stripped it and retrofitted the whole thing—stem to stern. Took him forever. But it is swe-et!"

Kate stopped and selected her words carefully. She didn't want to inadvertently influence Mike's recollection. But there was something specific she needed to know.

"Did Dr. Cooper mention a wedding or going to a wedding?"

Kate held her breath as Mike considered the question.

"Nope. Not that I remember."

Her heart sank. But she plodded onward. "Did he say what he was doing the next day? Or where he was going on the boat?"

"I didn't ask. And he didn't say. But he said something about leaving the past behind. No, I remember! He said it was 'finally time to leave the past in the past.'"

Chapter 15

"So Iris saw some signs of activity in the next cove early Saturday morning?" Ben Abrams summarized.

"*Sí*," Maxi confirmed. "From the shoreline up into the undergrowth and back. Lots of footprints and some drag marks."

Ben sighed, leaned forward in his office chair, and retrieved another chocolate crinkle cookie from the white bakery box at the front of his desk. He made short work of it. Two bites.

"For what it's worth, I already had Kyle Hardy check the cove Sunday morning," he said, after swallowing the last bit of cookie. "In light of whatever Cooper spotted there Friday. I wanted to cover all the bases. We're taking this seriously—I want you both to know that. And by seriously I mean man-hours, calls, and shoe leather following up on leads. But so far nothing—and I mean absolutely nothing—indicates any kind of foul play. It looks like the guy did what a lot of tourists do down here—left Coral Cay and went back to his own life. And, just between the three of us in this room?" He paused as both Kate and Maxi nodded. "No one was even aware that he was getting married," Ben continued. "Just the opposite. A few people who are close to him said he'd broken up with your friend Desiree, and she wasn't taking it so well."

"Zoey," Kate said, exhaling.

"No, not just her. Cooper's kids. The staff at the marine refuge he sponsors up the coast. Even some of the salts who hang out at the harbor. What nobody heard about was a wedding. Not the resort, not his family, not his coworkers. There was no car service hired to take Cooper or your friend Desiree to the beach that evening. And trust me, I called them all. Do you know we couldn't find a single justice of the peace in this end of the state who was booked to perform their wedding? And you don't want to know how long *that* took. I'm sorry, ladies. I know this isn't what you were expecting. But I can't find any evidence that there ever was going to be a wedding."

"Even if there was no wedding, that still doesn't explain Judd just vanishing," Kate said, leaning forward as she gripped the arms of the wooden office chair.

Ben paused, looked down at the cookie on the napkin on his desk, and sat back suddenly. "It really does," he said quietly. "If you've ended it with someone, and they can't or won't accept that, sometimes you have to make a clean break of it."

"Desiree's not crazy," Kate insisted.

"I'm not saying she is. And I'm not saying that Cooper didn't string her along or act like a jerk. I'm also not giving up on finding him and making contact. Because at this point, I'm curious. This happened on my island, on my watch, and I need to know that everyone involved is alright. But I don't think this is going to turn out the way you both hoped. And I think it might be time for your friend to face that, pack her bags, and go home."

"She wants to offer a reward," Kate said, sitting back and recrossing her legs. "For tips on Judson Cooper's disappearance or current whereabouts."

"Oh geez," Ben said, rubbing his face. "Any chance you could talk her out of that?"

Kate shrugged. "She's pretty determined. Ben, her gut is telling her that the man she loves—the man who loves her—is in trouble. I know you're meeting her at a bad time. But she's truly one of the most practical, levelheaded people I know."

Ben dropped both his forearms to his desk. Kate could see the exhaustion in his face. She was torn.

"Wouldn't some extra eyes looking out for Judson Cooper help?" Maxi asked. "I mean, someone will see him, phone it in, and this will all be *terminado*. Done."

Ben shook his head. "In a perfect world, sure. But this is the real world. Remember those yahoos who kept breaking into the backyard of your shop to dig for buried treasure? Picture that times a hundred. Because this time they don't even have to go anywhere or do anything. Just make a phone call."

"People will want to help," Kate reasoned. "Judson Cooper is a pretty popular guy. People look up to him."

Ben nodded in agreement. "They will. Most of 'em will be well-meaning. Well-meaning but mistaken. Never mind the days and weeks it will take us to sort through all the tips. And then there's the part she's refusing to consider. I haven't found any evidence yet that Judson Cooper is actually missing. If he's not, her little announcement could cause him some pretty big headaches. And it's not going to make her life any easier, either."

Maxi nodded. "I never thought of that."

"And you're right about one thing—a few extra pairs of eyes and ears could help us," Ben conceded. "But, trust me, a public appeal with a dollar figure attached isn't the way to get that. If you can't talk her out of it, can you at least convince her to hold off for a while? If I can make contact with the man and verify that he's really OK, I could at least put her mind at ease."

"I'll talk with her," Kate said. "I can promise you she doesn't care about anything except getting her guy back in one piece. But if you're saying this is counterproductive to finding him, I'll explain that."

"Thank you," Ben said. "I can't ask more than that. For the record, I don't think your friend's the least bit foolish. I just haven't been able to find any evidence that Judson Cooper didn't leave here voluntarily. He even settled his hotel bill."

Kate snapped her fingers. "If Desiree was planning to ambush Judd at the altar, she'd have hired a justice of the peace. That would be crucial. But she didn't. She left that and the limo to Judd. And, for some reason, he didn't follow through. Doesn't that prove that Desiree didn't plan the wedding on her own?"

Ben nodded. "Or she could have handed that part off to the resort, and they screwed up. But I see what you mean."

"Do you believe Judd was gaslighting Desiree?" Maxi asked, sitting forward in her chair.

"At this point," Ben admitted wearily, "I don't know what to think."

Chapter 16

"Maxi, this is the most delicious thing I've ever tasted," Desiree said, as she dug into her dinner enthusiastically.

"I can't believe you made enough for all three of us," Kate said, setting her plate and Maxi's on the bungalow's sunny dining table.

"More fun that way," Maxi said, trailing behind carrying two glasses of iced tea. "I knew you wouldn't have time to eat either. Besides, if I can eat two dinners, you can at least eat one."

"This is wonderful," Desiree said. "What do you call it?"

"*Picadillo*," Maxi said. "Sort of a cross between stew and sloppy Joe. And it's one of my favorites. This is *mi abuela*'s recipe. My father's mother. We serve it with white rice and fried plantains. With picadillo, the olives make it salty, the raisins add some sweet. And the rice just soaks up all the meaty flavor."

"I still say the plantains are the best part," Kate said between mouthfuls.

"That's what Miguelito says. The boy had three helpings."

"So, girls, anything new to add to our board?" Desiree asked.

"I talked with Mike Case," Kate said. "He's the one who drove Judson to the boat Friday evening. But your guy said not a peep about where he was going next."

"Well, if he wasn't planning to go anywhere, he wouldn't have," Desiree concluded.

"Did the boy offer up any clues?" Maxi asked.

"Well, there were a couple of odd things," Kate admitted. "Judd was asking about Harper Duval's place. Said he was curious about it. And I remember he mentioned it to me, too. Did he ever say anything about it to you?"

"That big house by the water? We went out there in the boat. A couple of days before we took you and Jack out. In fact, we anchored right offshore. Judd pointed up at the place. Said it was the habitat of a very rare species."

"Which one?" Maxi asked.

"That was the strange thing. He never got to tell me. We got an emergency alert on the radio, big storm moving in. We had to hustle back to the dock. I mentioned it later, and he laughed it off. Promised to tell me the whole story another time." Desiree looked down at her plate. "I should have pressed him," she said softly to no one in particular. "I should have made him tell me."

"You can't make a man do anything he doesn't want to," Maxi said. "Trust me on that one."

"Do you think that's it, though?" Desiree asked. "Do you think he discovered something out at that house, and that's why he was kidnapped?"

Kate shook her head. "Not necessarily, no. The other thing Mike mentioned is that Judd might have known Ken Salazar. Or known of him. Mike wasn't sure which."

"Why is that name familiar?" Desiree asked.

"The reality-show guy," Maxi supplied.

"That's it! I think he stayed at the Cascadian once or twice. Having some kind of work done on his condo. Seemed nice enough."

"Would Judson have met him then? At the hotel?" Kate asked.

Desiree shook her head. "This was a couple of years ago. But I guess it's possible Judd ran into him somewhere else. Judd does a lot of fundraising, so he knows a lot of high-profile people. But what does Ken Salazar have to do with any of this?"

"He's renting Harper Duval's house for the next few months," Maxi said.

"That can't be a coincidence," Desiree said, triumphantly. "What are the odds? We have to get in there. What if that's where they're holding him? Kate, he could actually be there!"

Kate and Maxi exchanged a look.

"We might actually have a way to do that," Kate admitted slowly. "To get into the house, I mean. But I don't think anyone's holding Judd there. Right now, they're filming a reality show there. Which means they have a house full of people."

"And cameras everywhere," Maxi added. "Plus oceans of wine to get people talking. So not a good place for secrets."

Desiree and Kate looked at her.

"I might have seen a few of his shows," Maxi said. "You know, while I was flipping channels to find something educational for *mis niños*."

"Still, the people at that house might know something," Desiree said. "And Judd might have stopped by there. Especially if he knows Ken Salazar. Or if he was worried about whatever rare species lives on that beach."

"He might have," Kate said. "Did Judd ever say anything about turtles?"

"Well, he's always concerned about the loggerheads," Desiree said, blotting the side of her mouth with a white linen napkin. "Poachers steal the eggs. And sometimes the babies. But the biggest threat is artificial light on their nesting grounds. Why?"

"It was one of the things that he and Mike talked about on the ride out to the harbor. I was wondering if it had to do with the cigarette boat in the cove."

"Judd is always doing battle with poachers. That's just who he is. He takes it personally."

"But when we saw the cigarette boat, it sounded like it was someone he'd encountered before," Kate pressed. "What was your first impression—did you think they were poachers?"

"Poachers or dumpers was what I thought at the time," Desiree said. "It could have been either one."

"Dumpers?" Maxi asked, her fork pausing above her plate.

"There are two kinds of criminals that really set Judd off. Poachers—who kill or steal what doesn't belong to them. And dumpers—the types who foul the land, air, or water. He believes that both of them are ruining the planet, and he'll go to war with either one. He actually keeps a running list of repeat offenders."

"I'd love to see that—and show it to Ben," Kate said.

"So would I," Desiree agreed, grimly. "Unfortunately, it's on the boat."

"We did manage to talk with Ben this evening," Kate said.

"Does he have any leads?" Desiree asked, her grip tightening around her fork.

Kate shook her head. "He's giving it everything he's got. And I told him about your idea of offering a reward for information. But he thinks that would hurt more than it would help. We had an incident on the island a few months ago. Money was involved. A lot of money. And it made things worse."

"Did they find the person?" Desiree asked, her voice cracking slightly.

"It wasn't that kind of case," Kate said quietly. "But the money—that made it harder. So much harder. I agree with him. At least wait a little while. See what Ben can come up with. And see if . . ."

"Is he really looking for Judd or just placating a crazy lady?"

"He's really looking, Desiree. In fact, he's still on the job right this minute. Even though he hasn't got any evidence of a crime yet, I get the feeling that this case is a priority. And for what it's worth, he knows you're not crazy."

"For what it's worth, I feel like I'm losing my marbles," she said, shaking her head. "If I met me right now, I'm not sure I'd believe a thing I said."

"You're in an impossible situation," Kate agreed. "But no one thinks you've lost it. And all of us are trying to help find Judd."

"I hate to even ask," Desiree said, pausing. "You've done so much already. Both of you. But you said you might have a way of getting into that big house above the beach . . ."

"Has she ever," Maxi said, twirling her fork. "All she has to do is agree to become a TV star."

Chapter 17

"When are the Coral Cay Irregulars meeting again?" Kate asked, as Maxi drove them back toward downtown.

With the Jeep windows down, Kate found the cool night air invigorating. A breeze blowing straight off the ocean carried the scent of salt water, as a symphony of frogs and crickets serenaded the night.

"Well, it was supposed to be the Sunday after next. But Barb hasn't settled on a venue. Minette's campaigning to host it at her place—which is super nice. Bridget and Andy offered the back room of Oy and Begorra. I told Barb if she wanted something outside, we could use my backyard at home, too. I even volunteered Peter to wait tables. Promised her he'd wear a tux with a bow tie and everything."

"So where did you have it before?" Kate asked.

"Well, originally, we were gonna have it at Barb's bookstore. Starting a mystery book club was her idea. She was gonna serve some cheese and crackers with wine. But once the word got out and we realized we were gonna have a few more people and a lot more food, Harp volunteered his wine cave. Now that he's gone, I think *La Presidenta* would love to move it to the bookstore permanently."

"But she also doesn't want to alienate any of the club members," Kate concluded.

"Yup. If I had to guess, I'd say from here on out, we're probably going to trade off," Maxi said. "So we're meeting somewhere in two weeks. We just don't know where."

"Something you and Ben said tonight gave me an idea," Kate started.

"Ben *and* I? I didn't think we agreed on anything. You and I were pretty much trying to talk him into something. And he was pretty much trying to talk us out of the same thing. So what was this super-good idea Detective Ben and I had together?"

"That we need a few more eyes on this—to find Judson Cooper. You made the point in Ben's office. And you were right. Ben even admitted it. He just said that attaching a monetary reward wasn't a good idea. So where do you think we could find a group of sharp-eyed people who see everything that goes on in this town and would help solve a mystery just for the sheer challenge of it?"

"I'm guessing the same place you find a bunch of people who love reading detective books and talking about them all the time. The Coral Cay Irregulars."

"Exactly. But for Desiree and Judson's sake, I don't think we can afford to wait two weeks."

"So we go around to the members ourselves and ask pretty please. We can approach *La Presidenta* first, to get her blessing."

"Rosie and Andre were at the wedding," Kate said. "They like Desiree—so I'm pretty sure they'll lend a hand. And Claire and Gabe were there, too—Claire's a big fan of Judd's. I'm thinking they'll pitch in."

"I tease Barb, but that girl's got a heart as big as Florida," Maxi said. "She's not going to turn away someone who needs help. Especially when whatever this is happened right at our doorstep."

"Counting you and me, that's at least seven."

"Make it nine. 'Cause you know Minette's not about to get left out of anything. And her Carl's an ex-police defective. He'll have a couple ideas on this. As long as we make it super clear we're turning everything over to the professionals."

"Definitely. I could tell by the way Ben looked tonight he's been working way too hard."

"*Sí*, but that's kind of what he does. It's not on you."

"Right now, Judson Cooper is a big part of his workload," Kate said. "And that kind of is on me. And he's right about one thing: We don't even have proof there was a crime. I mean, I trust Desiree's instincts. But Ben can't afford to. So if we could just give him a little more information—a little more to go on . . ."

Maxi dimmed her headlights for an oncoming car. Suddenly, the other vehicle swerved toward the center line. She gripped the steering wheel with clenched hands.

Kate saw the two passengers reach high and heave something at the Jeep. One of the projectiles clattered off the roof. The other landed in Maxi's lap with a solid *thwack*.

Laser-focused on keeping the Jeep on the road—and out of the other car's path—Maxi didn't even seem to notice she'd been hit.

As the car sped off, Kate heard hoots and laughter. She reached over and snatched the mystery object from her friend's lap. "A crushed beer can. You OK?"

"I'm super angry," Maxi said, still clutching the wheel. "Does that count?"

"I didn't catch the license plate, and I couldn't even begin to tell you what kind of car it was," Kate said. "Did you notice?"

"Just a green convertible. Three guys, I think."

"Should we call the police?" Kate asked.

"Nah, this area is cell phone limbo land. No signal. And by the time we get to the shop, those bobos will be long gone. Hopefully."

"Who would do something like that?" Kate asked, as she took a deep breath to try to calm her staccato heart rate.

"Someone with more beer than brains," Maxi replied. "I didn't recognize the car, so I don't think they're local. Could be tourists, or joyriders from the mainland. We get them sometimes. Blowing off steam. Not like this, though. Throwing stuff. Usually it's littering or speeding. And that's bad enough. Keeps Kyle and the guys busy from time to time."

"I know who might recognize that car," Kate said, turning the crumpled can in her hand, as she considered it. "And I just happen to be visiting him tomorrow about helping us find Judson Cooper."

Chapter 18

When Kate coasted up to Gabe's Garage on her retro five-speed bike, the mechanic was nowhere in sight. But evidence of his handiwork was everywhere.

The low-slung building's wood siding was freshly painted in a clean, white high-gloss, which contrasted smartly with the red-clay tile roof. The big bay doors—polished to a mirror shine—were shut.

A long window box overflowing with pink, yellow, and purple petunias set off the sparkling shop window. But the sign on the door was flipped to CLOSED.

Kate checked her watch: two fifteen.

The lime green tow truck that Gabe almost always drove was parked in the front corner of the lot. So, wherever the mechanic was, he was probably returning soon.

She had to hand it to Gabe; this was the cleanest garage she'd ever seen. But, living in New York for the last eight years, she hadn't really seen that many other garages.

She had a car. But in the city, she'd only driven it when

she left town on vacations—which were very few and
far between. And parking spots were almost as pricey as
rent. So when her sister, Jeanine, offered to make room
in her New Jersey home's three-car garage—for a fee—
Kate jumped at the chance.

In Kate's mind, it was a pretty fair deal. She wrote
Jeanine a check for a hundred dollars every month,
plus the cost of monthly detailing and twice-yearly trips
to the mechanic for oil changes and tune-ups. In return,
her brother-in-law, Dave, vowed to crank the engine and
drive it around the block at least once a week.

But her old reliable Toyota had barely gotten her to
Coral Cay before it broke down in a smoking heap on
Main Street. At the time, after two weeks of looking for
a job and nary a nibble, she hadn't had enough in her
checking account to even pay for towing.

Gabe had shown up out of nowhere. A mountain of a
man driving his distinctive tow truck, he had rescued her
from the tangle of angry drivers, hauled her car to his
shop, and stored it in his side yard for free. He'd also
nicknamed it "Gwendolyn."

His automotive diagnosis: profound neglect.

Despite cashing a pile of checks over the years, it
seems neither Jeanine nor Dave had taken the car anywhere near a mechanic. And based on the condition of
the interior—plus a bumper crop of mustard and catsup
packets with the odd French fry—Kate surmised they'd
been using it as an alternate car. Possibly for their au
pair, she suspected.

Over the past four months, Gabe had been tinkering
with the sedan in his spare time. "He loves a challenge,"
Claire confessed happily at one of their book-club meet-
ings. "And that car is as good as any Sunday crossword."

With a job—now a junior partnership—at a bakery
that was getting firmly back on its feet, Kate was slowly

repaying the mechanic's generosity. Though initially, he tried to refuse.

"Nope," Kate had insisted, placing the first check on the shop counter and pushing it toward the register. "You earned it. More than. So you can use it to help the next girl who breaks down on Main Street. Or just buy some more of Sam's sourdough."

As long as she was here, Kate reasoned, she might as well visit Gwendolyn. She wheeled the bike around to the grassy side lawn, put down the kickstand, and patted the white bakery box strapped to the back. It contained two wax bags, each with a big round of sourdough, fresh from the oven. Gabe's favorite.

Clean and shiny, her car looked better than it had in a long time. Almost as if it were sitting on a dealership lot. It sported four identical new tires with thick whitewalls, she noticed. The old ones had been cheap, mismatched, and worn, probably replaced piecemeal over the years by Dave.

"The old girl doesn't look too shabby, if I do say so," Gabe said, strolling from the area behind the garage. Wearing a sky-blue Hawaiian shirt, wrinkled tan Bermuda shorts, and his trademark wrap-around sunglasses, he could have passed for a tourist. Unlike a lot of the locals, he had a deep tan.

"The best part is a few little tweaks and she'll be good to go," he said proudly, pulling an oversized navy calico handkerchief from his pocket and mopping his ruddy brow.

"It looks wonderful," Kate breathed. "It doesn't even look like the same car."

The big mechanic grinned. "That would be Arnie. He does my detailing. Although I admit, I put a nice coat of wax on her myself."

"I don't think it had four new tires when I bought it."

He shrugged. "They were almost completely bald. I've seen pencil erasers with more rubber on them than those front two. Lethal. But now old Gwendolyn is solid. She may not be glamorous, but she'll get you where you want to go."

"I don't know, she looks pretty glamorous to me," Kate said, as she circled the car. "Even the chrome looks new. Shiny."

"Arnie. He keeps the exact process a proprietary secret. But if you hire him every six months or so for a touch up, she can look this good indefinitely."

"I don't know what to say. This is wonderful. I didn't even think it was possible."

"'Believe you can and you're halfway there.' With a lot of elbow grease, anyway," he added. "And FDR knew something about that, too."

"Well, it's nowhere near thanks enough, but I wanted to bring you a little something anyway," Kate said, as she untethered the bakery box and handed it off to Gabe.

"Is this what I think it is?" he said, bringing the box under his nose. "Oh man, I smell this stuff in my dreams. There's nothing like it."

Kate smiled. "Sam was just taking this batch out of the oven right before I left. So it's still warm."

"You don't have to tell me twice. I was just having my lunch. Late lunch thanks to Andy Levy's van. Got a shade tree out back, a big slice of Claire's lasagna, a thermos of iced tea, and now, thanks to you, some of this wonderful stuff. 'I must learn to be content with being happier than I deserve.'"

"I love Jane Austen," Kate said. "Lunch and a little light reading?"

"Always. Not the book club selection, though, so don't tell Barb."

"Actually, that was part of the reason I wanted to stop

by. At the wedding, Claire mentioned that Judson Cooper has been an inspiration. She said she really admires his work."

"Big-time. She always has. Even more so after moving here. When you're surrounded by water, you really come to understand the connection between land and sea."

The burly mechanic paused. "Did the guy ever explain why he missed his own wedding? Was there an ecological emergency?"

"No, he just disappeared. Nobody's heard from him since Friday night. Desiree's frantic. Ben's been trying to make contact. But Desiree thinks he was kidnapped. Judson's pretty comfortable financially—thanks to his inventions. So she believes there's going to be a ransom demand."

Gabe nodded. "Definitely preferable to the alternative."

"Desiree wants to offer a reward for information on his whereabouts."

Gabe put his hand to his forehead and shook his head. "Big mistake. Unless you want to bring out every kook, con artist, and grifter between here and the state line."

"That's exactly what Ben said," Kate admitted. "And while he hasn't uncovered any signs of foul play, he also hasn't been able to get in touch with Judson. Last anybody knows, the man sailed his boat out of the marina Friday night and no one's seen him since."

His mouth straightened into a grim line. "That poor lady."

"Ben's working all the angles, but he's hitting a brick wall. A big part of the problem is that there's no real evidence that Judd didn't just leave voluntarily. And I was thinking, we might not know where he is now. But we know Coral Cay was the last place he was seen. So if we could collect information from a few people who really know Coral Cay . . ."

"Then we might provide a few fresh leads to our stalwart detective friend," Gabe finished.

Kate nodded. "Exactly. I know you and Claire are really busy, so I understand totally if—"

"Please. If I bowed out of this, my lady would board the next boat back to jolly old England. For the past three days she's been wondering why a stand-up guy like Judson Cooper would miss his own wedding. So have I, truth be told. Count us in."

"Did you meet him while he was here?"

The mechanic shook his head. "Can't say I had the pleasure. Claire met him briefly, when they came to collect the bikes. But she and Desiree really hit it off. And I spotted him around town plenty."

"I'll stop by Claire's shop this afternoon," Kate promised. "We're going to set up a timeline for Judson's visit here. If we do it right, and get enough people involved, we should be able to account for most of his time on the island. And that might generate some leads."

"Let me look at some of my towing logs from the past week," Gabe said. "That'll jog my memory. See what I can recollect that might be relevant."

"Or irrelevant," Kate said smiling. "Right now we've got nothing. So even the smallest thing, no matter how insignificant, could help."

"Sounds like old Gwendolyn. Her problem wasn't one big thing. Just a lot of little things. Cumulative effect."

"That reminds me, you wouldn't, by any chance, have seen a green convertible racing around town? Maybe with three guys in it?"

"Not that I've noticed. Why? Is this related to Cooper's disappearance?"

"No, I don't think so. A trio of yahoos pelted Maxi

and I with empty beer cans on the drive back from Desiree's bungalow last night. We didn't get a plate number. Or even much of a description of the car. I figured if anyone recognized it, though, it might be you."

Concern clouded his face. "You guys OK?"

"We're fine. More rattled than anything. Well, *I* was rattled. Maxi was furious."

Gabe grinned. "Sounds about right. I'll definitely keep an eye out for a green convertible. A car full of drunken party boys is definitely something we don't need. Especially right now. I guess you heard about Ken Salazar."

"That he's filming at Harp's place?"

"Not just there. They're going to be all over the island. Some of the housemates even get jobs at local businesses. Last I heard, they were talking to Amos Tully over at the market."

"You think he'd consider it?"

"The show pays all the wages. So basically, it's free help."

Kate smiled. "OK, that would do it. Plus, after Teddy, I'm guessing he has a soft spot for reality TV."

Gabe grinned. "Amos won't divulge any of the details, but I get the impression his nephew Teddy did veerrry well on *Insanity Island*."

"Speaking of desolate island locations, have you heard anything about people visiting that cove next to Iris's cottage? The one that's part of the nature preserve?"

"You mean The Nose? That's what we locals call it."

"Why? It doesn't exactly look like a nose," Kate said, trying to recall the exact shape of the inlet as she'd seen it from the *Starfish*.

"Well, in the old days, when your pirate friend Gentleman George and his buddies were here, they gave it a proper Latin name—*Sinus Testudinis*. Over the years, the locals shortened it to '*Sinus*' and anglicized the pronunciation to get *sy*-nus. Then that became 'The Nose.' Which is the only thing I've ever heard it called. But on the maps, it's still officially 'Sinus Testudinis.' Turtle Bay."

"Turtle Bay?"

"Yup, that's part of the reason for the nature preserve. It's where those big loggerheads come to lay their eggs."

Chapter 19

Kate wrapped her bike chain around the bike rack outside of Tully's market and clicked the lock. She checked her watch. Sam had agreed to cover the shop for the afternoon. But she had to get back soon to bake, clean the bakery, and restock for tomorrow.

Surprisingly, Sam had also reconsidered the cookie class for Ken Salazar's "house guests."

"Not my cup of tea," he said, as he rolled the rack of sourdough out of the oven earlier that afternoon. "But folks seem to like it. Might spread the word. Get us a few more visitors."

Kate was floored. After talking with Desiree and Maxi, she wanted to teach the class. She still wasn't thrilled about teaching on camera. But she was curious to find out if Salazar knew Judd. And if the marine biologist might have called or stopped by the house on that fateful Friday evening. Maybe in relation to that "very rare species" that inhabited the grounds?

Still, she knew that Sam Hepplewhite was lukewarm

at best on the idea of getting involved with what he termed "Hollywood folks." So she'd decided to approach him later this afternoon—with a prepared list of ways that the on-camera exposure might benefit the bakery. Even with that, she expected the old baker would be a tough sell.

Now, out of the blue, he'd just changed his mind.

"Stop negotiating when someone says yes," her Girl Scout troop leader always used to say. So that's exactly what Kate did.

Even if she did have a million questions.

When she walked into Tully's market, Amos Tully was nowhere in sight. Instead, behind the counter was a twenty-something man she'd never seen. Tanned with sandy blond, heavily gelled hair, he was clad in a striped T-shirt, jeans, and a spanking new green apron—emblazoned with TULLY'S MARKET in large heavy white script. His name tag read TUCKER.

Odd, Kate thought. Amos wore a red apron occasionally, but it never had the store name on it. And name tags weren't needed in a small town where everybody knew pretty much everybody.

"Can I help you?" he asked politely. From the blank expression and the way he was staring out the window, Kate would have guessed he was more than a little bored.

"I'm Kate McGuire, from the Cookie House. I wanted to see Amos Tully. Is he here?"

"He's in the back," he said, gesturing vaguely toward the storeroom.

That's when it hit Kate. The reality-TV contestants. Tucker must be one of them.

"Hey, you work around here, right?" he asked, suddenly coming to life.

"Just down the block at the bakery. Why?"

"No bars on my cell," he said, waving the device in front of him. "So no texts. No FaceTime. No games. Not even calls. And Tully . . . I mean *Mister* Tully, just has that thing," he said, pointing to the landline on the wall. "I mean, what's up with that?"

"We're an island," Kate said lightly. "Cell service doesn't quite stretch everywhere. And downtown is pretty much a dead zone. So we use landlines."

"No cells? At all?" Tucker asked incredulously. "What about online orders? You know, ecommerce and everything?"

"A lot of the business owners have desktops. Either in their shops or at home." *Except for Sam*, she thought ruefully.

"Man, they said I had to get a job. But they didn't say it would be back in the Stone Age. This is some BS!"

Kate shrugged and headed for the back of the store. She pushed aside the red curtain, revealing Amos Tully's neat and tidy retail retreat, just off the storeroom. Amos stood—and gestured at the other chair.

Little more than a large closet, it was clean and comfortable. In one corner were a couple of cozy chairs and two small, low tables—the second one supporting a small old-fashioned box-style TV. And a battered filing cabinet shoehorned into the small space held all of the grocer's business paperwork.

If Tucker couldn't fathom a landline phone, Kate wondered what he'd made of the metal filing cabinet.

"Can't offer you so much as a cup of coffee," Amos said. "We're between pots right now. The young sprout was supposed to make some. But to hear him tell it, my coffee maker doesn't have enough buttons and doodads on it." The grocer lowered his voice. "I think he broke it."

"That's OK," Kate said. "I'm headed back to the

bakery pretty soon, anyway. I'll be baking tonight, so I'll have the coffeepot going all evening. And if you want to stop by later, I can stand you a cup and a few of those oatmeal raisin cookies. They've been pretty popular, so I'm baking up a big batch."

"Might have a few minutes. Need to have a word with Sam, anyway."

"I don't know if you've heard yet, but Judson Cooper's missing."

Amos nodded. "Did hear something to that effect. Runaway groom?"

"Not exactly. Desiree, his fiancée, is a friend of mine. I knew her back in New York. She's a good person. Solid and levelheaded. Anyway, Judson vanished the night before their wedding. No one's seen him or heard from him since Friday night. That's when his boat, the *Starfish*, sailed out of the harbor."

"Sounds like a job for Ben Abrams," the grocer said succinctly.

Kate nodded. "Absolutely. And he's working on it. Hard. The good news is Ben hasn't found any evidence of foul play. The bad news is he hasn't been able to contact Judson and make sure he's OK—that he left voluntarily. If he can do that, and Judson's fine, well, that's all Desiree wants to know. But right now, she doesn't know anything. Her guy simply vanished. And she's worried about him. Worried he's been kidnapped or hurt."

Amos hung his head. "That's rough," he said quietly.

Kate nodded. "Anyway, we're all trying to help. Desiree's working the phones. She's reaching out to people who know him. Maxi and I are talking to the folks on the island—the people who are plugged in and notice everything. We're trying to piece together a timeline of Judson Cooper's visit here. Especially those last few days before he disappeared. We're also spreading the word to keep an eye out. For him, for the boat, or just for something that might help Ben find out where he is now."

"I met him," Amos said proudly, straightening up in his chair. "Coupla times. Here and at the diner. Nice fellah. Brought his own market bag. Not many tourists do that. And I told him so."

"What did he say to that?" Kate asked.

"Said we're all just visitors to planet Earth—high time we started acting like decent guests. Told him he got that right."

"Did he mention what he was doing in Coral Cay?"

Amos Tully nodded. "Said he and his lady were here for a bit. That they were staying at one a' the resorts. But he was getting out to see the island. Some special places here."

"Did he mention where?"

Amos took a deep breath, and Kate could see the wheels turning in his mind. "Well, he mentioned Harp's old spread. Durned shame that. Now they're renting it out. Guess you heard?"

"What did Judd say about it?" Kate asked anxiously.

"Didn't say much of anything. Wanted to know what I knew. What the place was like. What the first owners were like." Amos paused. "I told him the truth," he said, his voice barely above a whisper.

Kate nodded. "What did he say?"

"Wasn't surprised. Got the feeling he might a' done a bit of research himself."

"Did he say why he was asking? Why he wanted to know?"

Kate heard the jingle of the shop door. And a scuffle, muffled. Then footsteps. A woman in heels.

Amos shook his head. "You know, he never did. But I—"

"Amos, are you here?"

Kate recognized Annie Kim's voice.

Amos jumped up and hustled out to the store, as Kate followed in his wake.

The pharmacist was standing in front of the counter staring at the door, a puzzled look on her face.

"Hey, Annie," Amos said, looking around. "You haven't seen a young man out here? 'Bout this tall, blond-ish hair and a green shop apron."

"Sounds like the guy who was running out of here when I walked in," she said, shaking her head. "Nearly mowed me down. He was carrying one of those big bags of potato chips," she added, pointing to a shelf display. "Muttering something about his phone. But he wasn't wearing an apron."

"This might explain why," Kate said, bending to retrieve a green apron that lay in a crumpled heap on the floor. It still had the name tag attached.

Chapter 20

Kate wheeled up to the Cookie House just as Andy Levy's yellow van was pulling up to the curb. He hopped out with two brown-paper carry-out bags.

"Don't tell me you're making deliveries now?" Kate said.

"Hey, from what Sam said on the phone, it was a spaghetti-and-meatball emergency," he returned, his face lighting up. "So two specials coming up. And you might recognize the garlic bread—we used Sam's baguettes."

"That smells wonderful," Kate said. "But I'd have been happy to pick it up."

"Nah, we need a bunch of stuff for the pub. Sam's holding it for us. So I had to come over anyway. But between you and me," Andy said, dropping his voice, "I think he was worried you weren't gonna eat dinner."

Kate looked up in fresh wonder at the gingerbread Victorian that was the Cookie House, glowing palest pink in the evening light. Purple flowers lined the driveway, and pink and white blooms framed the old-fashioned front porch. Courtesy of Maxi. And more spilled out of the upstairs window boxes—the window boxes outside Kate's own bedroom windows. Oliver had left his favorite purple Frisbee on one of the white benches that flanked the front door. And, inside, Sam was prepping for tomorrow and waiting for the dinner he'd ordered. For both of them. To make sure she didn't miss a meal.

She smiled.

"The carton on top's just meatballs," Andy said without missing a beat as they stepped across to the walkway. "That's for Oliver. Bridge made 'em special. Nice beefy gravy instead of marinara, and no garlic."

"He'll love that," Kate said, softly.

"Oh, and she told me about your friend. The marine biologist. He and his girlfriend ate at our place a few times. Usually late breakfast. French toast with all the trimmings."

"Did Judson ever talk about what they were doing on the island?" Kate asked, as she looped her bike chain around one of the porch columns.

"Just seeing the sights," Andy said, pausing beside the front door. "I remember one time he asked about Harp's house. I don't think his girlfriend was with him that time."

"What did he say?"

"He wanted to know what the plans were for the old place. I told him it was on the market. That was before they rented it out. You heard about that, I guess?"

"Yes, in fact, I'm going to be teaching a cookie class out there for the, uh, housemates," Kate said, opening the door for Andy. Remembering the sullen shop clerk from Amos Tully's market, she almost regretted the decision.

But they needed to learn more about Judd's connection to Ken Salazar—and his seeming fascination with that house.

"Cool! Well, if they want a cooking lesson, send 'em our way," he said, breezing into the shop. "But on second thought, I don't think Bridget wants to give away any of our trade secrets. That spaghetti pasta? She makes it from scratch. And fresh noodles taste worlds different than the kind you get out of a box, let me tell you. Same with the sauce. She starts simmering stuff the night before. So the flavor's deep."

"Evenin', Andy," Sam called, as he straightened up from polishing the glass bakery cases. "Got your stuff all fixed up in the back. The big boxes by the back door."

"Excellent! You want these on the kitchen table?"

"Yup," the baker said.

Kate followed Andy into the kitchen. "Do you remember anything else Judson talked about? Maybe spots on the island that he wanted to see?"

"Mainly, we talked about food and the Marlins," Andy said, as he deposited the bags on the table, already set for supper. "The guy's a diehard fan. A real foodie, too. But one afternoon—another time he was alone, come to think of it—I think maybe he and his lady had a fight. It was pretty late for lunch. And when I handed him a menu, he said it had to be really special because it was a peace offering."

"Do you remember what he said exactly?"

"Something about mending fences," he said, sinking into one of the kitchen chairs. "Or making amends. He said he'd done something really stupid, but he was gonna swallow his pride to set it right. Oh yeah, and he also said she'd be less likely to throw a lamp at him if he showed up with food—especially something chocolate."

Kate grabbed a cup from the cupboard, filled it with coffee. "Do you remember what day it was? When he told you that?"

"Let's see. I remember he asked about the special. It was this really creamy seafood stew Bridge made. We topped it with a nice buttery pastry crust. Pretty good, if I do say so. But you have to serve it piping hot, and the pastry's delicate. I was worried it wouldn't travel too well. So he went with two of the dill salmon salad sandwiches on challah rolls with a couple of Caesars, and a bottle of that lemon sparkling water. Oh, and two of those chocolate mousse cupcakes you make. The ones with the vanilla buttercream frosting? Anyway, if the special was the seafood stew, that was last Friday. Pretty late, too. Closer to dinner than lunch. 'Cause I remember thinking that when I was packing it all into a cold box for him."

"I don't suppose he mentioned what their fight was about?" Kate asked, setting the cup and saucer in front of him.

Andy shrugged, chewed on his lip, and grabbed the cup with both hands.

"Anything you can remember is going to help. Honestly."

"I know she's a friend of yours . . ." he started.

"We just want to help Ben get in touch with him. So that we know he's OK. The rest of it doesn't matter."

Andy heaved a deep sigh. "Well, he mentioned something about a ring. That it was a family heirloom. And he needed it back."

He took a long swig of coffee as his sneaker beat a nervous rhythm on the tile floor.

Kate could tell he wasn't quite finished. "But there

was more," she said quietly, as she heard Sam bustling in from the shop.

Andy nodded. "He said that life was too short to be with the wrong person. But thank goodness he'd realized in time."

Chapter 21

"Sounds like your friend's beau had more than a case a' the jitters," Sam said, as he used a chunk of garlic bread to clean the last traces of Bridget's homemade marinara sauce from his plate.

"I was with them earlier that day on the boat. Everything was . . . great. I'd have said 'perfect,' even."

Stretched out on the floor, halfway between the table and the back door, Oliver followed the back-and-forth of their conversation. He'd already made short work of his meatballs, Kate noticed.

Sam shook his head. "Relationship's like a bakery. Can't rightly tell what it's like from the outside."

"I guess," Kate conceded.

Privately, she had been struggling to process what Andy had revealed. Could Judd and Desiree have had an argument that afternoon that changed his perspective on the relationship? Was he just stringing her along until things got too "real," as Zoey had implied? Or did the sudden appearance of Lola Montgomery have something to do with his abrupt about-face?

And just how, exactly, could she broach the topic with Desiree?

A sharp rap on the kitchen door brought Kate back to the present. She looked over and saw Amos Tully framed in the glass. Oliver scrambled up and skidded to a stop in front of the door, wagging his entire back end vigorously.

"I invited him for coffee," Kate explained, walking toward the door. "The pot at the market conked out. And he needs to talk with you."

"You're just in time," Kate said, opening the door. "I'm just bringing out dessert."

"Can't stay long. Got to get back to the shop, but thought you might be able to use a little of this," the grocer said, handing off a cloth shopping bag, and bending to give Oliver a scratch behind the ear. "Young fellah looks good."

Kate opened the sack and was greeted by the strong scent of roasted coffee. She reached in to find two one-pound bags.

"Good beans," Amos said, walking into the kitchen and pulling out a chair at the table. "Ground them myself right before I left the shop. Nice, dark roast. And the one's got a little vanilla in it."

"Sounds perfect," Kate said, heading over to the counter. "I'll get the coffee going and get out some dessert, while you two talk."

"That kid from the resort show wrecked my coffee maker," Amos explained to Sam. "Had that thing twenty years. Was just getting broken in good."

Sam shook his head sorrowfully. "Durned shame. Mine's going on thirty years now."

"Ah-yup," Amos agreed, nodding. "They might try

and send that kid your way. Or one of the other ones. Sounds like a pretty sharp deal. Show pays all the wages and even got him some kind of uniform. Green apron with my store name in big letters. They said it would be like a billboard on TV. Free advertising. I shoulda known better. There's no free lunch. The sprout lasted three hours. Nipped out with not so much as a goodbye. Took a bag of chips and forty dollars from my register, to boot."

"Live and learn," Sam said. "Appreciate knowing the score, though."

"Thought you might," Amos said, as Kate slid a platter of oatmeal raisin cookies onto the table in front of him.

"You call Ben or Kyle?" Sam asked.

Amos shook his head. "I'm the one who put a total stranger in charge of my till. Didn't even check his references. Feel like a danged fool."

Kate scooped coffee into the machine, then paused. And spooned in some more. Something told her, with a night of baking ahead, a full pot would come in handy. Besides, she could turn the leftovers into iced coffee tomorrow. If there were any leftovers.

As the coffee maker gurgled and sputtered to life— and Amos and Sam had their heads together at the table—she selected a buttery coffee cake from one of the storage pantries, and slid it into the testing oven. As it warmed, the scent of cinnamon, butter, and brown sugar mingled with the aromas of coffee and vanilla. The perfect after-dinner treat.

A little sugar rush to kick off a late night of baking wouldn't hurt, either.

Oliver, sitting up straight and proud between Sam and Amos, listened in seemingly rapt attention as the two men debated various solutions to the problem of the light-fingered clerk.

"Woo-hoo! Anybody home?"

Kate recognized Minette Ivers's voice coming from the direction of the shop. She headed toward the front door, and found Minette and Carl standing on the porch.

"Maxi said you two were collecting information on Judson Cooper. Did he really jilt that poor girl at the altar?"

"Minette, baby—" her husband started.

"Hush, Carl. It's not like it's a state secret. And we're here to help."

Kate grinned. "How about a little dessert? I just put on a fresh pot of Amos's best vanilla roast, and I'm warming up a butter streusel coffee cake. And we've already got oatmeal raisin cookies on the kitchen table."

"I wouldn't say no to that," Carl said, with a weary smile. "Even if it does mean we're having dessert first."

"We can't stay—we just locked up the shop, and we're on our way home," Minette explained as the three of them walked into the kitchen. "But I talked with Maxi today. And from what she said, there's no time to waste. Oh, this kitchen always smells so good!"

Sam stood when they walked in. "Hey, folks, pull up a seat. I'll get a few extra chairs from the storeroom."

"I'll give you a hand," Carl said, following him up the stairs.

"Well, hello, Amos," Minette said. "How's everything at the market?"

"If one of those reality TV kids shows up looking for a job, don't fall for it," he said woefully, as he pushed the plate of cookies in her direction.

"Tell me about it," she said, picking up a cookie. "They approached my Carl when he was out there. A little heavy-handed, too. Said since they were 'giving' him so much work, surely it wouldn't be too much trouble to take on a few of them at the store?"

"What did he say?" Amos asked.

"He told them since they'd be dealing with vital plumbing and electrical equipment, they'd have to meet certification first, take a written test, and get a provisional membership in the local unions. Plus their own liability insurance."

"I had no idea it took so much paperwork to clerk at the hardware store," Kate said.

"It doesn't," Carl's baritone announced as he trooped down the stairs, two folding chairs hanging off each arm. "But I wasn't about to turn over my counter to a couple of unknowns. And I also didn't want to lose the biggest contract job we've had in a while."

"Wish I'd thought of that," Amos said.

"Don't you feel bad," Minette said, patting him on the hand. "How were you to know?"

"She's right," Carl said. "I think all those years on the job just make me more suspicious. Maybe too much."

As Carl and Sam put a few more chairs around the table, Kate carefully removed the rich, golden pastry from the oven, plated it, and sliced it up with a cake knife.

Sam grabbed the tray with cups, plates, and saucers and carried it to the table, as Kate followed with the cake plate and the coffeepot.

"Tell them what you told me, Carl," Minette prompted.

"Well, one of the things they had me do out there was to hook up CCTV cameras. Wanted eyes on the entire grounds. They said it was strictly for security, but I get the feeling they might also use some of the footage for their show."

"What makes you think that?" Kate asked, intrigued.

"The quality of the equipment and the resolution," he said, matter-of-factly. "You've all seen security footage on the news after a crime. It's grainy. And choppy.

Basically, you just want something that can record the fact that someone is on your property and give you a decent shot at an ID. When you have a problem, that's when a tech will pull a few frames and enhance it to produce a couple of recognizable photos. The rest of the time, it's running in the background, but you're never going to see the results."

"Makes sense," Amos said, nodding as he picked up a cookie and dunked it in his coffee. "Equipment's expensive."

"It is," Carl said. "And you'd be flushing money shooting TV-quality video twenty four-seven when you may never need it. That doesn't seem to bother these folks, though. They want every inch of those grounds covered. Or at least as much as humanly possible. And with the equipment they're using? You could send the feed straight to TV—it's that clear. Movie quality, even."

"Why do that unless they plan to use it on the show?" Kate mused.

"That's the only conclusion that made sense to me," he admitted, taking a swig of his coffee, as Minette put a big piece of the coffee cake in front of him. "Thanks, baby."

She patted his shoulder. "That's not even the best part. Tell them, honey."

"I saw your friend Judson Cooper out there," Carl announced.

"When?" Kate blurted. "What was he doing?"

Carl allowed himself to swallow a bite of cake. "The 'when' was last week. Monday. I was fine-tuning the security cameras. I looked up at one of the screens, and there he was. Strolling the grounds, big as life. Didn't even realize who he was at the time. Just that he looked familiar. It was only after I was talking with Minette this afternoon that the penny finally dropped."

"Any idea what he was doing out there? Could he be involved in the show somehow?" Kate asked, trying to make sense of it all.

"I don't think that's it. At least, I didn't see him talking with the producers or the crew. And they were around, believe me. When I saw him, he was walking the grounds, near the edge of the bluff. Like he was taking in the view."

"Looking out at the ocean?" Kate asked.

Carl nodded. "Up and down the beach."

"How did he seem?" she asked.

"Definitely upbeat," Carl said. "Buoyant. Grinning."

So maybe he'd found the "very rare species" he was looking for? And what would that mean for the TV show filming there if he had? Could he have shut it down? And did that have something to do with his disappearance?

"There's more to it, though," Minette said grimly. "And your friend might not like this part. I know I didn't. Eco-warrior or not, I'd like to give that man a good kick in the slats."

Carl smiled ruefully and swallowed another forkful of coffee cake, chasing it with a long sip from his cup. Then he sighed. "Let's just say your friend Judson wasn't there alone. He was there with a lady. And if she smiled any harder, I think her face would have split in two."

"Did they look like they were . . . involved?" Kate asked.

"What they looked was over-the-moon happy. But nothing obvious."

"Maybe it was Desiree?" Kate ventured. But as the words came out of her mouth, she knew that was wrong. The only time Desiree got near that house was when Judson pointed it out to her from the deck of the *Starfish*.

The ex-cop shook his head slowly, as he swallowed another mouthful of cake. "I've seen your friend around town. Cooper, too, for that matter. This wasn't her. This woman was younger. And she had red hair."

Chapter 22

After Amos left—with a box of oatmeal raisin cook-ies tucked neatly under his arm—Kate packed a dozen red-velvet cupcakes into a big white bakery box for the Iverses. As she taped the lid, she heard a soft rap on the shop door. She glanced over and spied Barb Showalter on the porch.

The bookstore owner waved and smiled.

"Maxi came to see me today," she said excitedly, as Kate opened the door and stepped back. "About Jud-son Cooper and your friend Desiree. They were in the bookstore a few times."

"Come on in," Kate said. "Minette and Carl stopped by, too. And you just missed Amos. We're having coffee and cake in the kitchen."

"As long as you let me buy a dozen of those cheddar popovers, if you have any left," Barb said. "That, plus a little of last night's stew is going to make a bang-up dinner. Doesn't matter what I put on them, it all tastes great. And with my kitchen skills, that's saying something."

"The way they're flying out the door, you're not alone," Kate confessed. "Sam baked a fresh batch this afternoon. I'll fix you a box before you leave."

"Solid," she said, following Kate through the shop into the kitchen.

"Hi, Barb," Minette called.

Carl nodded, as he popped the last bit of crumbly cake topping into his mouth with two large fingers.

"Hey, everybody," she returned. "Oh Carl, that John Grisham you wanted came in this afternoon."

Carl flashed a hasty thumbs-up as he reached for his coffee.

"Barb," Sam nodded, as the bookstore owner adjusted her slacks and settled into a chair.

Oliver, sitting beside her, looked up hopefully. She rubbed his back, and finished with an affectionate pat.

"Here you go, as promised," Kate said, slipping the bakery box to Minette.

"The kids are going to love these—especially this one," Minette said, nudging her husband. "So, Barb, did you meet that dog Judson Cooper while he was here?"

"Dog?" Barb asked, clearly perplexed. Oliver, beside her, cocked his head looking equally puzzled.

"Long story," Kate said quickly as she grabbed a clean cup and saucer from the cupboard. "We'll fill you in later. Did you happen to remember anything about his visit?"

"Well, I admit, Maxi's questions had me intrigued. I knew he and Desiree had been in a few times. I recognized him. And she introduced herself. But I had to go through my receipt logs to get the dates and times."

She unzipped her fanny pack, produced a small spiral notebook, and placed it on the table just as Kate slid a hot cup of coffee and a piece of coffee cake in front of her.

"Oh, that is gorgeous," Barb said, her face breaking into a broad smile.

"Tastes every bit as good as it smells," Minette admitted. "Although I had to try two pieces just to make sure."

"Naturally," Barb said, as she loaded the first bite onto her fork. "Oh man, this is good."

"I got the recipe from a cooking instructor of mine who used to be a pastry chef in Paris."

"Let me guess," Barb said between bites. "The secret is butter."

"As much and as cold as possible," Kate said. "See? You know plenty about cooking."

"I don't, but I was considering one of those cookie classes," Barb said.

"You should," Minette said. "I've been going to the Friday night one, and we have some fun. You should join us."

"Pop in at eight, and I'll save you an apron," Kate said.

"If I could make something half this good," Barb said pointing at her cake with a fork, "it would be worth it. Count me in."

"So what did you find out about Judson Cooper?" Minette asked. "Besides the fact that he left that poor girl at the altar and never looked back?"

Carl rolled his eyes.

Sam rose from the table. "Good coffee. Gonna get another cup. Carl?"

"Sure thing, I'll take some, if you're offering," Carl said, standing. "Minette?"

"I'm fine," she said. "Especially if I want to get a wink of sleep tonight."

"We don't know where he went or what happened

to him," Kate said softly to Minette and Barb. "He and Desiree were supposed to get married Saturday evening on the beach. At sunset. Judson even chose the spot. It was a place he loved. But his boat left the harbor Friday night, and no one's heard from him."

Barb nodded. "That's what Maxi said. That Ben's got the feelers out, but no news yet."

"Exactly," Kate said. "Desiree is a friend of mine from New York. She took me under her wing when I was starting out. Not just me. She helped a lot of us. Hospitality can be hard, especially when you're green. But she taught us the ropes. Watched out for us. And she became a friend. Now she could use some help . . ."

Barb waved her fork, as she swallowed another bite of cake. "Believe me, I understand. Count me in. Look, I don't want to seem alarmist, but could he have been kidnapped? The man's got to be worth a pretty penny."

"That's what Desiree's afraid of," Kate said. "It's the reason she's staying put on the island. She wants to be here in case there's a ransom demand. But it's already been four days, and nothing. Now I'm almost hoping he did just take off. At least that means he's OK. And I know that's what's weighing on her most."

"Well, I didn't really discover much that helps. I mean, your friend Desiree has great taste in books. And very eclectic. Classics and biographies, along with a few Golden Age mysteries. And a couple of best sellers, too."

"That sounds like her," Kate said. "She's curious about everything. And she loves books."

"She called them 'essential supplies,'" the bookseller recalled between bites. "Said they were stocking up for a cruise up the coast."

Kate nodded. "That was their plan for the honeymoon.

They were going to spend the night at the resort where they were staying, then take Judd's boat up the coast and stop off at a marine wildlife rehab center on the way. I was teasing her about it because she's always been such a city girl. But she was ecstatic."

"That was before that low-down excuse for a man got himself a red-headed hussy," Minette fumed.

Barb's eyes popped open. "Really? Geez, they seemed so good together."

"Mm-hmm," Minette said. "That's the way some men operate. It's all good until it isn't. Then they're out the door and long gone. I got lucky with that one," she said, nodding toward Carl, who was deep in conversation with Sam over the coffee maker. "But to hear his momma tell it, he was a real handful."

Barb looked at Kate, her eyes widening slightly.

Kate sighed. "Carl spotted Judson at Harp's old place last Monday. Carl was out there setting up a security system for the crew that's renting the place. Judd was with a woman. Not Desiree. And Carl said they were both—"

"Grinning like a couple of fools," Minette finished. "Man that age should know better. And don't even get me started about those reality houseguests," she said, waving her hand. "One of them was supposed to be working at the market. And instead he robbed poor Amos of forty dollars. Right out of the register. Took that *and* a bag of chips!"

"I think Amos is more upset that the guy broke his coffee maker," Kate said. "Apparently he'd had it for twenty years. And to hear him talk, it had at least another twenty left in it."

"This show could really help boost Coral Cay," Barb said, putting down her fork. "Showcase what visitors love about this island—and bring in a little new business. Especially in the off season. And it wouldn't hurt if we attracted a new shop or two to downtown, either. Harp's storefront is still empty."

The bookstore owner paused, leaning forward. "The truth is, this one was my idea," she admitted quietly. "I reached out to Salazar's production company. Invited them to consider us. When I heard back—that they had actually decided to film here—I was thrilled. So if their people are causing problems, it's on me to straighten it out. I didn't know about the incident with Amos. I'll have a few words with Salazar tomorrow and have him make it right. And if you hear anything else, good or bad, let me know, OK?"

Kate and Minette both nodded.

"Judson Cooper was out there," Kate said. "While the film crew was prepping the house. When you spoke with Ken Salazar, did he ever mention Judd? Maybe that he knew him or met him at some point?"

Barb shook her head. "I only met Salazar once. When they first landed here, after they rented the house for the season."

"Any idea who selected that particular house?" Kate asked.

"No," Barb said. "Salazar just mentioned in passing that they'd rented the place. At that point, he was more interested in local flavor for the show. Local sights, volunteer projects, interesting places, interesting people. A slice of life in Coral Cay. He was picking my brain for suggestions. When he asked where the kids might pick up part-time jobs, heaven help me, I sent him to Amos. I also mentioned Maxi's flower shop and volunteered my place, too. I know Maxi hires high-school and college kids—and I thought Amos might appreciate the help. Especially since Salazar said the show would foot the bill."

"And we know how our Amos loves a bargain," Minette said, shaking her head.

Barb nodded. "I feel awful now," she said, dropping her head.

"What about our disappearing groom?" Minette asked, scooting her chair closer to the table. "Did he ever talk about Ken Salazar?"

"Not to me," Barb said. "As far as I knew, their paths never crossed."

Kate looked back at the coffeepot and noticed that Sam and Carl had vanished. Along with Oliver. She hadn't even heard them leave.

"Took their coffee out to the front porch," Barb said, pointing. "It's a beautiful evening."

Minette shook her head and smiled knowingly. "More like it's all this talk about men and marriage."

"I don't suppose Judd or Desiree ever talked about *their* upcoming wedding?" Kate asked, crossing her fingers under the table. If the pair had chatted about it with levelheaded Barb Showalter, that would at least prove that the last-minute, low-key nuptials hadn't been a figment of Desiree's imagination.

"No, I had no idea," the bookstore owner said. "I mean, I wouldn't have been surprised. When I first met them, I remember thinking they were either newlyweds or they'd been together thirty years. They were that well matched. But neither one mentioned a wedding."

Barb ripped a sheet off the small spiral pad and handed it to Kate. "These are the dates and times they came into the store. Maxi said you guys were building a timeline."

"We are. At least, we're trying to."

"Well, for what it's worth, I never saw him with

another woman. But I did remember one interesting thing. Don't know if it's relevant, though."

"What's that?" Kate asked.

"Your friend Judson collected maps. Was absolutely fascinated by them."

"Historic maps or regular road maps?" Kate asked.

"That's what I found so interesting. They were one and the same to him. He put it down to . . . and I'm trying to remember his exact wording here . . . 'a uniquely human ability to communicate through pictures and symbols.'"

"Like a code," Kate said.

Barb nodded. "Exactly. He was bitten by the map bug when he was a kid. Uncle in the Signal Corps. Used to bring your friend Cooper his finds when he came home on leave. The two of them would pore over them together. Then as Cooper got more interested in boating and water, it just kind of grew from there."

"Did he look at any maps while he was in the shop?" Kate asked.

"Pretty much all of them. But he bought two. One was a road map of the island. I only sell a few of those. Usually to the new residents. Tourists typically don't keep to a schedule, so they just bump around. The other one he purchased was a historical reproduction that Claire made for the Pirate Festival."

"I remember those," Kate said, snapping her fingers. "She was leading bike tours along the beaches. To some of the pirate hot spots. She made the maps to show the tour stops and gave them to the cyclists. I remember she told me how she'd used tea to age the paper. They were beautiful."

"Works of art," Barb said. "And those were the little ones. This one was almost poster-sized. Completely hand-drawn. She used it in her window display. When

I learned she had still had it in the back room after the festival, I talked her into letting me put it up for sale in my shop. Your friend Judson spotted it. Studied it for the longest time. When he bought it, he told me he was going to get it framed and hang it in his office."

"That should make Claire happy," Kate said.

Barb nodded. "But when he was looking at both maps, there was one feature he kept referencing. In fact, at one point, he put them on the counter side to side and compared them."

Kate realized she was holding her breath. She unclenched the hands resting in her lap and willed herself to breathe evenly.

"It's a protected cove just within the preserve—Sinus Testudinis," Barb said. "What we islanders call 'The Nose.'"

Chapter 23

Kate rolled a rack of chocolate chip cookies into the big bakery oven and latched the door. Oliver, worn out from his hosting duties earlier in the evening, was sacked out under the kitchen table, snuffling softly.

Sam stretched his arms and yawned. "Time to call it a night," he announced.

"More than," Kate agreed. "I'll do a few more batches of cookies and turn in myself."

"Promise?" the baker asked gravely, as Kate read the concern etched on his face.

"Promise," she vowed.

"We'll do the rest in the morning," Sam declared. "'Sides, people like the smell a' baking when they come in. Lets 'em know we're the real deal. Not sneakin' packaged stuff in the back door, like some a' those places."

As Oliver snoozed peacefully, one paw resting protectively on Purple Frisbee, Kate sifted through what she'd learned earlier.

None of it made any sense. Everything seemed contradictory.

Judson and Desiree were happy. Judson wanted his ring back.

The couple was stocking up on books for their honeymoon cruise. Judson was swanning around with another woman.

Judson bought maps. But he already knew the island.

Desiree had met Ken Salazar, while Judson didn't appear to know him. But Judson visited Salazar's rental house.

Judson announced that a very rare species made its home near that same house. But the biologist seemed preoccupied with Turtle Bay.

Judson Cooper's extreme reaction to the strange cigarette boat. Drag marks in the sand.

Kate's head spun.

She remembered the trick her instructors used in culinary school after a kitchen drill. To help the students see order in the chaos of a busy kitchen and force them to reexamine every individual step—to take ownership for each move they'd made. Sticky notes on the refrigerator: what they did right, what they did wrong, what they needed to improve.

She opened a drawer next to the sink and rifled through it until she found a pen and a pad of yellow Post-it notes. She hastily scrawled each point she'd learned on a separate square of paper and pressed each to the refrigerator. Then she stepped back, trying to absorb the jumble.

Still nothing.

When the industrial oven timer sounded, Oliver raised a drowsy head. She bent and stroked his back, as he leaned into her. The pup's cream-colored hair was silky soft to the touch. He smelled like new-mown grass, oatmeal shampoo, loamy earth, and roses. Someone had been playing in Maxi's garden again.

"How about we do two more batches and call it a night?" she asked him. "Maybe a little sleep will help me make sense of this whole thing. I feel like it's one of those sudoku puzzles. And I have all the clues in the wrong boxes."

Oliver rolled onto his shaggy back. An invitation to a belly rub. Which, of course, he got.

Minutes later, after she'd opened the back door to let him into the yard, Kate scrubbed up at the sink.

Just as she was drying her hands, the phone rang. News about Judson Cooper? Desiree touching base? Or Sam checking up on her?

Kate grabbed the receiver from the wall. And heard voices on the other end of the line.

"No, Javi, little puppies aren't for show-and-tell."

"But, *Mami*, Matt doesn't believe I have a dog! He says George is 'magical.'"

"Imaginary?"

"He thinks I made him up! And he's my best friend!"

"I thought Marcus was your best friend?" Maxi countered.

"*¡Mami!* That was *last* year! He's not in my class this year. So he can't be my best friend."

"Well, maybe we can invite Matt over to play, and he can meet Mr. George," she said. "But he's still a puppy. He's not old enough to go to school. Now upstairs! *Vámonos*! It's way past your bedtime."

"And mine," Maxi whispered into the phone as Kate heard loud stomping on the other end of the line.

"Discord at Chez Más-Buchanan?" Kate asked smiling.

"Always. But no more than usual. Have you heard from Desiree today?"

"Yes, I called her this morning," Kate said. "She's determined to come with me to the cookie class at the reality show tomorrow. She wants to nose around and see what she can discover while I've got everyone occupied in the kitchen."

"That's not a bad idea," Maxi admitted. "What did you say?"

"I didn't. But I found out tonight from Carl that they've got cameras all over the place. Even the grounds. Which you had said was pretty typical for these shows. I just don't see how we'll pull it off without getting caught."

"But it would help to have an extra pair of eyes and ears, yes?"

"It would," Kate admitted hesitantly.

"So how about two sets of eyes and ears?" Maxi asked. "Desiree can look around, and I can watch her back."

"You'd do that? Can you afford the time?"

"Ah, you're very lucky," Maxi said. "I just happen to have a little hole in my schedule. Right after I frisk my youngest son to make sure he's not smuggling puppies to school, I have a couple of hours before I have to make deliveries. And the flowers are ready to go."

"We don't know what we're walking into, though," Kate said. "What if Judd discovered someone out there doing something illegal—something that impacted that rare species he mentioned—and confronted them? Now he's missing."

"All the more reason to go in a group. You'll be with the reality people on TV. And I'll be with Desiree. We know there are cameras everywhere. So we can't poke through people's stuff. But we can walk around and talk to folks and see what we can learn."

"That would be great. I don't know how to thank you."

"I wanna know what happened to Judson Cooper."

"So does half the island," Kate said. "And thanks to

you, we have a few new points for Desiree's board. In-cluding a few she's going to hate. But I still don't know what any of it means."

"So tell me," Maxi said.

Kate spent the next couple of minutes filling her in on the parade of friends who dropped by the bakery that evening and finished up with a description of the Post-it collage on the refrigerator.

"I gotta see that," Maxi said. "'Cause right now, all I got on mine is a grocery list from two weeks ago, the number for poison control, and a note from Miguelito begging me to buy something called 'Mega Cocoa Crunchy Super Pops.' And I'm just hoping those last two aren't connected."

Kate pictured her friend's warm, homey kitchen and smiled. "Maybe it'll make more sense to you. Because right now, I look at it and I just feel lost."

"Look at the bright side," Maxi said. "Today we found solid proof that Judson Cooper was out there at the reality-TV house. And tomorrow, we get to go there and investigate."

Chapter 24

As Maxi turned the Jeep onto a winding road that led up to the house on the bluff, Kate felt her stomach clench. Despite all that had happened, she still thought of the place as Harper Duval's house. The site of so many wonderful book-club potlucks when she first came to Coral Cay. And, later, the site of some things that weren't so good.

She wasn't in a hurry to revisit it anytime soon.

But Desiree needed her. And she wasn't about to let down her friend.

Riding in the back seat, Kate could see Maxi in the rearview mirror. She recalled their conversation earlier that morning—on the way to pick up Desiree—and felt a fresh stab of guilt.

They'd elected not to reveal what Judson told Andy Levy about wanting his ring back. Or the existence of the mystery redhead.

"If he asked Desiree to return his ring, then she already

knows," Kate reasoned at the time. "If he didn't, he may have changed his mind. Either way, it doesn't affect what we're doing this morning."

"Well, the redhead might," Maxi had said. "Especially if we run into her out there."

"I think we have to tell Desiree everything," Kate had replied. "All of it. But let's wait until we get back. The whole point of going out there is to stay under the radar and gather a little information. Could you be stealthy if you just found out Peter was happily going around town with another woman?"

"I'd be a heat-seeking missile of angry," Maxi had admitted.

"So we tell her later," Kate had concluded. "At the bungalow tonight. When she has time to deal with it privately, and we can be there for her. Not right before we pile out of a car into a house loaded with people and TV cameras."

Now as they drove up the twisty road, Kate was wondering if this was all a huge mistake.

"I know you don't believe he'll be there—at the house," Desiree said quietly from the passenger seat. "But I feel like we're at least getting close to him. Following his trail. You're sure your friend doesn't know what he was doing out here last week?"

"No, they didn't actually speak," Kate said. "Carl was inside adjusting security cameras. Judd was outside walking along the bluff. Carl didn't even realize who he was until yesterday. And from what Carl said, Judd wasn't interacting with Salazar or his crew, either."

"I wonder if they even knew he was there," Desiree mused, as she stared out the window.

"What do you mean?" Kate asked.

"Well, if he thought someone was breaking the law—concealing the existence of an endangered species or spoiling its habitat—it's possible he snuck onto the property without telling anyone."

"Trespassing?" Maxi exclaimed.

Desiree shrugged. "He's done it before."

"Would he go alone?" Maxi asked, making frantic eye contact with Kate in the rearview mirror. "Wouldn't he let someone know where he was? You know, just in case he got caught?"

"It depends," Desiree said. "If it was a spur-of-the-moment thing, not necessarily. He can be very spontaneous," she added.

"When he got back, he didn't mention anything about it to you?" Maxi prodded.

"Not a peep. Well, unless that's what he was trying to tell me on the boat a few days later. But we were interrupted. There was a storm coming."

"Truth" Maxi said under her breath.

"What?" Desiree asked.

"Here we are," Kate announced brightly, just as Maxi made the hairpin turn into the driveway. "The new temporary home of *Last Resort*. Everybody know what to do?"

"We help you carry in the equipment, then we make ourselves scarce," Maxi supplied.

"I brought Cookie House aprons for both of you," Kate said, as Maxi opened the Jeep's rear door. "That should buy you a little leeway to wander around a bit."

"If we get caught, we'll just say we got lost," Maxi said. "The place is *muy grande*. Humongous."

"It's beautiful," Desiree said, pausing to take in the view. "Very old Florida. I love the tin roof. And the big old trees."

"Believe it or not, this place is only about ten years old," Maxi said, as she slipped on the navy-and-white-striped bakery apron, tied the back, and smoothed it over her jeans. "On the outside, it's old-timey South Florida, right down to the Spanish moss in the trees. Inside, it's super modern. And really nice. But please notice the very green grass and flowers—*todo muy bonito*—courtesy of yours truly."

"It does look good," Kate said. "It looks loved."

"*Gracias*," Maxi said, taking a curtsy.

"You were out here, too?" Desiree asked. "You didn't see Judson out here?"

Maxi shook her head. "I didn't. But I finished up the yard before Carl started working out here. And it was all I could do to keep track of my crew. Teenagers. *¡Dios mío!*, a preview of coming attractions."

Kate looped a market bag over one shoulder and hoisted a heavy box of supplies onto her hip.

"What is all this stuff, anyway? Maxi asked.

"Ingredients and tools for the class," Kate said.

"They have at least two kitchens in there, that I know of," Maxi said, pointing toward the mansion. "And it costs *un montón de dinero*—a pile of money—just to rent the place. You mean to tell me they can't afford their own groceries and a couple of spatulas?"

"When you're in someone else's kitchen you have to bring everything you need," Kate said. "Because you never know what they have and what they don't. On the bright side, they're reimbursing me, and I bought as much of it as I could at Amos Tully's market."

Maxi grinned. "That'll show 'em. I wonder if your friend Tucker will be in class today?"

"Don't remind me," Kate said. "I wonder if Barb has called Salazar yet. I got the impression she was really upset."

"In that case, I'd hate to be him," Maxi said.

"One of the house guests caused a bit of trouble in town," Kate explained to Desiree.

"A whole lotta drama," Maxi summarized, as they trooped up the walkway.

Ahead, standing in the oversized doorway, Kate saw a young blond woman wearing a headset and carrying a clipboard. She stepped forward.

"Kate McGuire?"

"I'm Kate. I'd shake your hand but . . ." She nodded toward the box in her arms. "This is Maxi and Desiree. They're helping me get set up."

"I'm Aimee, Ken's assistant," she said smiling. "And I remember Maxi. You were out here to redo the gardens, right? They're really beautiful now. And they look great on camera."

Maxi beamed.

"Well, welcome to Conch House," Aimee added, with a wave of her hand.

"Conch House?" Kate and Maxi said in unison.

"That's what we're calling the house this season," she explained as she led them into the entryway. "For the show. Every house gets a name. Something in keeping with the local flavor. Makes it more distinctive for the viewers. This is South Florida on the Gulf, so Ken liked Conch House. We've got you in the main kitchen, this way," she added, gesturing. "I'll let you and your team set up, and then we have some papers to sign. Will you all be on camera?"

"Just me, I'm afraid," Kate said. "But I'll need their help to pack everything up and take it back after the class."

"Not a problem," Aimee said. "I'll get the two of you some tea and snacks while you wait."

"Thank you," Maxi said, as they emerged into the main kitchen.

With a double-height ceiling, clerestory windows, and folding glass doors across the back, it overlooked a

flagstone patio, the dunes, and the dark blue water beyond. The massive kitchen island covered in white
marble would make an ideal student work area, Kate
noted approvingly. The thick slab of veined stone was
ideal for rolling out pastry.

Skylights funneled sunlight to the back of the room,
which was immaculate, she noticed. Bright and almost
antiseptic, there was no place a speck of dust could even
hide.

But something was off.

The room seemed artificial, like a movie set. From
the bleached-wood floors and butcher-block counters
to the white cupboards with sparkling glass fronts and
matching panels concealing oversized appliances.

That's when it hit her. The smell.

The room reeked of furniture polish, wood oil, and
window cleaner, not food.

Well, with any luck she'd soon fix that.

"Has this room changed much?" Kate asked Maxi, as
she set a stack of cookie sheets on the island.

"It's mostly the same. But it used to be, I don't know,
more lively. Big splashes of color. Wire hanging baskets
over the island with oranges and lemons. Another with
hot peppers and dried herbs. Bright tiles that Caroline
used for putting under steaming pots. Lots of colorful
tea towels, too. And woven throw rugs on the floor over
there," she said, pointing to an empty kitchen table.
"Hot colors—red and yellow and fuchsia. Really pretty.
And there was always music. Salsa, classical, R&B. Just
small things. But it felt different."

Kate nodded, as her stomach fluttered again. What
was she doing here? Teaching a class to friends and
neighbors was one thing. But on camera to people who
probably didn't care whether their cookies came from a
bakery or a box? What was she thinking?

She glanced at Desiree, clad in her bakery apron, gamely unpacking a carton of supplies. That's why, Kate thought. Judson and Desiree. For them.

"I'd forgotten how big this kitchen is," Maxi whispered.

"I don't think I've ever been in here," Kate said in a hushed voice. "This room is bigger than my entire New York apartment—and some of the professional kitchens I've seen. It really is"—she stopped, trying to absorb it all—"incredible."

"Harper and Carolyn used the other one—the catering kitchen for the book-club potlucks," the florist said. "'Cause it's right next to the wine cave."

"They have a wine cave?" Desiree said, snapping to attention.

"Not a real cave," Kate assured her. "They just call it that. It's just a room on the other end of the house."

"You can't have a real basement in South Florida," Maxi explained. "The water table's too high. Dig down five or six feet and—boom—*agua*. But inside, this place looks just like a real wine cellar—with plastered walls and a stone floor and lots and lots of racks of wine. It's where our book club used to meet. Not too shabby."

"Could they be holding him in there? Judson? If it's an out-of-the-way spot . . ."

"I doubt it," Kate said. "It's not removed from the rest of the house, like a real basement. It looks different inside, but it's really just another room—surrounded by rooms. And from what Carl said, he was in and out of most of them running cables, beefing up the electrical system, and setting up cameras."

"But we can check it out," Maxi said softly. "If we're gonna accidentally get lost all over this house, we might as well start there."

"Thank you," Desiree said.

Aimee appeared again in the doorway and tapped her clipboard. "Ken's ready for you now in his office," she said. "You're in for a treat. You'll get to see the only room in the house that's off-limits to the cameras."

"We'll finish setting up," Desiree said, smiling.

"Yeah, we've got it here," Maxi said brightly. "You go get ready for your TV debut."

"Hi, Kate, welcome to Conch House," Ken Salazar said, extending his hand, as his brown eyes twinkled. "Thanks for doing this. I really think the kids are going to enjoy it. I believe you will, too. We have fun."

"It seems like a good opportunity," she said, smiling as she shook his hand. "To showcase the Cookie House."

His tan had deepened in the few days since he'd stopped by the bakery. Or it could have been bronzer. By contrast, Howie—who'd become a regular at the Cookie House—had a nasty sunburn that was just beginning to peel.

"Now if you have any questions on any of this, just say the word," Salazar said, slipping a two-page document on the desk in front of her.

Kate picked it up and scanned through it. The amount she'd managed to negotiate for teaching a class—printed in bold ink near the end of the contract—made her heart skip a beat.

"This is the contract I emailed over yesterday— standard boiler-plate stuff," Salazar said from his perch on the side of the desk. "Lets us use any of the footage you appear in. Promises we won't alter it to make you or your business look bad. We reimburse for any expenses. It also spells out that you don't get royalties. When it comes to the fee, we're one and done," he said, placing a check in front of her on the desk. "Unless, of course we decide to make the classes a regular feature. Then each time you teach, you get another check. Same amount. Sound good?"

"It sounds very fair," Kate agreed, doubly glad she'd accepted Maxi's offer to have Peter read through the fine print last night. The check in front of her would be a good start on an emergency savings account for the bakery. Something they didn't currently have.

Salazar handed her a gold pen.

She signed quickly and handed it back to him.

"Excellent. Aimee will make a few copies and have one for you before you leave," he said, as Kate deftly tucked the check into her jeans pocket.

"It's a beautiful house," she said, looking around the room. She missed the abundant collection of books that had lined the floor-to-ceiling bookcases. The library, while still beautiful, was spare. Only a few framed photos—Salazar and various friends, along with some scenic shots—littered the shelves.

"Yeah, we got quite the deal. Tremendous house. Just beautiful. But apparently not much demand for a place this size right now. Not locally, anyway. We just rented it for the season. But I could have picked it up for a song. Still might. I wouldn't mind having a winter place in Florida. New York gets a little dreary in January and February."

"Tell me about it," Kate said smiling. "This will be my first winter here. I'm really looking forward to it. Oh, and you might know another friend of mine who's down here, too. Judson Cooper?"

"The environmentalist? Never met him. He from New York?"

She cocked her head to one side. "As much as he's from anywhere. His work takes him all over."

"Mine too. But I have to say, this place, the people?

Great. Absolute salt of the earth. Yeah, Coral Cay is one of the nicest locations we've had in a while."

"Key," Kate said.

"What?"

She smiled. "The locals—they pronounce it 'Coral Key.' Like a key that opens a lock. Just to help you and the houseguests fit in," she said lightly.

"Right, sure. Now, let's go over the ground rules for this morning's contest."

"Contest?" Kate asked, puzzled.

"Oh yeah," Salazar said beaming. "This isn't public TV. We can't just broadcast a class, no matter how cute the teacher is. No, this is prime time. Top ten in the Nielsen's. We have to spice it up a little. But don't worry. You're gonna love what we've got planned."

Chapter 25

As her students wandered into the kitchen, Kate wondered how Maxi and Desiree were faring. She was also curious what would happen if Salazar ran into Desiree. Would he remember her? Or was she just one of the many "salt of the earth" people he'd encountered and forgotten over the years?

Awful as it sounded, she was really hoping he didn't buy this house. But then, if Judson had discovered a rare species on the grounds, there might not be a sale at all.

One of the houseguests skimmed an eye at Kate and elbowed his friend.

"OK, housemates," Salazar announced, clapping his hands. "Let's take our places around the work station. Now, you may notice that Tucker isn't here this morning. That's because he's lost his house privileges for the next forty-eight hours. Which means, yes, he'll be doing the grunt work at Conch House for the next two days. That's right, our friend Tucker will be scrubbing all the bathrooms, taking out trash, and doing your ironing. So if you need a little extra starch in your shirts, you know who to see."

The housemates giggled right on cue.

"Too bad, so sad for Tucker. Because he doesn't know what he's missing. Although he's going to smell it soon enough," Salazar teased.

The six girls tittered.

"That's right, because this morning, we're making cookies," Salazar enthused. "With a little help from our local guest, Chef Kate."

The cameraman swung the camera around and waved at Kate. Behind him, Aimee frantically pointed to her mouth. Kate hurriedly smiled for the camera.

"But here at Conch House, nothing is ever quite what it seems," Salazar intoned. "Because, while I can't wait to chill on the patio with a cold glass of milk and sample the results of your efforts, there's a little more at stake here."

Kate saw two of the guys stand a little straighter.

"That's right, this is a Conch House contest!" Salazar finished dramatically.

At this, three of the girls jumped up and down, while two more hugged each other. Several of the guys exchanged high-fives, as the rest of the group nodded excitedly.

"First, the treat—an entire day at the Playa Dulce resort! So while the rest of us are toiling away at the house, you'll get to kick back and chill around their salt-water pool, enjoy the swim-up bar, listen to live bands, and feast on five-star dining in your own private beach cabana. For you and the friend of your choice."

"Can I take the chef?"

"Behave yourself, Ryder," Salazar said, wagging a tanned finger. "Or Tucker's going to have some help with all that laundry."

The rest of the group giggled.

"Now, so that our winner can ride in style, he—or she—will have use of the sizzling hot Beemer in our Conch House garage."

One of the guys, wearing a red T-shirt and tan board shorts, gave a long, low whistle.

"Nice!" said another.

"But that's the treat," Salazar paused with a wolfish grin. "Those of you who are in it to win it know that's not quite all."

The housemates looked at one another expectantly.

"That's right," Salazar continued. "Win this competition, you could snag the biggest purse yet for your Conch House account. Fifty shells!"

One of the girls gasped and put her hands to her face, while someone else whistled.

"Fifty?" another girl squealed.

Salazar nodded. "That's right, housemates. And you know what that means. With Tucker out of the running, that could decide who becomes the leader of Conch House next week. So his loss is *someone*'s gain," he added meaningfully. "Ready to get started?"

As one, the housemates clapped and cheered.

"I'll take that as a 'yes,'" Salazar said, grinning. "Now our own Chef Kate will show you how to make . . ." Salazar looked at her.

"Sugar cookies," Kate supplied quickly, remembering to smile for the camera.

"Mmmm, sugar cookies!" Salazar said, rubbing his stomach. "My favorites!" "And at the end of our competition, you'll submit a half dozen of your best cookies for judging. Now you can get creative or keep it as simple as you like. Whatever you think will impress our panel. To keep things fair, we'll do a blind judging— none of the three judges will know who baked what.

That's between you guys and Chef Kate," he said, winking into the camera. "Now, I'm one of the judges. And you'll meet the other two when I come back in ninety minutes. But, in the meantime, let me leave you with one thought. Hard work and talent will be rewarded. Our winner will snag an entire day out at Playa Dulce, exclusive use of the luxury car, fifty shells—and the chance to be the next leader of Conch House. May the best man or woman win!"

Kate's stomach lurched. Salazar was leaving! He wouldn't be here for the class. Which meant, for the next hour and a half, while Maxi and Desiree banked on the producer being occupied in the kitchen, he could pop up anywhere in the house. And she had no way to warn them.

As Salazar strode purposefully out of the room, Kate prayed that—wherever he was headed—it wasn't the room her friends were scoping out right this very minute.

Chapter 26

"So do you know what the score is with Tucker?" one of the girls asked Kate. "Why's he on report? It's got something to do with his trip to town, but they won't tell us anything."

"I don't know," Kate said, crossing her fingers behind her back. "I'm just helping you guys improve your cookie-baking skills."

How could she warn Maxi and Desiree?

"Well, I slay at baking," a svelte, tanned brunette in a red sundress announced from the other side of the marble island. "Even my mom admits that my cookies are fire. So, no offense to you, but I'm just going to get started."

"If Daniella starts now, she'll get the oven first," fumed a tall, slim girl with a close-cropped Afro. "That's not fair."

"There are four ovens, Cecily," one of the guys said, pointing to two of the walls. "Check it out. Besides, if we have time to pick up a few tips, I say we do it."

"Do you think sugar cookies are really Ken's favorites?" asked a fair-skinned girl with tumbling waves of honey-blond hair. "Or was he just saying that? 'Cause with him, I can never tell."

"They actually are," Kate confirmed. "He was in the bakery earlier this week."

The blond smiled. "Then maybe I do have a chance."

An ugly thought invaded Kate's brain. As desperate as Desiree was to find Judson, what if Maxi couldn't keep tabs on her? And what would happen if Ken Salazar discovered one of her friends rooting through the house?

One of the guys snickered. "The prize Annabel really wants to snag isn't fifty shells. Or should I say, the prize she wants to *shag*!"

"Shut up, Jason!" Annabel shouted, punching him in the shoulder.

"Hey, guys, take it easy," Kate said, stepping toward them.

"Look, you don't know what we're going through," another girl added as she adjusted the red headband that held back her swingy, dark blond hair. "You have no idea what's at stake. Tucker's been house leader for all of three days, and he's making our lives miserable. Even on report. You think he's cleaning *our* toilets or ironing *our* clothes?" she asked, pointing to several of her girlfriends, who all shook their heads. "If he manages to put together enough shells to make house leader again—him or one of his bro squad," she hissed, eyeing a cluster of three boys across the kitchen island, "I swear I am so out of here!"

"Yeah, well good riddance, Candy!" one of the boys spat.

"You're right," Kate admitted quietly. "The truth is,

when I agreed to come here, I didn't know anything
about a contest—or the show, for that matter. I love to
bake. I co-own a bakery. Ken said he wanted me to give
you all a few pointers. For fun. A lot of people just enjoy
baking. It's relaxing. You think your own thoughts, enjoy the smell of the ingredients, experiment with flavors. And you can work out a lot of stress mixing and
squeezing dough."

"Meditation," said a lanky guy in jeans and a white tee.

"Exactly," Kate said "And, if you do it right, you get
a treat when you're done. Something you can share, if
you want. That's it. No contest. No prizes. No competition. Just enjoying the moment."

"Life's the journey," her new friend added, running
one hand over his cropped Afro.

Kate nodded gratefully.

"Well, while you losers are singing 'Kumbaya,' I'm
going to be sunning myself at Playa Dulce," Daniella announced. "And I'm not taking any of you. It'll be worth
it just to get away from all the whining and backstabbing.
Annabel."

"What's that supposed to mean?"

"It means, roomie, I don't buy your Little Miss In-
nocent act. And I also know you've been talking trash
about me since I arrived. Just like I know that my silver
dolphin ring didn't swim away on its own."

"Are you calling me a thief?"

"If the dolphin fits."

Annabel's nose turned red, as her eyes filled with
tears. "I've never stolen anything in my life."

"Don't mind her, honey," Cecily said, patting Annabel's shoulder, as she shot Daniella a dirty look. "Like
anybody would want anything that fits her big old fingers!"

Fingers! Kate realized she could text Maxi. Cell phone service may be iffy in downtown, but, thanks to Tucker and friends, she knew it had to work here.

"Hey, if you want to room with Klepto Annie, be my guest," Daniella spat. "But you better put a lock on your jewelry box."

"Enough!" Kate shouted, surprising herself. She took a deep breath, stepped forward, and placed her fingertips on the cool marble of the kitchen island.

"Ladies," she continued evenly, "the kitchen is for baking. If you want to argue, take it to another room."

The cameraman flashed Kate a thumbs-up.

"No chance," Daniella huffed, as she attacked the contents of her mixing bowl with a wooden spoon. "She's already taken my ring, I'm not letting her steal my resort day, too."

"OK, before we get started, I need to send a quick text," Kate said matter-of-factly, checking her watch. "Those who want to have some fun, bake sugar cookies, and pick up a few pointers—grab a baking sheet, a mixing bowl, a wooden spoon, and a spatula—and stake out a spot at the island. Those who don't, I won't keep you."

Chapter 27

"OK, Blue Oven team—Annabel, Candy, Cecily. Time to take yours out now," Kate said, smiling. "Good job!"

"They don't look brown enough," Annabel said.

"Not like your first ones, girl," Cecily said, grinning.

"They were good once I scraped off the charred parts."

"Sugar cookies—a lot of cookies, really—keep cooking even after you take them out of the oven," Kate said. "So you want to pull them out when they're just a shade or two lighter than you want. These look perfect."

"Not as good as *these* beauties," Daniella crowed, as she passed a hand over the platter piled high with perfectly formed golden-brown disks, studded with large crystals of colored sugar.

"I tint my own sugar," she bragged. "But that's not something you can just pick up. It takes skill. Otherwise, it looks gaudy."

Ryder and one of his buddies smirked.

Kate reflexively touched the phone in her jeans pocket.

She'd texted Maxi eons ago. Still no response. Did that mean that her friend was being cautious? Or that she hadn't gotten the message?

"OK, Red Oven team—Ryder, Jason, Cole—you're up in five minutes. Remember, every oven works a little differently. Since we don't know the quirks of these four, this is about the time you want to start watching those cookies constantly."

James was busily alternating three bags of royal icing. And he had a practiced hand with an offset spatula. When Kate looked over his shoulder, she saw that he was turning his cookies into baseballs. Complete with little red-icing stitches.

"OK, that's really cool," she said softly.

He beamed. "The smell reminded me of my gramma's Christmas cookies," he said, brushing a white smear of icing from his jeans. "We always decorate those with icing. That and the playoffs kinda gave me the idea. Since these things are round."

"I just might have to steal that," Kate said. "You don't know Andy Levy, but he and his wife run the pub in town. And he would absolutely love these."

"OK, it's almost noon and Mr. Salazar will be back any minute," Kate reminded her students. "Plate your best cookies and bring them up to the kitchen table. Keep the mistakes to eat later," she added. "They're still delicious."

It never ceased to amaze her that a group of people could follow the exact same recipe in the exact same kitchen at the exact same time, and every single batch would look completely different.

James's baseballs were a standout. Both realistic and uniform. But Kate had to admit that Daniella's cookies, coated with large crystals of colorful sugar that sparkled in the light, were pretty.

Annabel had finally conquered her tendency to over-bake the dough. Her latest batch was a tempting golden brown—even if they were a bit misshapen.

One unfortunate would-be baker got the butter too warm and was rewarded with thin, flat cookies that were slightly burnt around the edges. Kate recalled Maxi's story at the cookie class. She hoped—not for the first time—that her friends were managing to poke around unnoticed.

Cole attempted to draw detailed scenes freehand on his cookies with royal icing. They were colorful but un-recognizable. More Pollock than Picasso.

Cecily added pumpkin-pie spice to her dough, then topped the cookies with orange-tinted icing. And Kate couldn't wait to try one.

As the housemates milled around the table waiting for Ken Salazar, Kate carried a stack of used baking trays to the sink. She lifted the top pan, grabbed a rubber spatula, and scraped off the burnt cookie bits.

Candy and Cecily brought over their cookie sheets. As they each picked up spatulas, Kate moved over to make room for them at the oversized farmhouse sink.

"When did you guys start arriving at Conch House?" Kate asked.

"Sunday afternoon," Candy said softly, as she watched Kate's hands and copied her short, deft strokes with the spatula. "They gave us the evening to get settled in, learn what's where in the house, and hit the beach. Somebody even brought a guitar. And that was pretty cool."

Cecily nodded.

"But the next day, it all changed," Candy added.

"How so?" Kate asked.

"That's when the game started," Cecily said, glancing across the cavernous room where Daniella and a cluster of the guys were gathered around the large kitchen table talking and laughing. "Right off, Tucker was elected house leader."

"We all had a say, but it was, I don't know, like it had already been decided," Candy said. "Daniella and most of the guys voted for him. Anybody who didn't? He went after them. He's the one who changed up the room assignments and put Annabel in with Daniella."

"Daniella's been using her for a chew toy ever since," Cecily explained. "Making fun of her. Accusing her of taking stuff."

"We're all supposed to share the work and trade chores regularly," Candy said. "But he has Cecily and me on laundry duty for the week."

"While he and his friends lay on the beach," Cecily added.

"Yeah, forget the beach. We've barely been out of the laundry room in two days. I figured a couple of months working in a South Florida resort town would be fun. But this isn't."

"Nope," Cecily agreed.

"Now that Tucker's been sidelined, that should change, though, right?" Kate asked.

The girls shook their heads. "He's the 'golden boy,'" Candy said. "He'll wriggle out of it somehow. He's supposed to be out of the running for house leader next week, but it feels like he's still pulling the strings."

"You think the game is rigged?"

"More like Tucker and his buds have banded together," Cecily said. "I mean, it's allowed. Ken Salazar calls it 'gamesmanship.' As in whoever plays the game better wins."

"It sounds more like bullying than teamwork," Kate said.

Candy sighed. "Let's just say it's not what I expected.

At least if I had a resort job, I'd have some down time that would be mine. And a little cash. If this doesn't improve, I might just do that."

"Well, if you guys ever need to get away from this place for a little while, come see downtown. It's a whole different side of Coral Cay. And if you're serious about resort work, I know a few people. I can make some introductions."

"That would be awesome," Candy said. "Thank you."

"All right, housemates, the moment of judgment has arrived," Ken Salazar announced, strolling into the kitchen with a beatific smile on his face.

Kate took that as a good sign. At least it didn't look like the face of a man who'd had two people thrown out of his house for trespassing.

"And," the host said, pausing dramatically, and extending an arm toward the doorway, "I think you might recognize your two celebrity judges."

"OMG, it's Nikki and Siobhan!" Daniella squealed, as the room broke into loud applause, accompanied by whistles and hoots.

"Friends of yours?" Kate whispered.

Candy and Cecily shook their heads. "Nikki won last season," Cecily said under her breath. "Siobhan came in second, but just barely. It got plenty nasty, too."

As the judges circled the table, the housemates migrated back to the kitchen island, watching nervously.

"Oh, I want to try one of these first," Nikki said, picking up one of Daniella's colorful cookies.

"An early favorite for the win?" Salazar asked, examining them. "They certainly look good."

Nikki held the cookie up for the camera, broke it in half, and took a big bite. Suddenly, she started choking.

She hobbled to the sink and spit it out, rinsing her mouth then carefully blotting her lips with a paper towel.

The cameraman, Kate noticed, never stopped filming.

"That was awful!" Nikki exclaimed dramatically, running one hand over her spiky purple-black hair. "Totally vile."

Across the room, Ryder and Jason doubled over laughing.

Daniella turned on them. "You two! What did you do? What did you put in my cookies?"

She stalked over to the table and snatched a cookie from the platter. Breaking off a small piece, she popped it in her mouth.

Then she spit it into a paper napkin.

"Salt!" Daniella screeched, "You switched all my sugar with salt!"

"Not us," Ryder said, putting his palms up.

"Genius . . . though," said Jason said, struggling to speak while convulsing with laughter. "Wish . . . I'd . . . thought of it."

"Really?" Daniella marched over, yanked a pitcher of cold milk off the counter, and dumped the contents over both of them. "When you find out who *really* did it, you can give them that from me!"

Chapter 28

"So what's it like being a big reality-TV star?" Maxi asked as she, Kate, and Desiree hauled boxes of baking equipment back to the car.

"Put it this way, if we're lucky, no one will ever connect that show to the Cookie House. It's like *Lord of the Flies* in there."

"Yup, sounds like most of the ones I've seen," Maxi said.

"Not in a hurry to go back, then?" Desiree asked.

"Not in this lifetime," Kate admitted. "But that doesn't mean I won't cash their check. Honestly, I was never so relieved to see two people in my life. Once I realized Ken Salazar was loose in the house, I didn't know what to do."

"No worries," Maxi said breezily. "We got this spy thing down. Sit around and drink tea for a while until they forget you exist. Then just go where you want."

"That was pretty much it," Desiree admitted. "They

put us in some kind of den with iced tea and a bowl of nut mix. After that, we were on our own."

"Did you find anything interesting?" Kate asked, as Maxi swung open the rear door of the red Jeep.

"We found a young man sleeping in the laundry room," Desiree said, smiling.

"More like passed out," Maxi corrected.

"That would be Tucker," Kate said.

"The guy who stole from Amos?" Maxi asked.

"The same. And apparently he's a real piece of work."

"Well, when we saw him, he was working on his beauty sleep," Maxi countered. "If I'd known it was him, I'd have gone through his pockets for Amos's missing cash. 'Cause, believe me, that boy would not have noticed."

"Anything that connects to Judd?" Kate asked.

Desiree shook her head.

"We saw the wine cave," Maxi supplied. "'Course now it's just a cave. Not a bottle in sight."

"We even walked outside along the bluffs—where your friend spotted Judd," Desiree added. "But I didn't see anything. At least nothing that meant anything to me. But then, I don't know why Judd was here and what he was looking for."

"The cast mates didn't arrive here until Sunday afternoon," Kate said. "So that rules them out. And Salazar says he doesn't know Judd," Kate said. "Never met him."

"Do you believe him?" Desiree asked. Kate noticed fresh worry lines around her eyes.

"He's pretty slick, granted. But I didn't get the impression he was hiding anything. Self-centered, sure. Maybe a little manipulative. But I can't really picture him as a kidnapper. Not that that means anything."

"We talked to some of the crew members, too," Desiree said. "I'd thought if TV is anything like hospitality, it's the people who work behind the scenes who see everything."

"We couldn't exactly go around flashing a picture of Judson Cooper," Maxi added. "But we asked about visitors to the site. Or 'set,' as they're calling it now. *Nada*."

"I was so hoping we'd find something," Desiree said, staring back at the house as a breeze ruffled the branches of the ancient pin oaks. "Just a breadcrumb to help us follow his trail."

"I was thinking about that," Kate said. "Carl may have seen Judd here. But that was just one time. And it was almost ten days ago. There's another spot on the island that Judson mentioned frequently—and more recently, too. He even looked it up when he was buying maps at Barb's bookstore. And it was the same place we spotted that cigarette boat. I'd like to make The Nose—Turtle Bay—our next field trip."

"OK, *Corazón*, but you're gonna need a boat. Part of the reason that bay is so pristine is that pretty much the only way to get out there is by water. Unless you want to invade Iris's house."

"I'd kind of like to leave her out of it," Kate admitted. "Seeing as we don't know what we're dealing with—or who'll be watching. Although, the idea of going there with a group is smart."

"So what sea-loving veterinarian do you know who might ferry a few of us out there?" Maxi asked, grinning.

"Jack's got a boat?"

"A little motor boat, but yeah."

"You're right," Desiree said, her face lighting up. "He was telling Judd and I about it last week on the *Starfish*. He picked it up it for marine rescue work, and it seats eight. Oh, let's go out there today! If Jack can take us, wonderful. But if he can't, we can rent a boat at one of the marinas."

"Make it for after work, and I'll go with you," Maxi said. "That is, if I get all my deliveries done. And we can probably find a few of the Irregulars who'll go, too." She tapped Desiree's shoulder. "Show her the other thing."

Desiree opened her purse, and took out a palm-sized black-and-orange object encased in a Ziploc bag. She held it aloft.

"What is that?" Kate asked, puzzled.

"A distributor cap," Desiree said, smiling. "A little trick we used at the hotel from time to time to make sure guests didn't drive when they were impaired. Without this, the car won't start."

"Yup," Maxi added. "And this one goes to a brand-new, poison green BMW convertible. One with a back seat full of crumpled beer cans."

Chapter 29

"Call while you were out," Sam announced when Kate walked into the bakery. "Doc Scanlon. Left the message on the fridge. Couldn't make hide ner hair of those other notes, though."

"Ooo, do I sense a little romance in the air?" Delores Philpott cooed.

"It's about young Oliver, I expect," Sam said. "You want some a' that challah? Just came out of the oven 'bout an hour ago. Got whole wheat, too."

"I'll take a loaf of the regular," Delores replied. "Sliced, if it's not too much trouble, Sam. But you have to admit," she added, without pausing for breath, "those two would make a very cute couple."

Kate hadn't meant to leave her Post-it notes on the bakery's refrigerator. She looked at the scattering of yellow scraps again, hoping that something would click. Nothing.

Where was Judson Cooper? If he had just sailed away—voluntarily—why hadn't anyone heard from him?

Even if he and Desiree had broken up, why would he leave her without so much as a letter? That was just cruel. And what about the other people in his life—his children, his friends, his business partner? Even if Desiree had been a deranged stalker, certainly he'd have still been in touch with them?

Unless he really had reached out to them. And had asked them not to say anything.

Kate shook off the thought. Ridiculous.

She snatched the yellow slip with Jack's number, lifted the phone from the receiver, and dialed.

"Coral Cay Animal Clinic, may I help you?"

"Hi, this is Kate McGuire. I'm returning a call to Ja . . . ah . . . Dr. Scanlon."

"Hi, Kate, this is Becky. Doc's at the coffee maker. Hang on."

After half a minute of classical music, Jack's baritone filled the receiver.

"Kate, this is a nice surprise! How are you? And how's Oliver?"

"We're both fine, thanks. I was just wondering, you haven't by any chance heard from Judson Cooper, have you?"

"Nope, not a word. When I got back into town this morning, Andy Levy told me no one has. Not since Friday night."

"That's the problem. Desiree's going out of her mind with worry. Ben's still trying to make contact with him—just to make sure he's OK. But so far, nothing. It's like he's dropped off the face of the earth."

"Well, he always has been a bit of an absentminded professor."

Kate sighed.

"What can I do to help?" he asked gently.

The story came tumbling out in a verbal waterfall. No overt signs of foul play, but plenty of speculation and worry. Trying to trace Judd's movements. The biologist's fascination with Turtle Bay. The maps. The cigarette boat. The list of past criminals he'd confronted.

"I had no idea," Jack said, when she paused. "I'm sorry I just took off for the seminar. Judd recommended the class, ironically. Triage for distressed marine mammals. I should have stayed to help."

"At that point, we didn't know anything," Kate said softly. "I think we all thought we'd have heard something by now—even if it was a ransom demand. But it's been five days and nothing. We'd like to go out to Turtle Bay. Just to look around. But apparently you need a boat to get out there . . ."

"Which I just happen to have. When do you want to leave?"

"Could you do it this afternoon? After work?"

"I've got Mrs. Hardy's schnauzer at three. She's doing great, so it's just a quick checkup and blood draw. Barring any emergencies, I could have the boat gassed up and ready to go at four thirty. Would that work?"

"That would be great, Jack. I can't thank you enough for this."

"No worries. Judd and Desiree are friends of mine, too. I want to help. The boat's at Broken Creek marina. You want meet up there?"

"There's one other thing . . ." Kate said, hesitating.

"Now you sound like my pet parents at the end of an appointment. That's when they usually fess up and tell me the real reason for the visit. Like Mister Whiskers has taken to nibbling socks, or General Patton is afraid of thunderstorms."

"General Patton?"

"Mr. Squires' bulldog. But you didn't hear that from me. And the way the storms roll through here, I don't blame him."

"We think someone might have been visiting Turtle Bay recently. From what Iris noticed, likely more than one person. So we don't know exactly what's going on out there."

"Which is why we need to check it out, right?"

"I just wanted you to know what you were getting into," Kate confessed. "Anyway, there will probably be quite a few of us on the trip," Kate said. "Just for that very reason."

"Sounds like a good strategy," Jack agreed. "The boat seats eight. But in a pinch, I'm sure we can squeeze in a few more."

Chapter 30

"I'm surprised Minette didn't come," Maxi shouted over the roar of the engine as Jack's boat knifed through the deep blue water.

"Somebody has to watch the store," Carl explained. "And between you and me, I'd rather have her as far away from all this as possible. Not a great idea to poke something that could turn out to be a hornet's nest."

"Is that what Ben said?" Kate shouted.

"He said Kyle's already been out to The Nose," Carl said. "After Cooper took . . . uh, disappeared," he added, a quick glance in the direction of Desiree, who was seated up front next to Jack. "But he didn't see any harm in it. As long as you all weren't wandering around out there alone."

"He asked you to come," Kate said.

"Suggested it might be prudent," Carl confirmed. "Unofficially, of course. The place is beautiful. But it's also desolate. And treacherous. All manner of creatures out there."

"Snakes?" Kate asked.

"Yeah, but I'm more worried about the two-legged variety. They've been known to use the cove from time to time. And they're a lot more dangerous."

"From the pirates on, The Nose has always been a magnet for smugglers and criminals," Maxi shouted above the engine noise and the wind.

"Well, thank you for coming along," Kate said, gratefully. "Even if you are humoring us about finding a lead on Judson."

"Wasn't Sunny coming?" Rosie said, rubbing Oliver's back through his life jacket as he stretched out at their feet. "Her mom lives right down the beach."

"She's driving out to give Iris a heads-up," Barb said. "She'll meet us there."

"OK, folks," Jack said, turning. "Based on the maps, the tides, and the position of the shoals, I think I can get us within about seven yards of the shore. But we're going to have to walk the rest of the way. So I hope everybody's all right with getting their feet wet."

Maxi rolled her jeans to just above the knees, and Kate followed suit. Barb, Carl, Desiree, and Jack had opted for shorts, Kate noticed.

"I ditched my heels for running shoes, because I knew we'd be walking the beach—but this thing," Rosie said, waving a hand over her plum-colored skirt, "is dry-clean only."

"We'll go first, so you can see how high the water comes," Maxi said. "If you have to, just roll up the waistband."

The antique-store owner peeled off her sneakers and dangled them casually from one hand by the laces. "How's she doing?" Rosie asked, nodding toward Desiree, who was deep in conversation with Jack.

"Amazing, really," Kate said. "She's not giving up.

She just keeps going. Doing whatever she can to find him."

"Has Ben Abrams got any new leads?" Barb asked, leaning toward Carl.

"Nothing he shared with me," Carl said. "But if he'd heard from Cooper, he'd have told us."

"And here we are," Jack shouted, throwing the engine into reverse, then cutting it. "As soon as I drop the anchor, we can give it a go."

"A couple of ground rules, first," Carl said gravely. "Most important, we all stick together. Nobody goes wandering off." He turned to Desiree. "Anywhere you want to search, we'll search. But we do it together. And when we start losing the light, we leave. No arguments. If we have to, we'll come back tomorrow. Everybody understand?"

They all nodded.

"And this is one time I'd put our young friend Oliver on a leash," he added. "He catches the scent of something interesting in that underbrush, he might go charging off. And we'd have a heck of time trying to follow him."

"All set," Maxi said, producing a bright yellow lead from her fanny pack.

Jack climbed down the ladder and jumped off. Kate was relieved to see that the water came only halfway to his knees.

"We're anchored right at the drop-off," Jack shouted. "When you come off the ladder, take a big step toward the shore and you'll be in shallow water."

As Desiree climbed down the ladder, he stood off to one side and offered her a hand.

But before Maxi could clip the leash onto Oliver's collar, the pup scrambled to the bow and leapt into the water.

"Oliver!" Kate screamed, as she and Maxi lurched to the front of the boat. Kate leaned over the bow, holding her breath. The half-grown pup was excitedly dog-paddling in the deeper water below.

"Funny how the puppy who can't wait to get out of his bathtub is the same puppy who can't wait to jump into the sea," Maxi said.

Carl shook his head. "Dog's got a mind of his own. As soon as we get to shore—"

"We'll clip the leash right on," Maxi finished, brandishing the lead.

"Well, at least someone's enjoying our outing," Kate said, relieved.

As they waded through the warm water toward the beach, Kate saw Sunny Eisenberg waving from the shore. Sleek and ageless, the yoga teacher was a walking advertisement for her classes.

Oliver, apparently finished with his swim, bounded through the shallow water up onto the beach, where he gave himself a vigorous shake. Then he loped over to Sunny, and raced around her in the sand.

"Have you been waiting long?" Jack asked.

"Just a few minutes," Sunny said, offering the pup a treat from her pocket. "Mom sends her best. She wanted to have you all in for tea and sandwiches. But it's so late, we realized you'd be racing daylight to get back."

Maxi took advantage of the momentary distraction to clip the lead to Oliver's collar. Laser-focused on Sunny, the pup didn't appear to notice.

"Please tell her thanks anyway," Desiree said. "That's really kind of her."

"Of course, dear," Sunny said, slipping another treat to an enraptured Oliver. "Now, Maxi said you wanted to see where Mom spotted those footprints. They were this way, down the beach."

"I'm just as happy we're not dragging Iris into this business," Carl said quietly to Kate and Jack, as they trailed behind the group. "I seriously doubt we're going to find anything to do with your friend Cooper out here. But if some bunch of miscreants has been using the cove recently, I don't want to lead them back to her place."

Kate and Jack exchanged glances.

"Look, I hope Judd did just sail off for a few days of R&R," Jack said lightly. "But it's kind of odd that nobody's heard from him. And he's apparently a little obsessed with this beach."

"That would make sense," Carl said, swatting at a mosquito that had landed on his brown forearm. "It's where those big turtles come to lay their eggs. Then when they hatch, there's a whole wave of 'em all at once heading for the surf. Ever seen it?"

Kate and Jack shook their heads.

"Dangdest thing I've ever witnessed," he said, smiling. "Little things can't be much bigger than a silver dollar. They come out fighting, though. Motoring toward that water for all they're worth."

As they caught up with the group, Barb pointed toward a circle of rocks and stones with charred wood in the center. "Looks like the remains of a campfire," she said.

"That's it exactly," Sunny said. "It's one of the things Mom checks when she walks the beach in the mornings. To make sure it's cool, and the fire's out. A couple of times, she had to douse live embers with sea water, if you can believe it."

"So why not just take the stones away?" Rosie asked. "It kind of invites a fire."

"Devil's compromise," Sunny said. "People camping out here always light a fire, whether we like it or not. And in the past, a couple of the fools put it so close to the trees they nearly lit the whole forest on fire. So Mom picked an optimum site just above the high-water mark and set up the circle. It's like a neon sign that reads, 'If you're going to lay a fire, this is the place.' And, of course, she keeps an eye on it."

"Smart," Carl agreed.

"No argument there," Sunny said, grinning.

"Has she seen any more signs of activity since Saturday?" Kate asked.

"A few footprints Tuesday morning. And it looked like someone might have lit a fire. Based on what she saw, it was probably just a couple of teenagers. The local kids love this spot. Of course, I have no idea why," she added lightly.

Oliver lurched forward, tugging Maxi with him. "C'mon, Mr. Oliver. Behave yourself. Or no more swims and treats."

The pup lunged for the fire pit. Maxi, thrown off balance, landed in the soft, white sand.

Trailing his leash, Oliver trotted around the stone circle, sniffing each of the rocks intently.

"Last bunch out here might have brought a dog," Carl said, extending a hand down to Maxi. "He's picking up the scent."

Jack smiled, as he retrieved the end of the lead. "That would be my professional opinion. You OK?"

"*Sí*, just surprised more than anything," Maxi said, brushing sand off herself. "He doesn't usually do that. The Oliver I know always likes his leash."

"Probably because it usually signals that he's getting to go out and spend time with his favorite people," Jack said. "But this time, he's already out on an adventure with his favorite people. So he wants to explore. Don't you, Oliver?"

Oliver looked up briefly, then went back to methodically sniffing the fire pit. To Kate, he looked like a dog on a mission.

"So he's not turning into a doggie delinquent?" Maxi quipped. "Or, even worse, a teenager?"

Jack laughed, as he handed off the yellow lead to Kate. "A teenager, maybe. A delinquent, never."

As the guys and Maxi trailed Sunny and Desiree along the beach, Kate reached down and gave Oliver a pat.

The pup looked up at her with bright eyes, then quickly turned his attention back to one of the stones he'd previously sniffed. He nudged it with his snout. And again. Kate bent and took a closer look. A large jagged rock. She pulled it away from the circle and rolled it over, revealing a long streak of dirt on the underside. Not dirt. Reddish. Rust?

Kate watched as Oliver backed off from the circle and nosed the loose sand. Suddenly, she caught a glint of something in the sunlight. Then it disappeared. Oliver pawed the dirt and whined.

She put a hand on his flank—both to calm him and steady herself—and reached beneath the warm, sugary sand.

Her fingertips brushed something smooth. She thrust her hand blindly into the sand banked up around the fire pit. What was it Carl had warned about—"all manner of creatures"? She pictured nests of spiders and scorpions as her hand closed around something cold and hard. She yanked it free and opened her palm.

Resting in it was a man's gold ring. Ancient looking. Set in the middle with a small ruby.

Kate had been so focused, she hadn't even heard Desiree steal up and sink down into the sand beside her.

Desiree plucked the ring from Kate's palm. She clutched it to her chest, uttering one long, anguished syllable.

"Judd."

Chapter 31

After that, everything seemed to happen in fast-forward.

Sunny ran to Iris's cottage and called the police. Ben and Kyle arrived in a speedboat. And two white crime-scene vans—one from the mainland—arrived with a squadron of sheriff's department vehicles, creating a bottleneck in Iris's driveway. As the sun sank into the gulf, crime-scene techs, police officers, and sheriff's deputies trekked back and forth across the sand like ants at a beach picnic.

"We don't know much, at this point," Ben explained, as Kate and her friends coalesced around Desiree. "You've identified the ring as Judson Cooper's . . ."

"He always wore it," she said quickly. "It's from one of the first dives he ever made. In college. The sponsors let him have it instead of a paycheck. He never took it off."

Kate saw Ben glance at Jack, who nodded.

"Yes, ma'am," Ben said, consulting a small notebook in his palm. "Now, I've called in people from some of the local sheriff's departments, and they're helping us conduct a search of the immediate area tonight. To look for Dr. Cooper But we're battling Mother Nature. Pretty soon it's going to be too dark to see anything, much less continue the search. So we'll have to come back first thing tomorrow. And that's when we'll do the grid search."

"Can we help?" Desiree asked. "With searching?"

Ben shook his head. "We'll have our teams literally cover every inch of this area. If he's here, we'll find him. If he's been here, we'll find evidence of that."

"We know he's been here," Desiree said, her face alight with hope. "That ring is proof. He's never without it. He's been here. And he might still *be* here!"

"And that's our working theory, ma'am. But it's also possible that someone took the ring from him—that he was robbed. And we'll follow that angle, too."

Desiree sank down onto a fallen log, as if her knees had given way. "I'd like to stay here tonight. At the cove."

"Desiree, you can't," Kate said. "It's not safe."

"If it's safe enough for the local kids, it's certainly safe enough for me," she said serenely, as Oliver planted himself next to her. "Besides, this is exactly what Judd and I have been doing for the last few months. Traveling all over the world. Sometimes we'd stay in hotels. But just as often, we'd pitch a tent in a field or on a beach. He's here. He's close. He's got to be."

Ben looked over at Kate. He cocked his head and made a subtle motion with his chin. She nodded.

"Rosie, Barb, Maxi—can you guys stay with Desiree for a minute?" Kate asked gently. "Desiree, I'm going to have a quiet word with Ben, and see what I can work out."

"I want to stay," Desiree responded, shivering through clenched teeth. "I know Judd. And I know I can help."

"Just give me a minute," Kate pleaded.

As Ben sauntered down the beach, Kate followed.

When he turned, she could see a mix of emotions on his face in the fading light. Concern. Determination. Guilt. He looked down at her, and his dark eyes softened.

"I know this is hard for her," Ben started.

"Beyond hard," Kate said. "And this is the closest she's gotten to a lead on Judd. You can't just expect her to pick up and go back to her hotel room."

"I can when the entire cove is a crime scene," Ben said quietly. "The stain on that rock? It's blood. I didn't want to say that in front of your friend, because there's a good chance it's Cooper's blood."

"You think he's dead?"

"No, I'm not giving up that easy. On him or her. I feel bad enough we didn't spot the ring or that rock when Kyle was out here Sunday morning. I should have come myself, instead of delegating."

"The stain was on the underside of the rock," Kate said. "You couldn't see it. I wouldn't have noticed it at all if Oliver hadn't been obsessed with it."

"Leave it to our Oliver," Ben said, with a slight smile. "We'll make a police dog out of him yet."

"If Desiree wants to stay on the beach, I could stay here with her," Kate volunteered. "Safety in numbers."

Ben shook his head. "I'm stationing a couple of the guys out here all night. In shifts. They've trained for this kind of thing. But I can't leave civilians at a crime scene. Even if you two are making more headway on this case than I am."

"So it's officially a case now?"

He nodded. "Judson Cooper is officially a missing person. Missing under suspicious circumstances. And he's famous enough that this one could get ugly."

"What do you mean?" Kate asked.

"Some people try to attach themselves to high-profile cases. Makes them feel important. Part of something exciting. Your friend Desiree's phone's going to start blowing up. She's going to have people banging on her door. Well-meaning tipsters. Reporters. People with camera phones looking to make a quick buck from the tabloids. Fake psychics. Con men. When she's at her most vulnerable. You want to help her? Set up a rotation of folks to stay with her. To run interference. Tonight and for the next couple of days. She still at that resort?"

Kate nodded.

"Good. It'll be harder to find her there. I'll have a little word with the management. If we have to, we'll reregister her under a different name. Tell her to use her cell for friends and family only, and just ignore everybody else."

"Could it be a kidnapping?" Kate asked anxiously.

"It could be," Ben said. "Honestly, I'm not ruling out anything, at this point. But I've never heard of a kidnapping where they grabbed someone and went five days and counting without a ransom demand. Any chance someone reached out to her without you knowing? Sometimes, they warn victims' families not to tell anyone."

"No chance. She doesn't have a clue what's happened to him. We only came out here because he'd mentioned this cove to a couple of people around town. And because we saw the way he reacted to that cigarette boat."

"I need your help," Ben confessed, taking a step closer.

Kate picked up the subtle spice of his aftershave in the cool night air. Bay Rum. He'd clearly dressed in a hurry, throwing a blue blazer over a yellow golf shirt and jeans. It was the first time she'd seen him in running shoes.

"I need to get her back to the resort quickly, before all hell breaks loose," he explained quietly.

"This just happened," Kate said, wrapping her arms

around her body to ward off the evening chill. "No one even knows about it yet."

"Unfortunately, that's not exactly true," Ben said, shrugging out of his blazer and draping it around her shoulders. "You see that small army working the scene? My guys I trust to keep their mouths shut. But the two sheriff's departments from the mainland? Not so much. One of their dispatchers is dating a TV reporter. Another deputy's married to a local newspaper editor. Frankly, I'm surprised they haven't shown up here already, but the night is young. That's part of the reason we need a guard detail here tonight."

"Part of the reason?"

"Just between you and me, Iris and Sunny offered to put Desiree up for the night. I declined on her behalf. Mainly, because she'll be better off back at the resort. Away from all of this. And also because I need to know that she's not contaminating the crime scene."

"She wouldn't do that!" Kate exclaimed, just as the klieg lights popped on, bathing the cove in an eerie, otherworldly glow.

"She already has," Ben said evenly. "The way she was cradling Cooper's ring? I'll be very surprised if we pick up any usable prints that aren't hers. Same with DNA. The truth is, we stand a lot better chance of finding Judson Cooper if we can ID who's waylaid him. And so far, your friend has single-handedly destroyed the best lead we have."

Chapter 32

"Look at the bright side," Kate said, dropping her overnight bag next to the mini sofa in the living room of the bungalow. "It'll be just like a slumber party."

Leaning forward on the settee, Desiree shook her head. "A slumber party no one in their right mind would want to attend. Honestly, I don't need a babysitter. Your detective friend is picking me up first thing tomorrow morning, so I can be there for the search. Even if he did say I had to stay on the beach under guard."

"Not a guard, an escort," Kate corrected. "They just want to keep you safe. Especially after word gets out Judson is missing."

"I know he thinks I messed up," she said, shaking her head. "Handling Judd's ring like that. And he's right. I don't know what I was thinking."

"I handled it, too," Kate said.

"You found it," Desiree said. "Thanks to you, we know

Judd was there. Recently. But when I saw that ring . . . right there in front of me, after so many days . . . I can't explain it . . ."

"You don't have to. And Oliver found it. I just pulled it out of the sand. Which probably didn't help, either. But we have some real leads now. That's the whole reason we went to the cove. Now there's a full-scale investigation underway. I know it's scary, but this is progress."

"I know, it's just that my goal was to actually find Judd. I had this fantasy that we'd discover him locked in some storage room at that big house on the bluff. Or sitting on the beach at the cove, just waiting for a ride home. Mentally, I know we're getting closer. But in my heart, it feels like I'm being pushed farther and farther away from him. Like I'm swimming in the ocean and I can't get back to shore."

A sharp rap on the door made them both jump.

Desiree grimaced. "Too much to hope that's him? Got lost on his way to the boat. 'Hi, honey, I'm home. What did I miss?'"

Kate checked the peephole, and swung open the door.

Maxi, holding two large brown-paper carry-out bags, quickly stepped inside.

"Three pub specials, ready to go. I can stay for dinner, but then I gotta get back. It's *Mami*'s mahjong night, so *mi amor*'s holding down the fort by his lonesome. Oh, and Bridget and Andy said hi, by the way."

"You didn't have to do this," Desiree said, taking the bags from Maxi and depositing them on the dinette table. "We could have ordered room service."

"And miss Bridget's turkey meatloaf?" Maxi asked. "And her butternut squash casserole with the sage bread-crumb topping? And the garlic mashed potatoes that

Andy makes himself? Let me tell you, that boy has a heavy hand with the butter. Super good. You bring dessert?"

"Chocolate icebox cookies," Kate said. "I cleaned out the bakery case."

"This smells heavenly," Desiree said, gratefully. "Funny thing is, for the first time in a couple of days, I'm actually hungry."

"That's a good sign," Kate said. As she set out the plates, a loud pounding on the door startled them.

Are you expecting anyone? Kate mouthed.

Desiree shook her head.

"I didn't see a soul out there," Maxi whispered. "And after what Ben said, I was super careful."

"Ms. Goldsmith, this is Brad from the front desk. We need you to open the door now."

Desiree shrugged, as she started toward it.

Kate held up her palm. "Let me do it," she hissed. "Just in case."

She glanced through the peephole and opened the door just a crack. "Ms. Goldsmith's indisposed. I'm her friend, Kate. May I help you?"

"It's a personal business matter," Brad said, matter-of-factly, tapping his clipboard. "It concerns her bill. I need to speak with Ms. Goldsmith."

"I'm in here," Desiree called.

Kate opened the door and stepped aside.

"Ms. Goldsmith, regrettably, you are four days in arrears on your stay. We need to secure some form of payment."

"Judd paid through Sunday morning," Desiree explained to Kate and Maxi. "That's when we were going to check out and sail up the coast."

"How about we take care of this tomorrow?" Kate

asked. "It's been a very long day, and Ms. Goldsmith has to be up very early in the morning."

"I'm afraid that won't be possible. We've already let this slide longer than we should have. I'm under instructions to secure a method of payment this evening or offer to transport Ms. Goldsmith to another establishment. Whichever is more convenient. But we have to retain your belongings until the bill is satisfied."

Desiree snatched her purse from the sideboard and pulled out her wallet. She extracted a black credit card and offered it to him.

Brad shook his head. "We've tried that one already. It was the card Dr. Cooper left on file for miscellaneous room charges. But it's been declined."

She paged through the wallet, pulled out another card, and handed it off to him. "This should take care of the bill and buy me a few more nights. Hopefully, that's all I'll need."

"I'll process this right away and bring you a receipt," he said, shutting the door softly behind him.

"Man, they're all heart," Maxi said, when they heard the latch click.

"I wonder why Judd's card was rejected," Kate said. "No one knows he's missing yet. Least of all, his card company."

"Come to think of it, that *is* odd," Desiree agreed. "They've been mentioning the bill for the past couple of days, but I knew I had Judd's card, so I wasn't worried about it. I've been so focused on finding him, I haven't been thinking about anything else."

"This place is super expensive," Maxi said. "How long can you afford to stay?"

"Counting the four days I've already been here on my own? Through tomorrow or the next day, maybe. Then I'm going to have to move some money from my retirement account. But, tonight we have a new lead on my guy, a very nice roof over our heads, and a dinner that smells delicious. So I'm going to be content with that."

Chapter 33

As the rising sun washed the sky in pink, Kate changed into jeans and a clean navy T-shirt and galloped down the stairs to the bakery kitchen. Oliver, sitting by the table with the purple Frisbee in his mouth, looked up hopefully.

"Fresh pot a' coffee on," Sam called, rolling a tall metal rack out of the oven, as waves of heat filled the room with a yeasty smell.

"That sounds wonderful," Kate said. "Desiree and I sat up talking half the night, so neither one of us got a ton of sleep."

"Got us stocked up on breads," Sam said. "But we could use some cookies, 'specially chocolate chip and some of those oatmeal raisin. Lunchbox favorites, I'm guessin'. You got a few resort orders, too. That Emerald Bay place needs a big fancy cake for one of their guests. Golden Sands wants cupcakes for a baby shower. And Palm Isle says they need two a' those tall coconut cakes for their dining room first thing Friday morning. Left the names and numbers on the icebox. And Andy called from the pub. Wants me to tell you he's gonna try out three dozen baseballs. Sometimes I honestly wonder about that boy . . ."

"So did you have a good time at Rosie and Andre's place?" Kate asked Oliver, as they padded out to the backyard.

She knelt and gently took the Frisbee from his mouth, rubbing him on the shoulder with her free hand. His plush hair was soft and silky. "Oh, somebody's had a bath," she said, lightly. "A nice brush, too. Am I smelling honeysuckle shampoo?"

Oliver looked up and away quickly. If he were a person, Kate would have said he was embarrassed.

"OK, I get the hint," she said. "We've got a few minutes before those cookies have to go in the oven. Let's see how far we can make this disc fly."

"Your friend made the paper this morning," Sam said, as he refilled his coffee cup.

Kate looked up from scrubbing her hands at the kitchen sink. "What did it say?"

"Not much. Said that biologist fellah is missing. And she was the last person to see him. They had some kinda dust-up. And it sounds like his kids are pretty worried."

"Judd and Desiree didn't have a fight," Kate said, as she reached for a spotless white towel on the counter. "I wonder where they got that from."

Sam shrugged. "Don't believe everything you read. Most folks know that."

"Did the story mention searching the cove?"

The baker nodded. "Found evidence of foul play. Didn't say what, though. How's your friend doin'?"

"Better. Ben is taking her out to the cove this morning, so she can be there during the search. She's hopeful."

Sam raised his cup and paused, a sparkle in his brown eyes. "Hope's mighty powerful."

Chapter 34

Maxi carried two coffee cups to the kitchen table where Kate had set out a plate of key lime crisps. "So have you heard any news from The Nose?" the florist asked.

"Not a peep," Kate said, as she poured thick, fragrant batter carefully into a cake pan. Four more, lined up on the counter, awaited her ministrations. "But it's not like that area has cell service. Desiree said she'd call as soon as she gets back to the bungalow."

"Five cakes?" Maxi asked.

"Just one. But five layers. This is one of the coconut beauties we saw when we had lunch at the resort Saturday. They want two more by tomorrow. For their dessert cart."

"Speaking of which, I hear that Lola Montgomery is still in town, and she's gonna be here for a while. But nobody seems to know why."

"Not even Delores Philpott?" Kate asked, smiling, as she moved down the counter and slowly filled the second cake pan with golden batter.

"Delores is good for finding out the 'what,'" Maxi said, waving her hand over her coffee. "But the 'why' she usually gets wrong. Nope, this time I went to a super-good source—Sunny."

"How does Sunny know Lola Montgomery's travel plans?"

"Sunny teaches yoga to all the big names when they come to town. And Lola's booked classes at the studio through next week. The girl even said she might be extending her stay in Coral Cay."

"Hmm, I'd love to know if her visit has anything to do with Judd and Desiree. Or maybe it's just a coincidence."

"No way," Maxi said. "Nothing that gets you within slapping distance of a serious ex is a coincidence. Trust me on that one. If you want to talk with her, we could become regulars at Sunny's beach yoga class. Even if Lola's getting private lessons, she's gonna take that one a couple of times, at least."

"I'm not sure Sunny would be too thrilled with us stalking celebrities at her yoga classes. Besides, I'd feel kind of weird asking Lola about Judd in public."

"So what did you have in mind?" Maxi asked.

"I was going for the straightforward approach. Judd's officially missing now. I thought I might call her at the resort, explain that I'm a family friend, and see if she knows anything that could help us. If she does, I can steer her toward Ben."

"Speaking of which, that boy is looking good. He's always been a snappy dresser. But a little birdie told me he's hitting the gym a couple times a week now."

"Sunny said that?"

"Nope, this one's Delores. Besides, I can't picture Ben doing yoga."

Kate smiled as she grabbed a rubber spatula and

scraped the sides of the bowl, pushing the mixture into the last cake tin.

"Did you see the story in the paper this morning?" Maxi asked, taking two cookies from the platter.

"I didn't, but Sam mentioned it. Why?"

Maxi shook her head. "Gossip spreads fast on this island. But that's the first time I've seen it hit the papers so quick. The story said Desiree and Judson had a real blowup the night he disappeared."

"But that's not true. We talked to Desiree. And Mike Case was there. I'd think he would have mentioned something."

"It's possible there wasn't much to mention," Maxi said, shrugging. "*Una mini discusión.* Just a little spat. Maybe he didn't hear it. It could have been over by the time he arrived. Or maybe he was too far away."

"But other guests heard it? And those bungalows are pretty far apart. I don't buy it. And I think Desiree would have mentioned it."

"If it was a big deal, you'd think somebody would have called somebody," Maxi said. "'Cause I can definitely see Brad marching out there, tapping his little clipboard. But if it was a small deal, maybe the neighbors don't think anything of it at the time. Later, they hear that Judson has vanished . . . poof. And suddenly they remember."

As Maxi sipped her coffee, Kate tapped each pan against the counter, to release any trapped air bubbles.

"I never did tell Desiree about the redhead Carl saw with Judd," she admitted finally. "I was going to break it to her last night. But she was so happy that they were finally doing a search. And, for the first time in days, she actually had an appetite. I just didn't have the heart."

"That doesn't sound like such a bad thing," Maxi said. "We still don't know who Ms. *Pelirroja* is. It could be nothing."

She paused and took a nibble of one cookie. Then a much bigger bite.

"¡Están divinas! This is amazing! So citrusy."

"It's the same recipe I used for Desiree and Judd's cake toppers. Minus the bride and groom decorations. Oh geez."

"What?" Maxi asked, sitting forward.

"With the new leads on Judd, I completely forgot. Remember what Andy heard? About the family heirloom Judd wanted to retrieve? What if that was the fight? What if Judd broke it off Friday night and asked for the ring back?"

Chapter 35

"The Cookie House, this is Kate."

"Ah, am I correct in assuming this is Kate McGuire?" a woman with a polished British accent politely inquired.

"Absolutely. How can I help?"

"This is Jane Hitchens. And I believe it's my employer who can be of some assistance to you. Ms. Lola Montgomery? She received your message and has asked me to invite you for tea. Would you be free this afternoon?"

Reflexively, Kate glanced at the clock. The cakes and cupcakes were on the cooling racks. She could prepare the frosting this evening and work into the night, if necessary.

"Yes, that would be fine. What time would be convenient?" she said.

"She's at Emerald Bay. In the Principessa Suite. Could you be here in forty minutes?

As Kate pulled up under the portico in Sam's ancient blue pickup truck, a valet appeared at her window.

"You lost? This is the Emerald Bay Resort and Club."

"I'm Kate McGuire. I'm supposed to meet a guest here for tea."

"In that case, just go on in to the front desk, and they'll let the guest know you're here," he said. "And if you throw me the keys, I'll valet this baby for you. Been a while since I've seen one like this. What is it, Chevy sixty-five or sixty-six?"

"I'm not exactly sure," Kate admitted, handing him the keys. "I borrowed it from a friend."

"Needs a little work," he said, thumping the roof. "But they sure don't make 'em like this anymore."

Which is pretty much exactly what Sam Hepplewhite said when he volunteered the truck a half hour ago.

"No fancy air-conditioning, but it's got a full tank," Sam had promised, handing her the keys. "And a clean bill of health from Gabe. Just had a tune-up. Crank down the windows, you'll be all set."

The lobby of Emerald Bay was as elegant as its well-heeled clientele. Fitted out in a minimalist dream of cream-colored marble and exotic hardwoods, it could have been a five-star hotel anywhere in the world. It even reminded Kate a little of the Cascadian. Only a few tropical touches—jars of shells, a few rattan chairs, a couple of bamboo tables, and woven palm fans hung as wall decorations—betrayed its South Florida location.

Unsure of what to wear for tea with a Hollywood star, Kate decided to keep it simple, opting for a cool sleeveless indigo dress and flats. And the guests breezing in and out of the lobby were clad in everything from swimsuits and beach cover-ups to business casual blazers and dresses.

She definitely fit in. And she was certainly no stranger to the hotel industry. So why was she nervous?

"I'm Kate McGuire. I'm here for tea with, uh, Jane Hitchens," Kate told the front desk clerk, employing the instructions the assistant had supplied earlier.

"She never registers under her own name," Jane had confided. "She mustn't. If she did, it would create utter chaos."

The woman typed a few words into the computer at her elbow and smiled. "Ms. Hitchens is expecting you. Gerard, take Ms. McGuire to the Principessa Suite. I'll phone ahead and let her know you're coming."

"Is this your first time on Coral Cay?" Gerard asked, as he pressed the call button in front of a bank of gleaming, stainless-steel elevators.

"No, I actually live here. I co-own the bakery downtown—the Cookie House."

"Heard that place is pretty good," he said, as they boarded the elevator.

Gerard deftly turned a key and hit **P** at the top of the button panel. "Haven't been there yet, though. I just started here last month. I live over in Milagro Springs. Killer commute."

"Has Ms. Hitchens been on the island long?" Kate asked.

"Well, she checked in here about two weeks ago. Haven't actually seen her, though. I just remember hauling her stuff up to the suite and thinking 'Thursday's a weird day to check in.' I mean, we get a lot of traffic on Fridays and Sundays. Mondays, too. But Thursday morning?"

"I wonder how long she's planning to stay?" Kate mused.

"No idea on that one. The reservation's open-ended. So they won't promise this suite to anyone else until she checks out. Could be tomorrow. Could be next year. She a friend of yours?"

"Business contact," Kate explained. "I'm meeting her for the first time."

"Ahhh, well between you and me," Gerard said, lowering his voice, "I wouldn't be surprised if she's refurnished the place—just from the amount of stuff. Five of those steamer trunks and ten suitcases. It's like she was moving in. And one of the maids told me she actually brought her own sheets. People, you know?"

Kate nodded, and focused for a few seconds. "Definitely. Well, if you get a chance, stop by the bakery before you head out sometime. We do a mean black-and-white cookie."

"Hey, those things are my very favorite. Nothing better. I might just have to take you up on that. Come to think of it, might make that commute a little easier, too."

Kate's stomach tensed as she knocked on the door. When it opened, she was face-to-face with Lola Montgomery herself.

"You must be Kate. I'm Lola. Please come in."

Kate had to stop her mouth from dropping open. In bare feet, wearing a man's white dress shirt with the sleeves rolled up, slim jeans, and just a smudge of eye makeup, Lola Montgomery looked as fresh and dewy as her screen personas, despite being in her early forties. She wore a delicate gold chain at her pale throat and a small emerald ring on her left hand. And, unlike the character she played in her last rom-com, the actress had swingy, shoulder-length red hair.

"Thank you for taking the time to see me," Kate said, her mind momentarily blank.

"Of course," Lola said in a throaty voice that was, thanks to her fame, oddly familiar. "Please come have a seat. I've set us up in the living room. I hope you don't mind green tea. I'm on a bit of a kick lately."

Kate looked over at the coffee table and saw a wicker tray with a striking white china teapot that could have found a home in a modern art museum. Idly, she wondered if it had come from the resort or Lola's own kitchen.

The actress poured tea into two small, handleless white cups. Cradling a cup in her hands, she relaxed into the adjoining small sofa and curled her legs beneath her.

"I heard the news about Judd. It's everywhere, of course. How can I help?"

"I was just wondering if you happened to see him while you were here? And if he might have mentioned anything that might be helpful?"

"So you know we're seeing each other?" Lola said, in her signature whiskey voice. "What did he say?"

Kate's stomach dropped. She had been dreading this. She knew next to nothing about Judd's personal life before Desiree. She wished Ben was sitting here instead. He'd instinctively know what to ask.

"Judd knows how to keep a confidence," Kate replied cryptically. "I was just wondering if he told you something that might give us a clue. Where he was going next? Places he wanted to visit? Things he wanted to do while he was here? Anything, really."

Lola took a sip of her tea and looked off into the distance. She sighed.

"You know how some people say you get one real shot at love? One person who fits better than anyone else?"

Kate sipped and nodded. "I have heard that," she said noncommittally.

"Well, Judd is mine," Lola said. "And, I'm his. It just took us both a while to realize it. Break-ups and make-ups. And most of that was me. I'm so much younger than he is. And a bit more dramatic," she allowed, smiling. "But he's a good man. Strong and patient and kind."

"How did you reconnect?" Kate asked, feeling as though she was tiptoeing through a minefield.

"I hadn't seen him in, oh, six months. We'd broken up. And I figured that was it. I headed off on location and just poured myself into my role. When the project finally wrapped, I was spent. Exhausted. I needed a rest. So I didn't tell anyone where I was going. Just packed everything and picked a dot on the map. Well, maybe it wasn't entirely random. Let's just say a dot on the map with first-class hotels and good room service. But a few days later, there's a knock on my door and there he is. Judd. Just standing there with this big grin on his face. It was like we'd never been apart. What can I say? He's the one great love of my life."

Lola sipped her tea and looked out the panoramic windows to the turquoise water beyond.

"Did he mention someone named Desiree?" Kate asked, holding her breath as she held her cup with both hands. "Someone he was seeing?"

"I think so," Lola said, nodding. "Not by name, of course. But he mentioned an entanglement. A miscalculation, he said. Supposed to be a bit of fun. No strings. Nothing serious. Unfortunately, it sounded like maybe she developed different ideas. But I had the impression Judd had come here for the same reason I had. To rest. Alone. That maybe she'd followed him?" Lola tossed her head, as if shaking off the thought.

"Like I said, that was just an impression more than anything," she said. "Judd would never say anything detrimental. He's an old-fashioned gentleman. You wouldn't think that would appeal to a modern girl like me. But it's oddly magnetic."

"The last time you saw him—when was that?"

"Friday. And from what I read in the papers, that was the day he disappeared."

Kate nodded. "Can I ask where you saw him?"

"Right here in this suite," she said, blushing. "And that's the only detail you're getting from me on that."

"Did he say where he was going next? Or did you make plans to meet over the weekend?"

She shook her head and her thick, glossy hair fell perfectly into place. "He said he needed to go off the grid for a while. And I think, I believe, it could have been because of her. He'd ended it. But I got the feeling she wasn't quite ready to let go."

"Any idea where he might go, if he was going off the grid?"

"He didn't say," Lola said huskily, her eyes welling up. "Somewhere in the boat, I think. I remember right before he walked out that door, he told me he loved me. He said he was so glad we were together—that we'd finally come to our senses. And that nothing—no one— would keep us apart now. And he made me promise not to worry. With everything that was happening to him, he was worried about me, can you believe it?" she said, quickly looking away, and swiping her eyes with a pale, fragile hand.

Kate poured tea into Lola's cup, then topped off her own.

"When he didn't contact you after a few days . . ." Kate started.

When Lola looked up again, Kate saw that her lashes were wet.

"I just thought he was doing what he needed to do," she said slowly, her voice raspy with emotion. "So I stayed here. Waiting. Now he's missing? Truly missing?"

Kate nodded. "Have you spoken with the police yet?"

"No, and I'm not sure I want to," she said softly.

"What do you mean?" Kate asked.

"I don't know where Judd is," Lola said. "I don't even

know where he went right after he left here the last time.
But the minute I step forward, this whole thing will turn
into a circus. And that's going to distract from finding
him."

Kate chewed on her lower lip. Lola was right. There
wasn't a thing she'd shared that would help them locate
Judd. And what she said about Desiree would hurt. A lot.
But if Kate didn't say anything about this little *tête-à-tête*, was that concealing evidence?

"You picked Coral Cay pretty much at random,"
Kate said finally. "But Judd seems to know the area.
When you were together, did he mention any particular
places?"

"You're right, he's crazy about this place," Lola
said, settling back into the sofa. "Because of the biodi-
versity. 'The world in microcosm,' he calls it. But no,
he didn't. Well, except for that cove. The one they're
searching today. He told me when this whole thing
was over, we'd go out there, spread a blanket on the
beach, and watch the turtles."

Chapter 36

"Bad news," Maxi said, looking up from her computer as Kate walked into the floral shop. "They didn't find Judd at The Nose. They even did one of those things where the deputies walk an arm's length apart. But they didn't find anything. Not even a soda can."

"Well, I've got some bad news of my own," Kate said, sitting on the sofa, as Oliver came bounding over and hopped up next to her. "I might have found our mystery redhead. And she says their on-and-off relationship was very definitely back on."

"No! OK, so we couldn't see her hair at the restaurant. But since when was Lola Montgomery a redhead?"

"Since her last visit to the hair stylist," Kate said, as Oliver playfully stretched out across her lap. "Or maybe always. I couldn't tell. But by the time we were lunching on the resort patio toasting Desiree's wedding, they had already rekindled their relationship and were planning to run off together. At least, that's what she's saying. And I don't see why she'd lie about it."

"That snake! So maybe we just let him stay lost, and find Desiree a better man."

"I know I have to tell her," Kate said. "It's better she hears this from a friend. But how? How am I going to break her heart?"

"You're not breaking her heart. Mr. Judson the Cheater did that. I say we tell her in person. Later, we can make a food run, too. When she called before, she sounded so tired. She probably hasn't eaten since breakfast. If then."

"We? Maxi, you don't have to do this."

"Hey, we girls gotta stick together. And Rosie's already out there. Besides, look at the bright side."

"Bright side?" Kate said, stroking Oliver's plush, furry head.

"If she doesn't have to wait around for him, she can check out of that super-expensive resort and save her money for something good."

"Somehow," Kate said, "I don't think she's going to see it that way."

When they knocked on the bungalow door, Rosie Armand opened it. Clad in a creamy silk blouse and a tan suit skirt with heels, she looked like she'd come straight from the shop.

"Step in quick," she said. "This place is like Bourbon Street at Mardi Gras the way everybody's coming and going. Reporters. TV cameras. Lookie-loos. I wanted to call hotel security, but Desiree doesn't want to make trouble."

"We might need the reporters and news people later to get the word out," Desiree called from the sofa. "The search this morning didn't find anything. But they're having a press conference that's supposed to start any minute."

"We've been flippin' channels, trying to catch it on the local news," Rosie explained.

"I brought cookies," Kate said, putting a large white bakery box on the coffee table. "Comfort carbs. Chocolate chip and orange madeleines."

"Desiree's got to be exhausted," Maxi said quietly. "We'll make a food run, after the news conference."

"No need," Rosie said. "We've got a kitchen full of casseroles and goodies. Bridget dropped off a deep-dish lasagna and some garlic rolls. Minette and Carl showed up with a baking dish full of her mac-and-cheese and a roasted chicken. Made me feel like a piker when all I brought was a big ol' platter of étouffée. And Barb stopped by with a garden salad and some stuffed baked potatoes we can heat up. We've got more food than we know what to do with."

"This is it, this is it!" Desiree called excitedly. Kate, Maxi and Rosie clustered around her and the TV.

As the cameraman zoomed in, Kate saw Ben Abrams looking serious at a lectern in front of the Coral Cay police station, flanked by Kyle and a few other local faces she recognized.

"Thank you all for coming. I'm Detective Ben Abrams. I lead the investigative division of the Coral Cay police department. As many of you now know, marine biologist Judson Cooper is missing. He was last seen taking his boat, the *Starfish*, out of Sullivan Harbor on Coral Cay last Friday night. We're asking anyone who's seen him or his boat since then to please call our offices. We're also asking anyone who may know where he was headed to please give us a call."

Kyle leaned over and softly said something to Ben, who nodded.

"Mr. Cooper, excuse me, Dr. Cooper's children, Liam and Sarah are here. And they'd like to say a few words."

Ben stepped off to the right, and a lanky man positioned himself at the lectern. A few inches shorter than Ben, he adjusted the microphone. His sandy brown hair was disheveled and his eyes were red. But Kate could see a marked resemblance to Judson Cooper.

"Liam," Desiree said, nodding. "I've never actually met him. But Judd's shown me plenty of photos."

"Good evening," he said clearing his throat. "I'm Liam Cooper. This is my sister, Sarah. This has been a really tough day for us. Our dad is missing. To you guys, to the world, Judson Cooper is this globe-trotting eco-warrior. And he is. He is all of that. But to us, he's dad. Our dad. He's got a collection of vintage T-shirts that he brags are older than I am. He can't sing to save his life, even though he thinks he can. And he's always working on his next invention. Because he believes that one person really can make a difference."

"That's true," Desiree whispered. "That's the Judd I know and love."

"And that boat he's on?" Liam continued. "He bought it as a wreck and fixed it up himself . . ."

Suddenly, a cell phone bleated. Ben reached into his pocket, pulled out his phone, and checked the screen. He stepped away from the gathering, and Kate saw him disappear into the police station.

Liam cleared his throat. "My dad's boat—the *Starfish*—he bought it as scrap. And he fixed it up himself. Sarah and I helped. It was a family project. That boat has carried him, and us, all over the world. So that my dad could help the oceans, the marine animals—and the people who depend on both. Now we're hoping that a few of you can help our dad. Help us to bring him home safely."

Sarah leaned in and whispered something. Liam nodded.

"There's more to this story. My father was human. And as we sometimes do, he got involved—briefly—with the wrong person. He ended it. He told her that. Very clearly, several times. But she didn't take it well. And she confronted him again the night he disappeared. I'd say they had a fight, but the truth is she threw a temper tantrum. We know this because she was so loud that it disturbed people in the nearby bungalows. Shortly after that, my father opted to go to his boat and called for a taxi. What happened next, we don't know. Did he get fed up with her antics and sail out of the harbor himself? Or did someone do something to him? Like I said, we don't know. And we need to. So along with leads on my dad, I want to hear what you know about this woman. Her name is Desiree Goldsmith. She's unemployed. She has no fixed address. She also got ahold of one of dad's credit cards and has been charging up a small fortune in the past few days. Jewelry. Designer clothes. Shoes. Limos. Champagne meals. And, until I cut off the card last night, she even tried to use it to book a hotel suite. Currently, she's staying at the Palm Isle resort, in bungalow 43, although we're not sure how she paid for that. Again, her name is Desiree Goldsmith, and if you know anything about her that could help us find my dad—my sister and I would be very grateful."

Maxi snatched the remote from the table and flipped the channel—just in time to catch another version of the press conference on another local news station. She quickly hit the POWER button.

No one said a word. Desiree leaned forward, her head in her hands. Kate couldn't tell if she was crying, embarrassed, or both.

"We need to get out of here now," Kate said gently, patting her friend's shoulder. "How quickly can you pack a bag?"

"I'm not leaving," Desiree said, sitting up straight and staring at the wall with weary eyes. "I maxed out my card to pay for this place through Saturday, and I'm not running away like a thief in the night. How dare they! How dare they stand up there and peddle those lies. Judson will be mortified."

Kate looked at Maxi, who shrugged.

"And where was your friend Ben?" Desiree said. "Why didn't he stop them?"

"Ben got a phone call halfway through the press conference," Kate said.

"Love to know what that was all about," Maxi murmured.

"We can ask him later," Kate said. "In the meantime, we have a bigger problem. Liam gave everyone your address. It's going to get pretty chaotic in about fifteen minutes or so."

"To be fair, it wasn't that great this afternoon," Rosie said, crossing her arms across her chest. "Half the people at that press conference have been out here already."

"Yeah, but now Lunkhead Liam has kinda put the spotlight on her," Maxi fumed.

"I went to see Lola Montgomery this afternoon," Kate said softly to Desiree. "She's claiming that she and Judd are back together. Could that possibly be true?"

Desiree shook her head. "No. No way. Judd wouldn't do that. He couldn't hide something like that. That man doesn't have a sneaky bone in his body."

"When you two were vacationing here, did he go off on his own much?" Kate prodded gently.

"Well, yes. But we both did. Then we'd meet up for lunch or dinner. Or hit the beach for a swim or a bike ride."

Maxi and Kate exchanged glances.

"Sounds like that man could have been two-timing you," Rosie said, shifting in her chair.

"No," Desiree said, calmly. "I know he wasn't. Just like I know what Liam was spouting in front of those cameras was total codswallop. I don't know why Lola Montgomery would say that. But I know my guy. And I know it's not true. Just like I know Judd didn't run away from our wedding. There's something going on here. Something I don't understand. But I'm going to get to the bottom of it. Because I have a feeling that's the only way I'm going to get Judson back."

Chapter 37

As a fingernail sliver of moon sailed across the velvety night sky, Kate whipped up a large batch of creamy coconut icing in the kitchen of the Cookie House.

As she blended the butter, sugar, and coconut cream with vanilla extract in the mixer, she wondered how so many people could see Judson Cooper so differently. Kind of like those sugar cookies the housemates baked at Conch House. The same recipe. The same ingredients. The same equipment. But widely divergent results.

Everyone she'd talked to about Judd seemed to be describing an entirely different person. To Desiree, he was a beloved fiancé and a loyal one-woman man. To Zoey, he was a brilliant business partner, but also a serial ladies man—leaving a trail of romantic wreckage in his wake. To Lola Montgomery, he was half of a tumultuous relationship, her one great love. To poachers and polluters, he was a vociferous opponent and an obstacle to their illicit activities. While to Liam and Sarah, he was a steady, loving father, and—if Judd himself was to be believed—a regular, ready source of money, too.

So who was the real Judson Cooper?

With a clean spoon, she tasted a smidgeon of the frosting, added a little coconut extract, and set the bowl back into the stand mixer.

Under the kitchen table, Oliver shifted, stretched, and rolled over in his sleep. Tuckered out from his day—and several sessions of Frisbee in the yard that evening.

If Judd had left on his own, he'd come back on his own. But his ring and the blood on the fire stone at Turtle Bay were signs that something had happened. Something bad. Kate couldn't picture devastated Desiree, tiny Zoey, or fragile-looking Lola as the cause of the violence.

And while Liam—or Liam and Sarah together—could have been responsible, Kate doubted it. The siblings seemed completely gutted by their father's disappearance. Even if they were lashing out at the wrong person.

That left Judson Cooper's real enemies: poachers and polluters. And that explanation made a lot more sense. Judd confronted someone at Turtle Bay. Possibly the same person he noticed earlier in the cigarette boat. The exchange got heated, and someone—probably Judd—was injured.

But why was his ring discarded in the sand? He'd worn it since he was a college student. Kate had seen it on his hand. And while it didn't seem overly tight, the ring wasn't loose, either. So how did it come to be buried in front of the fire stones?

She tasted the frosting again. The rich, sweet mixture tingled on her tongue. The balance of vanilla and coconut was almost perfect. She added heaping cups of coconut flakes, picked up a wooden spoon and finished blending it by hand—her secret for giving the cake its fluffy appearance.

Using a power mixer risked breaking down the coconut. But with a few good turns of the spoon, she could incorporate the shavings into the frosting just enough.

As he dozed, Oliver yawned and smacked his lips several times. Was that super-powered nose still on alert, even as he slept?

Kate grabbed an offset spatula from the counter, scooped up a generous helping of coconut frosting and, with quick, deft strokes, coated the top of the cake. Then she placed a second layer on top and repeated the process.

As the cake grew taller, Kate allowed her mind to wander back to the disappearance of Judson Cooper.

A ringing phone broke the quiet. She checked the clock. Nearly eleven.

"The Cookie House, this is Kate."

"Kate, it's Ben. I'm sorry for calling so late."

"Don't worry. I'm finishing up a couple of orders for tomorrow. I'll be up for a few hours yet. And you didn't bother Oliver. He just rolled over and went back to sleep."

Ben yawned. "Oh man, right now I wish I could do the same. I called your friend Desiree. To apologize for this afternoon. The press conference? It was not supposed to go that way. And I am definitely not her favorite person right now."

"You didn't know what Judd's kids were going to say?" Kate asked.

"Not in the slightest. When we went over everything beforehand. I told them that they needed to humanize their father. Share a couple of anecdotes that everyone would be able to relate to."

"The stories about the T-shirt collection, and his bad singing, and the boat," Kate said.

"'Yup. And that part of it was fine. Liam did what we needed him to do. Take his father off the pedestal and give the public a look at the real guy. Make him human.'"

"But then he went off script."

"'Fraid so," Ben admitted. "In a big way. He was never even supposed to mention Desiree. Or anyone. Just talk about his dad and ask the public for help."

"Had he asked you about Desiree?"

Ben sighed heavily. Kate could hear the exhaustion in his voice. "Yeah. He was worried she might have had a hand in the disappearance. They both were. I assured them that we'd looked into her and her background and found her to be totally credible. She was the first to sound the alarm that Cooper was gone—and she's been dogged in asking us to investigate."

"You told them that?" Kate asked.

"I did, although they didn't like hearing it. It sounds like they didn't like your friend Desiree from the word 'go.' But when I pressed him on it, Liam admitted his father had never said a word against her, either. But hey, don't let facts get in the way of a good feud."

Kate sighed. "The blood on the stone . . . is it Judd's?"

"Human and consistent with Judson Cooper's blood type. But that's all we have for now. I'm going under the theory that it is his. Hence the press conference that went so well today. I'm going to be kicking myself over that one for a long time."

"You didn't know Liam would do that."

"I picked up on some hostility there," Ben said, his voice husky with regret. "Toward Desiree. And toward me for not arresting her first and asking questions later. I should have stayed within grabbing distance of that mike. Just to be safe. My old sergeant used to say that limelight is like alcohol. You never know how anyone's going to react. So small doses only, and always keep an eye on 'em."

"What was the phone call?"

"Between you and me? I think it was a setup. The number that popped up was the crime lab. We put a rush on the blood. So I pick up, and they tell me it's urgent. Have to talk to me now—it can't wait. Critical new information. Fine. That's when I moved inside to get a little privacy. Then the woman tells me they need me to hold for just a minute. Five minutes later, I'm still holding, and she hangs up. When I call back, the lab clerk tells me that the results aren't back yet. And he swears nobody called me."

"You think the call was to lure you away from the press conference?" Kate asked.

"I think the Cooper siblings played me like a big bass drum. And if I could prove it, they'd be cooling their heels in the Coral Cay jail."

Chapter 38

"Thanks for giving me a ride out to the resorts," Kate said as she sipped coffee from a paper cup in the back seat of Maxi's Jeep. "Sam's truck isn't exactly built for hauling delicate desserts. And after being up most of the night, I'm probably in no shape to drive."

"You just keep drinking that *Café Cubano*," Maxi said, smiling at her friend's reflection in the rearview mirror. "Trust me, that stuff can wake the dead. After we finish, how 'bout we check in on Desiree?"

"I'd love that," Kate said. "If she's up to it, I want to update her crime board. We have a few new leads. A little more yarn. And I keep hoping that putting all the information in one place will help us somehow make sense of it."

"What I can't make sense of are Liam and Sarah. Saying the things they did. Did Ben ever say what was up with that phone call he was so hot to take?"

"I'm guessing whatever it was, it had to be important," Kate said, vaguely.

"*Ay*, I know it's not Ben's fault that Liam went after Desiree like that. But I might have mentioned the press conference to a certain lawyer I know. Just to see if Desiree could sue Liam. For all the nasty things that lunkheaded boy said."

"And let me guess, the best prosecutor in South Florida said no."

"The best prosecutor in all of Florida. And *sí*."

"I'm beginning to wonder if Liam Cooper had some legal advice of his own," Kate said. "Everything he said was technically true. Desiree and Judd were traveling the world. She sold her New York place, and her stuff's in storage. So she has no actual address. She took early retirement. Which technically makes her unemployed. And Judd gave her the credit card to use for bopping around town and wedding prep—things like the dress, and our brunch, and those earrings from Rosie and Andre's shop. So she was using it."

"But he was so slimy!"

"Exactly. He presented it in a way that invited people to think less of Desiree. To see her as unbalanced or a schemer. And possibly a kidnapper."

"If I were Desiree, I don't think I'd want to marry into that family," Maxi said, putting her right hand on one of the cake boxes in the passenger seat as she turned onto a narrow road flanked by dense undergrowth.

"The credit card!" Kate shouted.

"What about it?"

"The other night, when Brad showed up at the bungalow, Desiree tried to give him Judson's credit card," Kate said.

"Well, yeah, that's one of the things that made the lunkhead so mad."

"If you were breaking up with someone—telling them you weren't going to marry them—wouldn't you make sure you got your credit card back? Or at least cancelled it?"

"Especially those black cards," Maxi said, nodding. "'Cause an angry ex could do a lot of damage with one of those. Especially at that resort."

"Exactly! But Judd didn't do that. He just left for the boat. Casually talking about turtles with Mike as he rode out there. And we know the card worked the next day because that's when Desiree picked up the antique earrings at As Time Goes By and bought us brunch. The card didn't stop working until a few days later. When Liam cancelled it. He said so at the news conference."

"But what about the fight?" Maxi asked. "The shouting match the neighbors heard Friday night between Judd and Desiree?"

"What about it? No one from the resort mentioned it at the time. And Ben's people were all over there asking questions the night after Judd disappeared. Right after he didn't show up for the wedding. But sometime between then and Wednesday afternoon, this story pops up about a loud argument between Judd and Desiree. I smell a rat."

"You think *el raton*'s name is Liam? *Corazón*, if they're working that hard to throw Desiree under the bus, it sounds like those two rotten kids are guilty."

"Guilty or just stubborn," Kate said. "From what Desiree and Judd said, they've always hated her."

"Judd said *that*?" Maxi exclaimed.

"No, Desiree said that. Judd said they're just afraid he and Desiree are going to spend all of his money."

"OK, I'm no big, fancy lawyer, but that kinda sounds like a motive."

As the Jeep zipped along a raised boulevard from one end of Palm Isle toward Desiree's bungalow, Kate stared out the windshield at the busy harbor beneath them. Café Cubano or not, now that she'd made her deliveries, she could have happily dozed off in the warm car.

"Those coconut cakes were really pretty—and so tall," Maxi said. "And I loved the rainbow-colored cupcakes."

"Five layers. It was a real kick to see it on the resort's dessert cart," Kate admitted. "They bought one on the Q.T. to sample, and they must have liked it."

"What's not to like? Five layers of cake and all that good coconut frosting. How do you top that?"

"Well, don't tell anyone, but I'm experimenting with a chocolate version."

"OK, I definitely want to be your taste-tester. And I think I'm gonna need a few more classes at Sunny's."

"It's nowhere near the—Stop the car!"

Maxi braked, and Kate braced herself.

As soon as the car stopped, Kate unfastened her seatbelt and scrambled out of the car. Running across the street, Kate leaned over a waist-high stone wall, hand to her forehead against the glare, searching the water beyond.

"Are you OK?" Maxi asked when she joined her moments later. "Are you sick?"

"I saw it! Or thought I did. Running along right out there," Kate said, pointing.

"The *Starfish*?"

"No, the cigarette boat. I swear it was right there. But by the time I got over here, it was gone. Or maybe I just imagined the whole thing. Sleep deprivation."

"You know what I don't understand? How does anybody tell one cigarette boat from another? They all look alike to me."

"In the case of the one Judd spotted that time, I suspect it might have been the people he recognized, as much as the boat. I got the feeling that, whatever it was, he didn't want to scare Desiree. Or us. Or that maybe he wanted to make sure he was right about whatever he thought was going on."

"Poaching or dumping," Maxi said.

Kate nodded.

"Then it's got to be poaching."

"What makes you say that?" Kate asked, swiveling to look at her friend.

"Well, The Nose—and the preserve, in general— is home to all kinds of unusual creatures," Maxi explained. "That's why it's there. But the super-important part? Those deputies Ben called were all over that cove and they didn't find anything. No trash or chemicals or anything. So if Judson Cooper saw a bad guy he knew doing something out at the cove, it means they were probably poaching."

Chapter 39

Kate knocked. The door opened instantly.

Maxi and Kate stepped quickly inside, as Desiree slammed the door and flipped the deadbolt.

"So how bad has it been?" Kate asked.

Desiree shook her head and smiled. "Don't ask. Every time that door opens, cameras appear like magic. I swear one man really did jump out of the bushes. But thanks to your friends, I haven't had to order room service."

"They're your friends, too," Maxi said, flopping down on the couch.

"I don't know how long they're going to want to be friends with an unemployed drifter. At least, that's pretty much Liam's description of me."

"Well, your friends—and they are your friends— know that's not true. And this one," Kate said, pointing a thumb at Maxi, "has already talked to a lawyer about whether you can sue Liam and Sarah for slander."

"Really?" Desiree said, tearing up.

"My husband, Peter. He's a local prosecutor. But he said it's probably not a super-good idea."

"That's OK," she said patting Maxi's arm. "I wouldn't want to, anyway. It would just make things worse. All I want is to get Judd back. Still, I can't believe you asked."

"Well, yeah."

There was a soft knock on the door.

Desiree whirled around. "Not again!"

"It's Zoey," Kate said, looking through the peephole.

"Thank goodness! Definitely let her in. She's been so sweet. She called last night after the press conference to see how I was faring."

"Hi, Zoey, come on in," Kate said. Spying a man in the street with a camera attached to a long lens, she slammed the door. "We need to call security. There's a guy in the street with a telephoto lens."

"He was here before," Desiree said, waving her hand. "Or one of them was. That's why the drapes are shut."

"Man, that is wild," Zoey said. "One minute, he wasn't there and the next minute he just popped up behind me."

Zoey's hair was disheveled. Her eyes and nose were red. And Kate noticed she was wearing two different sneakers. Clearly, Judd's disappearance was taking a toll on his business partner, too.

"Look, I hate to be the bearer of bad tidings, but I heard there's going to be another press conference," Zoey announced.

"Do they have any news to announce?" Kate asked. "I don't think they've discovered any new information about Judd, have they?"

"No idea," Zoey said, quickly checking her phone before shoving it into the pocket of her wrinkled skirt. "Somebody in the next bungalow mentioned it when I was down at the pool. I have zero idea what it's about. But I figure if it's important, it'll make the noon news. I was going to try and catch it, and I thought you'd want to know."

A loud rapping on the door startled them.

"Do you think it's Mr. Telephoto Lens?" Maxi hissed.

"Ms. Goldsmith, this is Brad from the front desk. I need you to open the door."

"I'm paid through tomorrow morning," Desiree said softly. "And I transferred enough money from my retirement account to stay at least another week."

Desiree marched to the door, squared her shoulders, and threw it open. On the street, they could hear the mechanical whirr of the camera as the photographer clicked off multiple shots.

"Ms. Goldsmith, this is simply unacceptable," Brad said, gesturing at the photographer. "Your presence here is creating a disruption that's making it impossible for the other guests to enjoy their stays. We've received multiple complaints, and I'm afraid we're going to have to ask you to leave."

"If your security folks were doing their jobs, that guy wouldn't have been able to get in here," Maxi called over the sofa.

"Our security officers have been working double shifts since that fiasco on the news last night. Mentioning the resort by name was bad enough. But this can't be allowed to continue. It's simply not fair to the other guests."

"I'll pack my things, and leave this afternoon," Desiree said.

"Desiree, no," Kate started.

But her friend put her hand up. "It's OK. I understand. And he's right. It's been awful for me. And I can't imagine what it's been like for the other guests. They didn't sign on for this."

"Neither did you," Maxi said.

"I really am very sorry," Brad said, as he turned to leave. "But I believe this is for the best. For everyone concerned. Of course, I'll process a refund for tonight's stay."

"That boy is all heart," Maxi said as Desiree shut the door. "He's got me seriously rethinking my vacation plans."

"Wow," Zoey agreed, pulling out her phone again. "That was slightly brutal."

"Please tell me I was never that bad when I was at the Cascadian," Desiree said, sinking into the sofa and putting her head in her hands.

"You were a marshmallow, and you know it," Kate said.

Zoey grabbed the remote and started flipping channels.

". . . and for that we take you to Coral Cay with the latest bizarre twist in the mysterious disappearance of Judson Cooper, renowned marine biologist, inventor, and philanthropist. Carmen Morales is on the scene. Carmen?"

Her eyes glued to the screen, Zoey dropped the remote and absentmindedly chewed on a thumbnail.

"Yes, Ashley, well, as we found out this morning, there is a lot more to marine biologist Judson Cooper than just a love of fish. It was revealed today that the multi-millionaire scientist and inventor is also in a relationship with screen actress Lola Montgomery. And Miss Montgomery held a press conference earlier this morning."

"Of course she did," Desiree said softly, rubbing her forehead.

"You want me to try another channel?" Zoey asked, her eyes glued to the screen.

"No, I want to hear this. Let's see what the woman has to say for herself."

The video switched from a crowded beach in the resort area to the inside of a large conference room. Downstairs at the hotel, Kate surmised.

Another lectern, this time, with Lola Montgomery flanked by a small group of men in suits. Assistants, body guards, or hotel staff? Kate wondered.

"Miss Montgomery has a few remarks and then she has to leave," said an unidentified man in a gray suit, who appeared to be running the show. "So I'm afraid we won't have time for any questions."

Lola Montgomery was wearing a slim navy dress. With her hair up and half her pale face hidden under enormous sunglasses, she looked both fragile and magnetic.

"Thank you all for coming," she said in that familiar husky voice, pausing to take a deep breath. "This isn't easy for me. So I'm just going to try and get through it as quickly as I can. As you already know, Judson Cooper has gone missing."

Kate saw Desiree flinch as Lola said Judd's name. She patted her friend's hand reassuringly.

"What you may not know is why he was here on this island to begin with," the actress continued. "He came here because of me. To be with me. This is the man who, if I'm honest, is the one true love of my life. We've spent an idyllic time on this beautiful island. And now he's missing." She paused, gripping the lectern with white knuckles.

The man in the gray suit said something to Lola that Kate couldn't hear. The actress shook her head and waved him off.

She took a deep breath, composed herself, and started in again. "I'm here today to ask anyone—everyone—out there who might have seen something to step forward. Share what you know. What you've seen or heard. Even if you're not sure." The throaty voice faltered.

Lola removed her sunglasses, and Kate noticed the same light touch with the makeup that she'd witnessed yesterday. And the same damp eyelashes.

"He's my guy, but Judson Cooper belongs to the world," she continued, smiling bravely. "We need him. And if we all work together, I know we can bring him home."

With that, Lola Montgomery—looking radiant and relieved—was surrounded by her personal coterie and whisked quickly from the room, as the assembled gallery shouted questions after her.

"Ms. Montgomery, any truth to the rumor that Cooper's kidnappers were really trying to capture you?" a male reporter challenged.

A piping female voice cut through the din, "Ms. Montgomery, is it true you're carrying Judson Cooper's baby?"

Chapter 40

After Zoey left, Desiree hauled her two suitcases and a backpack into the living room.

"That should be everything," she announced. "I want to grab my yarn board from the kitchen, then go through the place one more time, just to make sure I haven't forgotten anything. Oh, and don't let me forget all that wonderful food in the fridge."

"You really don't have to do this," Kate said.

"I think our Mr. Brad would disagree. Besides, the whole point of staying in a hotel is to be welcome. No matter what else is going on in your life. But I'm definitely not wanted here. And when it comes to the comfort of the other guests, that little turnip is right. They don't deserve this, either."

"Are you headed home?" Maxi asked.

"No way," Desiree said. "Not until we find Judd. I figured I'd rent a car and find a little motel on the mainland. Check in under another name and just pay cash."

"You could stay at my place," Maxi said. "We've got

plenty of room, and the food's *buenísima*—if I do say so myself."

"I can't do that to you," Desiree said, smiling. "I've been keeping some strange hours lately. And I'm trying to maintain a low profile, but there's no guarantee. You've seen what this place has been like the past few days. And you've got a family to consider."

Desiree turned to Kate. "And before you offer, no, I absolutely am not going to stay with you at the bakery. You're already hiding that adorable half-grown bear cub you call a dog. Besides, I'm used to being on my own."

"What if you rented a place?" Kate asked. "Here on the island? Maxi, is there anybody who's looking for a boarder?"

"Well, Delores Philpott was talking about renting a room for a while. But nobody took her up on that one, *gracias a Dios*. Delores has a big heart but she also has a lot of cats," Maxi explained. "Besides, the minute you landed there, everybody in town would know. She's kind of our *Radio Bemba*—gossip central."

"What about renting a house?" Desiree said. "Something small? Maybe out of the way? It wouldn't even have to be on the island if it was close by."

"Like a beach house?" Maxi asked. "You might be able to find something this time of year. And it would still be cheaper than this bungalow. We could call Sylvia Hardcastle. She's a real estate agent—she'd know what's available."

"You don't need to rent a car," Kate said. "How do you feel about a slightly abused Toyota sedan, lovingly refurbished by a friend of mine right here in Coral Cay?"

"I can't take your car!" Desiree exclaimed.

"Not take—borrow," Kate said. "And I haven't used it since I moved here. Downtown I walk or bike."

"And we carpool a bunch, plus Sam's got a truck,"

Maxi said. "Man, I wish I could have seen the looks on their faces when you pulled up at the resort in that thing."

"The valet said it was a classic."

"Really?"

"Well, what he actually said was that they don't make them like that anymore."

"OK, that's true," Maxi said, grinning.

"I don't know what to say," Desiree said, wiping her eyes with her hand. "But thank you. Both."

"I'm just so glad you're staying," Kate said. "I know this past week's been a nightmare. But I had another idea that might help while you're here. And it virtually guarantees you won't have to worry about any more cameras."

"Kate McGuire, don't tell me that you're finally moving out of that bakery?" Sylvia Hardcastle said as she reached across the messy desk to shake hands.

"Just temporarily," Kate said, placing a small white bakery box in the middle of the desk as an offering. "A few peanut butter cookies," she explained. "Fresh from the oven."

Sylvia dipped her hand into the box, pulled out a cookie, and waved it under her nose. "Love these things," she said, taking a small bite. "Takes me straight back to childhood."

"Your mom made them?"

"Nah," she said. "Mom couldn't boil water. She was a corporate girl. Executive. But our school used to make these every Wednesday. Spaghetti for lunch with a little roll and some kinda green salad. And a peanut butter cookie. Those lunch ladies could cook, let me tell you. Loved Wednesdays. And I still love peanut butter cookies. So, what's 'temporarily'?"

"We might be doing some work to the apartment upstairs," Kate said. "I was wondering if it might be a nice time to try something different. Just for a couple of weeks. Especially if you had something on the beach. Maybe something snug and cozy?"

"You do know that 'cozy' is real estate lingo for 'tiny'?"

"I'm counting on it," Kate said, laughing. "As long as it comes with a price tag to match."

"Rent with an option to buy?" Sylvia asked, leafing through a large, black ring binder with one hand as she munched on a cookie with the other.

"I'm only looking for something for a few weeks, tops. And I thought you guys were completely computerized."

"We are. But I consider myself an old-fashioned matchmaker. And having the listings in a book just helps with that. More tactile somehow."

"I spend my days mixing and kneading dough. I can relate."

"Heard a rumor that might interest you," Sylvia said, looking up from the binder just long enough to snatch another cookie from the box. "Seems that Harper Duval's old place is under contract."

"The store or the house?"

"The house. But I'm working on the store—that one's my listing. Got a few live ones, too."

"I'd heard they'd leased the house for a couple of months," Kate said. "For a reality show."

"Nah, this isn't a lease," she said, waving the cookie dismissively. "It's a sale. To some corporation. Don't know what they want with it, but I guess we'll find out."

"Hey, now here's a cute little place," Sylvia said, turning the book and pushing it across the desk at Kate. "Not on Coral Cay. Just across the bay, though. And right on the beach. Limited stay only. The owners will be back in five weeks. So that's your maximum. One bedroom and plenty cozy, if you know what I mean. But tons of natural light, and it's fitted out really well. It's got a great kitchen and a beautiful spa bathroom. Steam shower. Sunken jetted tub."

"It sounds perfect," Kate said. "I'd love to see it."

Sylvia checked her watch. "I've got a showing in ten minutes. How about I give you the keys, and I'll pick them up later at the Cookie House? Phone me after you see it. If you're interested, I'll bring the paperwork and trade it for a check."

Chapter 41

Kate breezed through the shop and nearly collided with Oliver. The big pup raced around her in circles, before planting himself at her feet. Or, more accurately, on her feet.

"I missed you, too, you know that?" she said, rubbing his silky flanks and scratching under his chin, as he gazed up at her with mischievous, twinkling black eyes.

She walked into the bakery kitchen to find Sam enjoying a late lunch. As Oliver settled himself beneath the table, Kate saw Sam surreptitiously slip the pup a tidbit.

"Busy morning," Sam said. "Bit of a lull now. I expect it's the heat. Locals won't do their shopping for a few hours yet. Cool of the evening."

On Sam's plate, Kate noticed half an open-faced ham-and-cheese melt alongside thick slices of juicy late-summer tomatoes. And the baker had placed a large pitcher of iced lemonade on the table.

Kate grabbed a glass from the cupboard and joined him.

"Sylvia just called," he said, his face tense. "Said she'd be by around five with your lease. You movin' out?"

"It's for Desiree," Kate explained, topping off his glass, then filling her own. "She needs another place to stay now that Judd's kids are making trouble. So I'm renting a house for a few weeks in my name. But she's actually paying for it. I told Sylvia I needed a place for a while because we were thinking about doing some work to the rooms upstairs."

"Gotcha," he said, his face relaxing into a smile, as he slipped another morsel to Oliver, who thumped his tail in appreciation.

The shop bell jingled, and Sam started to rise from the table.

"Let me take it for a while," Kate said. "Afterwards, I can get a little baking done during the lull."

"That works," Sam said happily.

She walked into the shop to see a familiar face on the other side of the counter.

"I don't suppose you could spare two dozen of those chocolate crinkle cookies," Howie asked hopefully. "And if you have any, I'll take a half dozen sugar cookies to butter up the Boss Man."

Kate was relieved to see that his sunburn had finally settled into a nice tan. And he seemed upbeat.

"They don't call us the Cookie House for nothing," she said lightly. "I think I can rustle up a few. Hey, did you hear they sold the home where you guys are filming?"

"Nope. But no surprise there. They don't tell us working stiffs anything. Who bought it?"

"I was hoping you knew," Kate said, rapidly assembling a small bakery box, and then a larger one.

"Well, I know Salazar was making noises about snapping it up at one point. He's loaded. But he hasn't said anything about it lately."

"I think you should sample one of these, just to make sure they're still good," Kate said, scooping up a cookie with wax paper and passing it across the counter.

"Like a wine tasting? I could get used to this," Howie said, grinning. "But you'd have a lot fewer cookies in that case."

"So how's everything going with the show?" Kate asked. "Is everyone behaving themselves?"

"Same old, same old. Some of the kids are really sweet. You can't help rooting for them, hoping they'll do well. That James is a good egg. He's actually got a part-time job down at the bookstore. And Candy and Cecily snagged gigs at one of the resorts. They love it."

"But a couple of those kids?" He shook his head sadly. "Total hellions."

"That was kind of the impression I got when I was out there," Kate said, gathering crinkle cookies from the case and putting them into the larger box. "Tucker was giving some of the girls a hard time."

"Tucker's always giving someone a hard time," Howie said. "Between you and me, that's why he's on the show. The kicker was when he swiped my coolers."

"You're kidding!"

Howie shook his head. "I have a few of 'em so that I can always have one clean, chilled up, and ready to go. When we film, we can be out in the heat and the sun for hours. I've got a whole kit—hat, sunscreen, cooler, water bottles. Then one of the coolers goes missing, and I mean it vanished. All the kids swore up and down they hadn't seen it. Then a second one disappears. So in my off hours, I do a little trolling through some of the footage. Big surprise. Tucker. And he had them stashed under his bed."

"Why? What did he say?" Kate said, selecting six sugar cookies and placing them in the smaller box.

"Says he had no idea they were there. Said it wasn't him. I had the little creep dead to rights on film. Coming back late at night with one in each hand. Beer run, I guess. Or a little party on the beach. He insisted it was one of the other housemates pranking him. Some prank on him—they're my coolers. And they were filthy. I mean, it's a beach town, so a little sand on the outside is normal. But there was a coating of wet sand all over the inside, too. How do you even do that? Took me forever to clean 'em."

"Will Ken send him home now?" Kate asked, hopefully, as she sealed each box with tape and passed it over the counter.

"No way," Howie said, handing her a credit card. "By all the metrics we have so far, Tucker's going to be one of the most popular characters on the show. Some viewers will love him, most will love hating him. Either way, the guy is ratings gold for Salazar. And Tucker knows it."

"Did he get a reprimand, at least?"

"Salazar took him aside and gave him a stern word of warning. Off camera. Basically told him to go forth and sin no more. Or, at least, not get caught. And we can't mention anything about what happened to the other housemates. Ken has a thing about not letting unrelated, off-camera incidents contaminate the competition inside the house."

"The 'golden boy,'" Kate said softly, remembering Candy's words.

"Yup, you got it. It's Tucker's world, apparently. And the rest of us are just living in it."

Chapter 42

"Are we official?" Desiree asked, peeking her head over the swinging doors of the bakery kitchen.

"Sylvia left about fifteen minutes ago. We're signed, sealed, and delivered," Kate promised. "I told her I'd already moved some stuff in this afternoon."

"Oh good," Desiree said. "I was a little nervous about spending too much time there, in case she came to check up on the place. So I haven't been back since we dropped off my bags and stocked the fridge."

"Where have you been all afternoon?"

"Let's just say I was taking a Judson Cooper tour of Coral Cay. And I came up with a few things. Have you got time to chat? I even brought the corkboard."

"Good, I wanted to work on that this morning," Kate said. "But we never really had time. For now, I've just been sticking everything up on the fridge. But it doesn't make any sense. At least, not yet."

Corkboard under her arm, Desiree walked over and studied the door of the stainless-steel refrigerator. "You weren't just humoring me—you're really doing this," she said, a note of awe in her voice. "I thought I was just turning into a crazy woman. But this is . . . wonderful."

"Not just me," Kate said. "A bunch of us have been working on it. And with everything that's been going on, we didn't get to update it."

"What's this?" Desiree asked, pointing to a line of yellow sticky notes off to one side.

Kate smiled. "I call that section 'unexplained weirdness.' Strange things that have happened in the past few weeks. But we don't necessarily know if they're connected to Judd."

"Conch House sold?" Desiree read from a note.

"Sylvia told me that this afternoon. It wasn't her listing, so she doesn't know much. But apparently some big corporation bought it."

"That can't be good news for Judd. Or that rare species he was talking about that lives there."

"That's what I thought," Kate said. "I don't know if it's related, but maybe we should at least consider it. And see if we can get a little more information on the company that bought it."

"¿Qué pasa? What's up, girls?" Maxi said, swinging through the back door. "Oh good, the yarn board. We wanted to work on that this morning. Before the Evil Brad showed up."

"See, I told you," Kate said, patting Desiree's arm. "She thought we were just humoring her."

"Here," Maxi said, gently taking the board from Desiree. "Let's put this guy up on the counter where we can see it." She adjusted and readjusted the board until she got it to stand upright. "Ay, just like that. ¡Muy bien!"

"What does this one mean?" Desiree said, pointing at the refrigerator. "'Dirty coolers'?"

"Sounds like a band," Maxi said. "One that plays club music super loud."

Kate recounted Howie's story about his stolen coolers, as she snatched up the sticky notes from the refrigerator and repositioned them on the corkboard.

"That's just weird," Maxi said.

"That's pretty much what Howie thought," Kate said. "Apparently he's now keeping them under lock and key. Literally."

"There's something about that that seems familiar," Desiree said. "But it's not coming to me right now."

"Something about coolers? Or Conch House itself? Maybe something you noticed when we were out there?" Kate asked, as she studied the board.

"I don't know," Desiree said, dejected. "It's like the memory is close, but I just can't seem to grab ahold of it."

"When's the last time you ate?" Maxi asked.

"I have an entire kitchen full of wonderful leftovers," she said. "But I was afraid to hang around since we hadn't signed the paperwork yet. And I really didn't want to get tossed out again. Then I sort of got caught up in what I was doing—revisiting a lot of the places Judd and I saw while we've been here."

"So why don't I make us a couple of omelettes, while you can tell us what you remember," Kate said, opening the back door and leaving it ajar. "I have it on good authority there's some first-class ham in the fridge."

As Desiree recounted her travels, Kate chopped spring onions and diced Swiss cheese and ham. She cracked the eggs and whisked them to a frothy yellow, added salt, pepper, and a generous pour of cream. She put four skillets on the stove and sliced a pat of butter into each.

"Four at a time?" Maxi asked. "And why four?"

"You'll see. We used to do omelette stations in the

restaurants all the time. For the customers—and for the staff, when we'd missed a meal."

"Remember Omelette Surprise?" Desiree asked.

"That was fun," Kate said, swirling each pan in turn, as the smell of warm butter drifted across the kitchen.

"What's that?" Maxi asked.

Kate smiled. "It was something we'd do at the hotel when the staff was hungry, and we couldn't get home anytime soon. Basically, it's what we're doing now. You look in the fridge or the pantry. And whatever you have leftover, that's what goes in the omelette. Some days it was beef bourguignon, other days it might be baked apples. That was the surprise."

Kate poured the eggs into two pans. A half a minute later, she filled the other two. With a wooden spatula, she worked the first pans, tilting them as needed. She finished up by giving them liberal helpings of ham, cheese, and scallions.

Then she moved to the second two pans, working them in tandem. While the last two omelettes cooked, she folded the first two with her spatula and plated them. She added two thick slices of fresh tomato to each, and slid the plates in front of Maxi and Desiree.

"Just let me know what you think," she said, proudly.

As they tucked in, Kate finished the second two omelettes. One with all the trimmings, the other simply with ham and cheese.

Oliver appeared at the back door, as if summoned.

Kate cut the ham and cheese omelette into quarters, and again into eighths, sliding the pieces in his bowl.

As he gave the offering his undivided attention, she grabbed her own plate and joined her friends at the table.

"OK, this is seriously the best omelette I've ever had," Maxi said. "You better not let Bridget and Andy know you can cook like this. They'll hire someone to come over and break all your frying pans."

"Bridget and Andy have nothing to worry about. Besides, the secret is butter and cream. And somehow, I have a feeling they already know that one."

"This is scrumptious," Desiree agreed. "You always had talent. But I think you've risen to a whole new level."

"It's just a few eggs," Kate said, between bites.

"It's more than that," Desiree said. "You're happy. And it comes out in your food."

Oliver looked up, and if Kate didn't know better, she'd have sworn he winked.

"So did you remember anything we can add to the board?" Kate asked, as she cleared her dishes.

"Mainly, I remembered how much time Judd and I spent together. Yes, we'd each go off occasionally. But it was never for long. I don't know what Lola Montgomery is trying to do, but I know she wasn't seeing Judd. He wouldn't have had the time.

"We came to the same conclusion," Kate said, as Maxi nodded. "And I feel more than a little guilty that I went to see her."

"Why? You were looking for leads on Judd," Desiree said. "Heck, I'd have visited her too, if I thought she knew anything."

"Her performance at the press conference?" Kate said slowly. "I think I caught the dress rehearsal. Right down to the halting voice and the wet eyelashes."

"OK, that is super shady," Maxi said, as she finished off the last bite of tomato on her plate.

"She'd have done it regardless," Desiree said. "If it wasn't you, she'd have run her lines with one of her entourage. The lady needs her time in the spotlight, and that has nothing to do with you. That's just who she is.

I'm furious that she took advantage of Judd's situation. And even more furious that anyone is taking her seriously. But Judd said it was almost like she couldn't help herself. She had to be the center of attention. And if you're in a relationship, that gets old pretty quick."

"Do you think she could have kidnapped Judd?" Maxi asked quietly. "Or had somebody take him? Maybe if she was jealous?"

"I doubt it," Desiree said. "From what little Judd's said, and what I've witnessed the past few days, I honestly don't believe she ever thinks about anything besides herself. And possibly her next role."

"So you want to cross Lola Montgomery off the suspect list?" Kate asked.

"Let's leave her in that side pile," Desiree said smiling. "Unexplained weirdness."

"I meant to ask you," Maxi said. "Are we still having cookie class tonight?"

"Cookie class!" Kate said. "I completely forgot about it."

"And how much sleep didn't you get last night?" Maxi prodded.

"I had a couple of cake orders, so I kind of pulled an all-nighter," Kate explained to Desiree.

"Don't worry," Desiree said. "We can meet up tomorrow to work on this. I also want to tag up with that detective to see if he has any new information."

"Why don't you stay and join us?" Kate said. "Not for the cookie part. I mean, you can bake if you want to. But the women who are coming? You've met them. They've all been working on helping us compile a timeline for Judd's visit—trying to remember anything that might have a bearing on his disappearance."

"You mean stay and work on the board?" she asked.

"Why not?" Kate said, as she grabbed a spray bottle and paper towels. "We can still do the class."

"These women—they all want to help," Maxi said.

"You don't know it," Kate said as she cleaned the counters, "but Sunny and her mom offered to let you stay at their cottage on the cove the evening we found Judd's ring."

"Your detective friend vetoed that one?" Desiree asked.

Kate nodded. "Apparently civilians and crime scenes are a bad mix."

"Well, he was very kind when he took me out there the next morning. And he didn't have to do that. Even showed up with breakfast sandwiches and coffee."

"That kinda sounds like Ben," Maxi said. "The man does like his food."

"Are you sure they still want to help?" Desiree asked anxiously. "With what Liam and Sarah are spreading, they might want to keep their distance for a while."

"Just the opposite," Kate said. "But hey, we'll ask them when they get here. My guess? You'll have more help than you know what to do with."

"Plus," Maxi said, rubbing her hands together, "*someone* promised that tonight's cookie recipe would have something to do with melted chocolate."

Chapter 43

Barb Showalter was the first to arrive. Oliver greeted her fondly, and remained in the bakery shop, curled up in front of the door.

"That's some guard dog you've got there," Barb said, laughing as she walked into the kitchen.

"More like a doorman," Maxi said. "We're going to get him one of those cute hats and a jacket with that gold trim."

"He knows he's not really supposed to be back here now," Kate explained. "But he doesn't want to miss the party. Especially when he knows everybody."

Kate heard the shop bell and looked out to see Minette, Sunny, and Rosie greeting their canine gatekeeper.

"I don't suppose we can slip this boy a little treat?" Rosie drawled, when she walked into the kitchen. "He was looking at me with those hungry puppy eyes."

"He's fine for now," Kate said. "He literally just polished off dinner."

"Cooked table-side," Maxi said, grinning.

"Girls, you know Desiree," Kate said.

Her friend, stationed at the corkboard, gave a friendly wave.

"Hmmm, this looks familiar," Minette said, standing next to Desiree in front of the board. "My Carl worked a lot of these in his day. Never seen one with yarn before. Is this for your man?"

Desiree nodded. And Kate saw her swallow hard.

"We've been gathering information from everyone in downtown to compile a timeline of Judson's disappearance," Kate said. "And all of the details you guys have shared. Now we're trying to put it together in one place. And trying to make some sense of it. I was wondering if maybe during cookie class or after, you guys would want to help us fill it in a little."

Minette put an arm around Desiree, whose eyes were welling up. "I know my Carl would love for me to come home with some new cookies. But I'm thinking we might just need to skip that today, and do this instead."

"Absolutely!" Sunny chimed in. "And high time, too."

"Locked in a bakery with a mystery to solve," Rosie said. "Count me in."

"Well, this is my first cookie class," Barb said. "But I'm thinking no time like the present."

"Thank you," Desiree said, her eyes glistening. She shook her head and wiped her eyes with her hand.

"Baby, we are going to do everything we can to bring that man home," Minette said. "Don't you worry."

"Let's put this where it will do us the most good," Sunny said, picking up the board and carrying it to the kitchen table, where she propped it up in a chair. Then she arranged the chair so that it was front and center. "There, that's better. Now we can all focus on it while we strategize."

"That's perfect," Kate said. "I'll get a platter of cookies to fuel us."

"I'll brew us a big pot of strong coffee," Maxi said.

"Sugar and caffeine," Rosie said. "Now that's some brain food I can endorse."

"So was Lola Montgomery having a fling with Judson Cooper?" Rosie asked, reaching for another cookie from the tray.

"Girl, hush," Minette hissed, nodding toward Desiree.

Desiree shook her head. "No, that's OK. Believe me, after the past few days, I'm not easily embarrassed. And with you girls, no secrets. Everything on the table. Anything that can help us find Judd is fair game."

"We believe, based on the credit card and the time frame, that Lola Montgomery was spinning a story," Kate said. "Something else I realized—she said that she heard a knock on the door, opened it, and Judd was just standing there. But when I went to see her, I had to give my name at the desk. They confirmed she was expecting me and called to let her know I was coming up. Then I was escorted by a bellman who had to use a special elevator key to access her floor. So there's no way anyone just dropped in on Lola Montgomery."

"Makes a more romantic story," Maxi said. "Like something out of one of her movies."

"Exactly," Kate said. "And I think that's all it is—a story. But for the life of me I can't understand why."

"That's because you don't read the scandal sheets," Rosie said. "Her last movie tanked. So bad it couldn't even be released. Then she spent three months on location in Eastern Europe filming a horror flick. I'm hearin' it's such a stinker, it probably won't be released, either. At least not over here."

"Why, Rosie Armand, you mean to tell me you read the gossip columns?" Sunny teased.

"I may have skimmed a few of the headlines," she admitted, blushing.

"No shame in that," Sunny said, with a wave of her hand. "Knowledge is power. No matter where it comes from."

"I love those magazines," Minette rhapsodized. "Such pretty clothes. That's why I like watching the awards shows."

"So she was doing this just for the attention?" Barb said in disgust.

"Ben warned us about people trying to attach themselves to the case," Kate said. "I just never dreamed one of them would be a household name already."

"We also found out a corporation's buying that big house on the bluff—the one where they're filming the reality show," Desiree said.

"Harp's place," Maxi said. "Somehow, I can't bring myself to call it Conch House."

"Why would you?" Sunny asked.

"It's what they named it for the show," Kate said. "Ken Salazar thought it gave the place local flavor."

"Balderdash," Sunny said. "The architecture and location give it local flavor. Naming it is just pretentious."

"Judd mentioned that the house—whatever it is— was home to a very rare species," Desiree said. "And I think he was concerned about it. We know he'd been out there."

Maxi looked at Kate.

"Carl saw Judd out there the Monday before he disappeared," Kate said quietly. "He was with a women—a woman with red hair. At first, I thought it might be Lola Montgomery, but we've pretty much ruled that out. I pushed Lola several times, but she never mentioned that house. In fact, she couldn't name one single place they'd been together. Desiree, do you have any idea who the redhead might be?"

"Not in the slightest," she said, glumly. "Zoey—she's Judd's business partner—has dark blond hair. And his daughter Sarah, well, you've seen her. Hers is more of a light brown. It could have been someone from one of the wildlife centers. Or another biologist that he trusted. But I don't know."

"I wonder if she has anything to do with the corporation that's buying the place," Rosie said.

"Well, I for one would like to know a lot more about that corporation," Minette said. "Who are they, and why are they buying a house here?"

"You want to look into that?" Barb said, her pen hovering over a small notebook. "Just make a few phone calls, talk to people, and see what you can discover?"

Minette grinned. "I most certainly would," she said, straightening herself in her chair. "You can't be married to a detective all these years without learning a thing or two."

"With any luck, you'll find that mystery redhead, too," Maxi said.

"You mentioned his fellow biologists," Kate said. "Anyone he'd call if he found something interesting on this island?"

Leaning into the kitchen table, Desiree cradled her coffee cup with both hands. "It would depend on what he found. But maybe someone at the rehab center up the coast would know. We were supposed to head up there on our honeymoon, so they might talk to me."

"Good girl," Sunny said, patting Desiree's arm.

"OK, so we've got Desiree calling the rehab center

and checking with local biologists," Barb said, making notes. "And Minette's going to track down that corporation. So the corporation doesn't stand a chance."

"Darn right," Minette said.

"Sunny, have you or Iris noticed anything or anyone at The Nose since all the commotion the other day?" Barb asked.

"Not a soul," Sunny said, tucking a stray lock of her short champagne blond hair behind one ear. "Not so much as a wayward backpacker."

"That's good, at least," Maxi said, lifting a cookie from the platter. "Wait a minute, what about the cigarette boat? Kate thought she might have seen it this morning, right offshore from Palm Isle. The same one you guys saw the day your guy disappeared."

"Are you sure?" Desiree asked.

Kate shook her head. "I thought I caught a glimpse of it. For a split second. From the car. When I ran over to the seawall for a better look, it was gone. I could have been imagining it."

"I know a couple of people at the marinas," Barb said. "I could chat them up a bit."

"That would be great," Desiree said. "Thank you. If it helps, the one we're looking for is black. And I think it had red stripes down the sides."

Barb jotted down the description in her notes. "Anything else? Driver male or female? Any passengers?"

"We were too far away," Kate said.

"We could barely see the boat," Desiree added.

"Got it," Barb said. "Let me see what I can find."

"Desiree, when you and Judd got engaged, did he buy a ring or was it a family heirloom?" Kate asked.

"I don't think Judd has any family heirlooms," Desiree said, smiling as she held out her left hand to the group. "He actually had this made special."

"Ooo, that is nice," Rosie said, leaning in.

"That is some pearl," Maxi said, turning Desiree's hand to catch the light. "Is it pink?"

Desiree nodded proudly. "We bought it from a lady who dives for them. In Japan. She was particularly pleased with this one. It's not huge, but it's perfectly round. And she said the faint pink color reminded her of the clouds at sunrise."

"It's beautiful," Sunny said, examining it closely. "Exquisite."

Desiree beamed. "I had no idea he was having it made into a ring. Or that he'd use the ring to propose. But every time I look at it, I think about him and all the places we've seen together."

"Did he ever mention any other jewelry?" Kate asked. "Maybe a ring that had been in the family?"

"Not that I remember. Judd's family wasn't wealthy. 'Solid middle class' is how he always describes his upbringing. Why?"

"Andy Levy at the pub talked with Judd. The day he disappeared, actually. It was late afternoon, and Judd had stopped in for a takeout lunch. Salmon salad sandwiches and chocolate mousse cupcakes."

"That wasn't for me. Late afternoon, I was at the resort spa. Getting ready for the wedding the next day. By the time I was finished and Judd got back, we were both famished. I remember we went out for a big dinner, then took a walk on the beach. Did Andy say anything else?"

"Keep in mind this is Andy Levy," Maxi said, as Rosie nodded. "The boy is magic with food, but as a witness—I'm not so sure."

"Amen," Minette said.

"All he said was that Judd was worried he was going to make someone angry. But that she was a lot less likely to throw something at him if he showed up with chocolate. Andy claims Judd said he was going to ask for a ring back. Because it was a family heirloom."

"This is the only ring he ever gave me," Desiree said. "And it's the only one I ever wanted."

"Could he have given Lola a ring?" Barb asked. "Back when they were dating?"

Desiree paused, considering the question. "No, I know he didn't. He once told me that when it came to proposals, he was batting a thousand. Two for two."

"Does he get along with the ex-Mrs. Cooper?" Minette asked, a note of suspicion creeping into her voice.

"Emily? Extremely well. Of course, she's happily remarried and living in Connecticut. Has been for years. The new husband's in finance. Or is it insurance? Anyway, they're very comfortable. And she's not a redhead. She's blond. Platinum blond. I've seen the Christmas photos she's shared with Judd."

"Those kids of his would know if there's a family heirloom kickin' around," Rosie said.

"They most certainly would," Desiree agreed. "But I can't exactly ask them."

"Maybe Ben could," Barb said. "You know, just say it's come up in the course of the investigation."

"That might not be a super-good idea," Maxi said, warily. "We'd have to tell him everything. And Andy says Judd said something about life being too short to spend with the wrong person—and thank goodness he came to his senses."

"We need to tell him," Desiree said. "It's OK. I know Judd wasn't talking about me. And this is a clue. A big, fat honking clue."

"OK, so someone needs to talk to Ben," Barb said, pen poised over her notes. "Any volunteers?"

"I can do that," Kate said. "There was something else I wanted to ask him about anyway."

"Got it," Barb said, scribbling. "What else can we tackle from that board?"

"I'm going to tackle getting us a few more cookies," Kate said, picking up the almost empty platter. "Anybody want a refill on coffee?"

"*Sí*, and I'm on it," Maxi said, stretching as she stood up.

As Kate set a big platter of cookies on the table, Rosie pointed to one oddly misshapen one. "What's that?"

"Oh, sorry, that's not supposed to be there," Kate said. "It's an experiment. Wafer-thin, turtle-shaped sugar cookies. In honor of the loggerheads. But it's still in the experimental stages. Very experimental."

"Turtles!" Desiree shouted, her eyes wide. "That's it. That's what I was trying to remember earlier. When you were telling me about the dirty coolers."

"Slow down, honey," Minette said lightly. "Some of us are going to need a road map to follow this conversation."

"When poachers dig up turtle eggs! I remember Judd told me about it once. Sometimes they'll pack the eggs in coolers filled with sand. Usually sand from the same beach as the nest. They want to keep the eggs warm. But it doesn't really work. What was it he said? 'Mother Nature won't be fooled.'"

"One of the cameramen from the *Last Resort* had a couple of his coolers stolen," Kate explained to the group. "By one of the housemates on the show. When he finally got them back, they were coated inside with sand."

"Was it that little jellyfish who quit on Amos?" Sunny asked.

"Quit and stole forty dollars from his cash register," Minette fumed. "That boy's a straight-up thief!"

"His name's Tucker," Kate said. "And yes, he's the

one. Howie—the cameraman—got Tucker on film, coming back one night with the coolers. And he found them stashed under Tucker's bed. That's what the sticky note on the board with 'dirty coolers' means."

"If he's the poacher, and he was on that beach, he could have something to do with Judd's disappearance," Desiree said.

Kate nodded. "We definitely need to call Ben."

Chapter 44

"Please tell me this isn't what it looks like," Ben said, sitting at the bakery's kitchen table with a fresh cup of coffee in front of him.

Kate said a silent thank-you to whomever had moved the corkboard out of sight.

"We're taking a cookie class," Minette said.

"And these would be the cookies that you made?" he asked, pointing to the platter on the table.

"Nope. That's a little snack," Minette said.

"Just being neighborly, since we knew you were comin'," Rosie added.

"Far be it from me to look a gift cookie in the mouth," he said, selecting a sugar-dusted chocolate crinkle cookie and an orange madeleine from the platter. "But if you ladies have spent the evening baking cookies, why does this kitchen smell like ham, onions, and coffee?"

"Score one for the detective," Sunny said. "Now Ben, we need your help."

"At your service," he said. "I'd tip my hat, but it's over there on the counter. What's up?"

"We think one of the housemates on *Last Resort* is stealing turtle eggs from The Nose," Kate said.

"Let me guess. Tucker."

"No grass growing under him," Sunny said, helping herself to a chocolate chip cookie.

"Have you heard about this already?" Maxi asked.

Ben shook his head. "Nope. It's just that that little twit has been a constant thorn in my side since he got here. And a little birdie told me that three of the kids from that house were tearing around in a poison green convertible, chucking cans at unsuspecting drivers."

"We only caught a fleeting glimpse of the car," Kate said. "And we didn't recognize it until later. It was the one the housemates get to use when they win a competition."

"How did you find out about it?" Maxi asked.

"Gabe," he said, swallowing a bite. "He's the one they called yesterday when the thing wouldn't start. Lo and behold the distributor cap was missing. You wouldn't know anything about that, I guess?" The detective paused, a cookie poised above his coffee cup.

Maxi reached for another cookie. Desiree smiled blandly. Looking down at the table, Kate could feel her face turning pink.

"No? Well, in any event, let's just say my guys have become a very obvious and visible presence on that stretch of road. Ticketed your friend Tucker for speeding once already. So I think his days of joyriding and can chucking are over. At least I hope so. Now tell me about the turtle eggs."

As Desiree explained how poachers package their illicit cargo, Kate refilled everyone's coffee cup.

"And you know it was Tucker how?" Ben asked.

"He stole the coolers from a cameraman on the show," Kate said. "But there are cameras everywhere in the house. Even outside on the grounds. The guy went through the footage, and he found Tucker coming back one night with the coolers. Tucker even stored them under his bed."

"Love to know what night that was," Ben said.

"Howie is the cameraman. He could tell you. But he wasn't really supposed to tell anyone. I don't want to get him fired."

"He just happened to tell you?"

"He comes into the bakery. We were chatting. Commiserating, really. When I was out there teaching a class, I got a front-row seat to what it's like for some of the houseguests."

"So you know some of these kids?"

"Well, I spent a few hours with them," Kate said. "We talked."

"Any that you trust? Specifically the boys?"

"James," Kate and Barb said in unison.

"He's been working in my store the last few days," Barb explained.

"What's he like?" Ben asked.

"Nice," Barb said. "And hardworking. Comes in early. Stays late. Tell you the truth, I think he might be avoiding going back to that place."

"He's kind, and he's smart," Kate said. "He's also the one who came up with the idea of decorating sugar cookies like baseballs. For the playoffs."

"How does he get along with the others?"

"There's a clique that's trying to establish some sort of hierarchy in the house—Tucker and his crew—but James isn't part of it," Kate said. "He goes his own way."

"That's my take on it exactly," Barb said. "I think he wants to win the competition. But I don't think he banked on the outrageous behavior he'd have to put up with to do it."

"Who else have you talked to about this?" Ben asked.

"Just the people in this room," Desiree said. "We literally put the pieces together tonight and called you."

"Good. Ladies, this is a solid lead. But if we're going to make the most of it, I need a big favor. I need you to keep this information inside this room. For Judson Cooper's sake. That means not a word to anyone. Not even mothers, or husbands or"—Ben cast a quick sidelong glance at Kate—"or boyfriends, or whatever. Promise me?"

They all nodded, as Maxi skinned an eye toward Kate.

"Any idea where James is right now?" Ben asked Barb. "I'm guessing back at the house?"

"Actually, he's at the shop," Barb said. "We've been staying open later on Friday and Saturday evenings, to catch the after-dinner crowd."

"Can you bring him here?" Ben asked. "Or better yet, relieve him at the shop and send him over here? Tell him you need him to pick up some cookies?"

"I suppose I could. But why?"

"If Tucker is really selling turtle eggs, I have a little idea that might help us catch him in the act. But I'm going to need an inside man."

Kate led a slightly confused-looking James into the kitchen, as Oliver peered underneath the swinging doors. "It's OK, these are friends of mine. James, this is Desiree and Maxi. And that's Ben Abrams. He's a police detective, and he's the one who needs your help. Would you like some coffee?"

"Sure, but I don't see how I can help," he said, folding his tall lanky frame into a chair and adjusting his black T-shirt.

"Well, for starters, you can take these away from me," Ben said, smiling as he pushed the platter of cookies across the table. "I'm trying to watch my figure."

James helped himself to a peanut butter cookie, as Kate slid a mug of coffee in front of him, along with a plate and a paper napkin.

"How do you feel about Tucker?" Ben asked.

"He's a jerk. But he's probably going to win *Last Resort* this season. Why?"

"Would you like to take him out of the running?" Ben asked.

"I'm not gonna cheat," James said, planting his sneakers on the floor and sitting up straight.

"Does Tucker cheat?" Ben asked, sipping his coffee.

James shrugged, as he devoured the cookie and reached for another.

"Does he seem to have a lot of cash?"

"Flashes it whenever he can," James said, swallowing a mouthful of cookie. "Funny thing is, when he landed here, he was bumming stuff off everybody. Two days later, he's got a wad of bills."

"He's still got it?"

The cookie vanished. James brushed his hands on his jeans and reached for another. "He did. You guys gave him a speeding ticket last night. He says the fines are gonna clean him out."

Ben nodded. "Good to know. And I would never ask you to cheat. Just the opposite. We need to set things right. And that's where I need your help."

James shrugged again.

"At the house, do they ever talk about what happened out at the cove near the nature preserve?"

"You mean the search for that guy who disappeared? The marine biologist?"

Ben nodded.

"Yeah, some of Tucker's friends were talking about it. Tucker seemed kind of hacked off."

"Good. When you go back tonight, I want you to mention something you overheard in town. At the diner. You heard a couple of uniformed officers talking. They were saying how the police finally finished up at the cove this afternoon. They didn't find a thing, and they're just glad they don't ever have to go back out there again. And you don't have to say it to Tucker. Maybe say it to someone else when he's within earshot."

"Then what?"

"That's it," Ben said, casually checking his watch as he finished his coffee. "And, unless I miss my guess, that will be more than enough."

Chapter 45

Kate opened her eyes and glanced at the clock on her bedside table: 4:05 a.m.

Oliver, curled up at the foot of the bed, snuffled softly.

"OK, you get enough sleep for the both of us," she said softly to the fuzzy, slumbering form. "It's Saturday morning, and I've got some baseballs to bake."

After a quick shower, she threw on a navy T-shirt and jeans, and stepped lightly down the stairs.

Looking around the spotless kitchen, Kate was glad she'd cleaned up last night. Now she could enjoy the fun stuff. She plugged in the coffee maker, and flipped the ON switch. Nineties model or not, Sam was right. It still had plenty of life left in it.

As the machine gurgled, the smell of coffee filled the room. Kate pulled a strawberry yogurt from the fridge and wondered if Ben's trap had netted any results. Like a wily Tucker.

Oliver padded down the stairs, turned around three times, and curled up under the kitchen table.

Later as the pink and gold clouds danced on the horizon, she rolled a rack of sugar cookies out of the oven. The fragrant scent engulfed the kitchen. She rolled in the next rack—this one with trays of peanut butter, peanut butter chocolate chip, and classic chocolate chip (her personal favorite).

Oliver, standing by the back door, whined softly.

"Of course," she said, flipping the deadbolt and opening the door. The pup raced across the dewy grass like a spring colt.

Back at the counter, she mixed up a batch of royal icing, then divvied it up between three pastry bags. Most of it would remain white. But to form the stitches and pattern on her baseball cookies, she also needed a portion of it in red and some in soft gray.

Oliver bounded back into the kitchen and lapped noisily from his water bowl.

"Would you like a little something to go with that?" she asked. "I just happen to have a couple of those sausage swirls you like," she said, removing two of the large rounds from the rack and putting them gently into his bowl.

"Wouldn't say no to one a' those myself," Sam said, wheeling in the back door. "Tried one the other day. Mighty tasty. Thyme's a nice touch."

"There's fresh coffee in the pot. I'll have us stocked up on cookies by the time we open the doors. And we've got plenty of sausage swirl biscuits. Now that you mention it, I might have one, too."

"Was thinkin' these might make good breakfast food," Sam said, pulling two off the rack and putting them each on a plate. "Kids goin' to school, people drivin' to work. We could make 'em in a couple of flavors. Maybe one with a little cheese and tomato sauce, a little basil. Put 'em in the case. See what happens."

Kate smiled. A few months ago, Sam was in a rut. The Cookie House, despite its name, sold a dozen different kinds of bread. Only bread. Because while Sam was a standout baker, his late wife, Cookie, had been the pastry maker.

But after nearly going out of business and a short stint in the local jail as a most unlikely murder suspect, the baker was rediscovering life. And throwing himself into his business again.

"Nice idea," Kate said. "I can bake up a test batch this afternoon. Let people try them, and see what they think."

"Oh, meant to give you this yesterday," he said, handing her a thick cardboard folder with a bank logo. She opened it to find a sheaf of papers, a debit card, and six books of checks, all of them with the Cookie House name and address.

"Opened that savings account you wanted," Sam explained. "They made up two a' those packets. That one's yours. Account's in both our names. I put a bit a' money in it, too. Had a little something squirreled away."

"This is great," Kate said, smiling. "Now I can just drop by and deposit that check from the reality show. How did you manage to put me on it, too? I thought we'd both have to take a lunch break next week and dig up five kinds of ID."

"One business partner's the same as the other, as far as anybody cares. Showed 'em our paperwork, and that was it."

"This calls for a cookie with breakfast. So how would you feel about splitting a baseball?"

The next few hours were a blur. Local customers started trickling in at seven thirty, even though the shop didn't officially open until eight.

"I just wanted to be sure we could get a birthday cake

for Tuesday," Sally Jessup explained when she showed up at quarter to eight. "Oh, and three dozen of those baseball cookies."

"How old is Eddie going to be?" Kate asked.

"Eight. And we'll have nine little monsters terrorizing our neighborhood for the afternoon. Followed by a hotdog cookout, cake, and ice cream."

"I heard," Kate said laughing. "Maxi says Michael's been talking about it all week."

Sally shook her head. "At this point, I almost need two cakes. One that says 'Happy Eighth Birthday Eddie!' and a second that reads 'I Survived My Son's Eighth Birthday Party.'"

The phone rang nonstop. At one point, Kate and Sam traded off manning the shop and answering the phone.

"At this rate, we're gonna have to close early," Sam said, gleefully, when he cut through the kitchen to restock the peanut butter chip cookies. "Won't have nothing left to sell."

"Hello, the Cookie House. This is Kate."

"Well, my friends in Coral Cay believe me, but Judd's friends at the rehab center are a whole other story."

"Why?" Kate said. "What happened?"

"The staff at the marine rehab center," Desiree said, "they won't talk to me. I left a couple of messages this morning. To various people Judd's mentioned from time to time. But the only call back I received was from the center's attorney."

"Yowch! What did they say?"

"He said if anyone wanted to call me, they were free to do so on their own time. But they didn't know where Judd was, and if they had any information to share in the future, they'd forward it directly to the proper authorities. And his parting shot? He was formally requesting that I stop phoning, as my calls are—and I quote—'a source of angst and a distraction from the center's important day-to-day mission.'"

"Wow. Just wow. Are you all right?"

"I am *steamed*. That was the place I was going to spend my honeymoon, for Pete's sake. That's how much I believe in their important day-to-day mission."

"It sounds like someone might have had a word with them," Kate said.

"Liam and Sarah."

"Most likely. I'm so sorry. You want me to call? You can tell me who to contact."

"Once they find out what it's about, you'll just get the same phone call."

"Wait a minute! What about Jack? They know him. He's actually done some volunteer work up there."

"Kate, that's brilliant. I'll call his clinic now. I know he's got to be slammed on a Saturday, but maybe he can squeeze in a phone call or two on his break. Or even after work. Hey, stop that!" Desiree screeched. "Get away from there!"

"Desiree! Are you OK? What's happening?"

"Just had to close the drapes," her friend whispered into the phone. "I hope you're in good with that real estate lady, because our friends with the cameras are back."

"Oh geez," Kate said. "Let me come pick you up. I can borrow Sam's truck."

"No, no, I'm fine. I'm inside, they're outside. Besides, you have a bakery to run, and I have more calls to make. It's just that I don't know how they even discovered I was here. I was so careful driving back—checking the rearview mirror to make sure I wasn't being followed. I haven't told a soul where I am. How on earth do they keep finding me? I feel like I'm being hunted."

Chapter 46

"So what's the lady of leisure doing today?" Maxi asked, lifting a large glass vase of sunny yellow mums and vibrant orange tiger lilies onto the top of the bakery case.

"Those are beautiful!" Kate said. "What's the occasion?"

"They're magical stay-awake flowers. Since I know you got about four hours sleep last night."

"Look who's talking. You were here until the bitter end. And then you had to drive home."

"Well, if *mi padrino* asks, this is our latest cross promotion—flour and flowers."

"Come into the back, and I'll show you the sketch for Eddie Jessup's birthday cake. And you can try a baseball cookie."

"Andy's selling out of them at the pub," Maxi said, strolling into the kitchen and retrieving two coffee cups from the cupboard. "He's even got a little sign on the counter: 'Batter up! Get your baseball playoff cookies here!'"

Kate grinned. "James definitely deserves a reward for these," she said, arranging a few of them on a plate. "He's the one who designed them. And they're a hit—oh, blast, now Andy's got me doing it."

"Bad puns are contagious," Maxi said.

"Sally Jessup wants five dozen of them for the birthday party."

"Suddenly, I'm thinking that Miguelito might need a chaperone," Maxi said, carrying the cups to the kitchen table. "You know, just to make sure he behaves himself. Not so I can sit back in a lawn chair and be served coffee and cookies."

"I mean, we can't keep them on the shelves, and neither can Andy and Bridget," Kate said. "Even if they are a little labor intensive."

"Ay, all those tiny red stitches," Maxi said, studying the front of her cookie. "That would drive me loco."

"But James is the one who came up with the idea," Kate said, snagging one for herself. "He should get something from it."

"Like a design fee?"

"Exactly! I get the feeling there's a reason he's on *Last Resort*, and it's not for the thrill of competition."

"Those shows give out big piles of money to the winners," Maxi said. "Not that I've ever watched them, of course."

"Of course."

"So some of the contestants use the shows to earn money for school or pay off student loans," Maxi said, dunking the baseball in her coffee. "Plus, if you're a popular character, you can get other gigs on other shows. So it kinda becomes a career."

"I'll talk to Sam tonight," Kate said. "It won't be

enough for a scholarship, but the Cookie House is going to pay its first ever design fee."

"Oh, these are so good!" Maxi said, happily. "Definitely worth sitting through a kid's birthday party."

"Hey, girls," Barb said, sticking her head over the kitchen doors. "Wait a minute, isn't this where I left you two about sixteen hours ago? Don't tell me you pulled an all-nighter?"

"Not me," Maxi said. "But I think she might have."

"Not even close. Come on in, I'll get you a cup. And you can try our latest taste sensation: baseball cookies."

"I bought one of those at the pub yesterday—after lunch," Barb said, pulling out a chair. "It was going to be my three-o'clock snack. Never even made it out the door."

"We used James's cookie design, and my recipe," Kate said. "How is he, by the way? Have you heard anything on you-know-who?"

Barb shook her head. "Total radio silence. And James wasn't scheduled to work today, so I haven't heard from him. I just hope he's OK. Some of those housemates are brutal. Oh, but I have a little news on the cigarette-boat front. Not that it's particularly helpful."

"I'm afraid to ask," Kate said.

"Remember how you said you might have seen one yesterday near Palm Isle, but you weren't sure? Well, I'm pretty sure you did. But it may not have been the one Judson Cooper recognized."

"I'm telling you, all of those things look the same to me," Maxi said.

"And it turns out there's a reason for that," Barb said. "There's a cigarette boat regatta here this weekend. On the island, but just across the bay on the mainland. And black with red racing stripes is a very popular color combo."

"So what I saw yesterday was probably just some weekend boater enjoying a morning on the water," Kate said glumly.

"Owners are bringing them in from around the world to show them off. And they have all kinds of competitions and prizes. Races, precision-driving demonstrations, you name it. The things are also called 'go-fast boats' because—you guessed it—they can go really fast."

"They really knocked themselves out coming up with that one," Maxi said, hoisting her coffee cup.

"I'm still asking around," Barb said. "I have a friend at one of the marinas who's pretty plugged in to local scuttlebutt when it comes to boats. But she's been out captaining a fishing charter since Sunday. She gets back tomorrow, so I'm hoping to hear something then."

"What's worse than looking for one go-fast boat in a great big sea?" Kate asked.

"Looking for one go-fast boat in a sea of identical go-fast boats," Maxi said, as the three of them clinked coffee cups.

Barb shook her head. "Gives a whole new meaning to the phrase 'hiding in plain sight.'"

Chapter 47

Kate had just rolled another rack of sugar cookies out of the oven when she heard the tinkle of the shop bell.

"Afternoon, Doc," Sam said. "How's everything at the clinic?"

"Busy," Jack Scanlon said. "Man, this place smells great. So what do you recommend?"

"Can't go wrong with chocolate chip," the baker said. "Just out of the oven."

"Melty chocolate? Say no more. I'll take a dozen. And I heard you guys have some sausage swirl biscuits? I'd love a half dozen of those to try out at the clinic."

"You got it, Doc. Kate came up with the recipe for young Oliver. He really likes 'em. 'Course I do, too. Good for humans and dogs."

"In that case, make it a dozen," he said, handing off his credit card. "That might be my dinner. By the way, is Kate here?"

"In the kitchen," Sam said, pointing. "Go on back. I'll

fix up your order. Get yourself some coffee. Just brewed a fresh pot."

"Thanks, that would be great."

Jack walked through the kitchen door and stopped. "Howdy, stranger," he said, breaking into a wide grin.

"Howdy yourself," Kate said.

"Look, there's no easy way to say this. I got a call from Desiree, and it sounds like she's under siege."

"Oh geez," Kate said.

"I offered to come and get her, but she insisted she was fine," Jack said. "She didn't sound fine. I asked if she could slip into the garage and just drive away, but the beach house doesn't have a garage. And it sounds like they have her surrounded. Not in a dangerous, gunfight-at-the-O.K.-Corral kind of way. Just really unnerving. I'd like to make a rescue run, but I don't even know where she is."

"I do," Kate said, pulling off her apron. "Sam, can you hold down the fort for thirty minutes?"

"Don't see why not," the baker said, appearing at the kitchen door. "Doc, here's your card and your order. You tell that Desiree to hang in there."

When Jack's Range Rover reached Desiree's house, it was bedlam. Neighbors—at least Kate assumed they were neighbors—had formed a loose ring around the perimeter of the property, occasionally taking selfies in front of the house. Four photographers with more serious lenses were staking out the front yard.

Kate saw a local news van at the curb, with a reporter setting up on the lawn.

"Looks like the car is a lost cause," Jack said softly. "We're on the mainland. Does that mean you can get a cell signal out here?"

"Your guess is as good as mine," Kate said, pulling the phone from her purse.

She tapped a couple of buttons. "Yes!" she said, triumphantly.

"The backyard, what's the terrain?"

"Grass up near the house, then it turns into sand as it nears the beach."

"Perfect," Jack said. "Tell her to grab what she needs and go to the back door. We'll pick her up there."

"You won't get stuck?" Kate asked.

"That's why I bought this thing," he said, patting the gearshift. "Most times, an animal can come to the office. But when they can't, it helps to have a car that can go anywhere. And this baby was built to drive through the bush. So I figure it can handle a suburban backyard."

"Desiree, it's Kate. Jack and I are right outside. We can pick you up by the back door. Can you throw together an overnight bag?"

"I never unpacked. Give me a minute, I'll get my stuff. But where are we even going?"

"We'll worry about that later. First, we get you out. Oh, and Sam says hi. Actually, his exact quote was 'Tell her to hang in there.'"

"Now you're making me cry," Desiree said. "Still a lot better than what I've been doing all afternoon. OK, all set. Tell Captain Jack I'm by the back door. There's no furniture on the patio, so he can drive right onto that."

"Around the back and pull up onto the patio," Kate relayed to Jack. "She's just inside the door."

Jack headed up the driveway, and took a wide turn as they came to Kate's car. After all of Gabe's hard work, she hoped Gwendolyn would be all right.

Clear of the car, Jack took a hard left, picked up speed, and brought the SUV to a stop within two feet of the house. He popped the door locks.

Desiree locked the house, threw her bags into the back seat, and scrambled into the car.

"You might want to duck down so they can't see you," Jack said. "Better they think you're still inside than try to follow us."

He hit the door locks again and shifted into gear, driving forward to come out on the other side of the house. Much to the surprise of the neighborhood welcome party.

"Thank you both," Desiree said, from the floor of the back seat. "I was just going to stay there and ride it out. But I'm really glad I don't have to. Should we go back for your car?"

"It will be fine," Kate said, hoping she was right. "Once this bunch clears out, Gabe can tow it back to Coral Cay. Who are all those people, anyway? And what are they doing?"

"Neighborhood lookie-loos," Desiree said. "Don't tell Rosie, but at least two of the guys with telephoto lenses are from the scandal sheets. I know because they actually slipped their cards under the door. The news van just arrived. I don't know what that's all about."

"Did you find out anything from your friends at the wildlife rehab center?" Kate asked, glancing over at Jack.

"I wouldn't go as far as calling them friends," Jack said. "Although I really enjoyed spending time there. But no. No redheaded biologists or rescue types that they know of in this part of the state. At least none that matched Carl Ivers's description. In fact, the only two they could recall were a seventy-five-year-old bio professor from Tampa and a fifty-year-old weatherman who pitches in on his vacations. OK, ladies, where do we want to go now?"

"There's a cute little motel just down the beach road. I passed it a couple of times today. The Pink Flamingo. I'm going to check in there."

"You'd said you wanted to talk with Ben, too," Kate said.

"How about we get you checked in now, and you can drop off your bags?" Jack suggested. "Then we'll all drive back to Coral Cay. That way you can touch base with the investigation. And this evening, when you're ready to head back, I'll give you a lift. Or, if Gabe retrieves Kate's car, you can drive."

Desiree nodded as she pulled herself onto the seat, buckled up, and ran her fingers through her disheveled hair. "That would work. Jack, thank you. I mean it."

"No sweat."

"I'd like to know how anybody knew you were here," Kate said.

"Could the real estate lady have said something?" Desiree asked.

"Sylvia? I never told her. As far as she knows, I'm renting the place for myself."

"I'm guessing she knows now," Jack said, smiling. "Along with the rest of the world."

"Yes, I'm going to have to make some serious apologies there," Kate said.

The white gravel crunched as Jack swung the Range Rover into the parking lot of the Pink Flamingo. Obviously built in the sixties, the motel either had been meticulously maintained or recently renovated. It was tidy, clean, and welcoming. And it made the most of its mid-century kitsch. A giant neon pink flamingo perched above the office.

"Why don't I check in?" Jack said. "That should give you a little extra privacy. Since no one's looking for me."

"As long as you let me reimburse you," Desiree said. "And I mean today."

Jack threw up his hands in mock defeat. "Anything you want. I'm just the chauffeur. Seriously, do you have a preference on rooms? Upstairs or down? Near the ice machine or not?"

"It honestly doesn't matter. At this point, I just want a hot shower and a soft bed."

"Got it," Jack said, climbing out of the car. "Be right out."

"Have I said 'thank you' lately?" Desiree asked softly when he was gone.

"No need," Kate said, turning to face the back seat. "That's what friends are for."

Chapter 48

When Kate, Jack, and Desiree clattered in to the bakery, Sam was handing a large bag to Margaret Kim.

"Tell Leonard I said hello," he said. "And see what he thinks o' those sausage swirls."

"If it's got meat, he'll love it," she said. "So you got big plans for Saturday night?"

"Takin' in a picture. Then thought we might stroll around downtown."

"Well, you didn't hear it from me, but the ice cream shop has a new flavor," she said. "Cinnamon apple."

"Wouldn't say no to a scoop of that. Much obliged, Margaret."

"Any time, Sam. You be good!"

"Bye, Mrs. Kim," Kate said, as Jack stepped back and opened the door for her.

"Thank you," she said brightly, waving at Kate. "Such a gentleman!"

"Nice to see you, Desiree," Sam said. "Kate, you have a visitor in the back."

As Kate strolled into the kitchen with Jack on her heels, Ben was sitting at the table working on a cup of coffee. He raised his cup.

"Hi, Ben, we were just about to call you," Kate said.

He looked at Kate, over at Jack, then down at his notebook on the table, as he retrieved a pen from his blazer pocket. "Did I hear Ms. Goldsmith out there?"

"Right here," Desiree said, walking into the kitchen.

"I just wanted to bring you up to speed on what we've found so far," Ben said, standing and gesturing for her to take a seat at the table.

When Desiree pulled out a chair, Kate and Jack followed suit.

"First things first," Ben said. "We got back the lab results on that blood from the cove. It is Dr. Cooper's."

"Oh," Desiree said softly. The syllable sounded like air suddenly rushing out of a balloon.

Kate put her hand on her friend's, as Desiree gulped a few deep breaths.

"Did it . . . tell you anything?"

"Only that Dr. Cooper was at the cove. Unfortunately, it can't tell us when. And it was his blood alone, so we don't know who was with him. But they were able to determine that it was a very small amount. And that's good."

"Your other investigation . . ." Desiree started, haltingly, as she wrapped her arms around herself, shivering.

"You all were right. Tucker was stealing turtle eggs."

"He confessed?" Kate asked, slipping out of her chair and stepping lightly to the coffee maker. She filled a cup, spooned in a generous amount of sugar, and topped it off with a long pour of cream.

Ben shook his head. "Not at first. We picked him up with two of his buddies from the house—Ryder and

Jason. Those two—and the film from the house—pretty much clinched the deal for ol' Tucker. He played the 'it's not me' routine for all it was worth. Then we explained that interfering with a protected species means federal time. The Feds have got a better than ninety percent conviction rate, and you serve the full sentence. That's when he decided to play ball."

Kate sat the cup gently in front of Desiree. "Drink this. It'll warm you up."

"Anyway, he named his handler: Tate Ardsley. Turns out the Feds know all about him. They call him 'Fagin,' because he always uses a crew of local kids to do the actual thefts. Targets teens and twenty-somethings who are looking for a little quick cash. If they get caught, no skin off his nose. He disappears and pops up somewhere else. He's probably the one your guy recognized that day you were out in the boat."

"Do you think he has Judd?" Desiree asked quietly.

"No ma'am, I do not," Ben said. "Ardsley's manipulative and greedy, but he's not violent. Never has been."

"What if Judd threatened him, threatened his operation?" Desiree asked.

"Ardsley's MO is to vanish. Go to ground. Which is what he did this time. But the Feds just picked him up. With Tucker as a witness, he could finally do some serious time."

"And Tucker skates?" Kate asked.

"That's up to the Feds," Ben said, cocking his head to one side. "My impression is that he'll get a better deal but still see the inside of a prison."

"I know some people at Conch House who will be very happy to hear that," Kate said.

"Don't think there's going to be a Conch House much longer," Ben said. "After we showed up with a warrant for their tapes and three of their prized players, I got the definite impression that Ken Salazar was folding his tent and heading off to more hospitable climes. I believe he mentioned Barcelona."

"So Judd's disappearance didn't have anything to do with the turtles?" Desiree said, clutching her coffee cup with white knuckles.

"I'm afraid not. From what the Feds shared, Ardsley was at the cove Friday in a cigarette boat confirming the presence of several turtle nests. Judd saw it and, from what you said, he was going to report it. But for some reason, he didn't."

"Because he disappeared," Kate said.

Ben shook his head. "Not quite. Judson Cooper saw Tate Ardsley at the cove Friday just before one o'clock. But Cooper didn't vanish until Friday night. Friday afternoon, we know he picked up a late lunch to go from the pub. And Friday evening he and Ms. Goldsmith had dinner at the resort followed by a nightcap at a beach café. Servers at both places confirm that. And the resort has a record of ferrying him out to the *Starfish* that night. He had more than nine hours after seeing Ardsley at that cove to say something. But he didn't."

"But Judd was so anxious to alert the authorities that he cut our trip short," Jack said. "That doesn't make sense."

"It doesn't," Ben agreed. "And that is our latest mystery."

Chapter 49

In the quiet before sunrise, Kate's mind felt like a hamster spinning round and round on a wheel. Finally, she gave up on the idea of sleeping. Since her mind was busy, she'd throw her body into gear, too. If she couldn't find Judd, she could at least clean the shop.

She sat up and yawned, as Oliver opened one drowsy eye.

"Would you like to help on cleaning detail?"

The eye closed, and he stretched out across the bottom of the bed.

"Message received," she said, stroking his soft back. "Growing puppies need their beauty sleep."

On Sunday, the Cookie House was closed. And Sam was taking a well-earned day off.

As she plugged in the coffee maker, she hoped Desiree had a peaceful night in her new digs. At least her neighbors at the Pink Flamingo wouldn't be taking selfies on the lawn.

Twenty minutes later, fortified by caffeine and a thick

slab of Sam's sourdough with butter, she vowed to clean the shop from top to bottom.

As she gathered the cleaning supplies, her mind kept drifting back to the problem at hand.

Liam and Sarah had been oddly silent. Other than possibly tipping the photographers to Desiree's presence at the beach house. But how would they have known where she was?

Kate wiped down the counters. She spritzed the cases with cleaner and scrubbed out the insides with paper towels. Then she polished the glass until it shone like a jewel.

Zoey, too, seemed to be in wait-and-see mode, though Kate sensed ever-widening cracks in her cool-girl veneer. Still at the resort herself, Zoey checked in dutifully with Desiree to see if she needed anything. But, like the people Jack had talked with at the wildlife rehab center, Zoey didn't know of anyone Judd might have contacted regarding an endangered creature on the bluff. Much less any wildlife experts in the area who had red hair.

Lola Montgomery had given a flurry of tearful interviews in the past twenty-four hours without ever leaving her penthouse, including one short segment for a network morning show. The actress never said anything concrete. Just that Judson Cooper, her one true love, was missing. And she was heartbroken.

The three women—Desiree, Zoey, and Lola—couldn't be more different. But, for whatever reason, they'd all been part of Judd's life for a time.

Kate grabbed the mop and bucket and went to work on the shop floor. As her arms ached, she pushed harder, exorcising the stress and angst of the past week.

Oliver watched her from the bakery doorway.

"Just shining up the old place," she told him. "So we can do some baking this afternoon. More sausage swirls."

Seemingly satisfied, he disappeared into the kitchen.

As the floor dried, Kate resolved to give the kitchen itself a deep cleaning. She opened the back door for Oliver, who happily bounded outside.

Kate cleared the counters and loaded up the dishwasher. Opening one of the drawers near the sink, she discovered the folder Sam had brought her from the bank. Which reminded her of the check from Ken Salazar.

Mentally, she slapped herself. She still hadn't deposited it. This afternoon, she vowed. Besides, where else but Coral Cay could you visit a drive-through ATM on a bike?

She removed the debit card and retrieved the small backpack from under a lower cupboard. Putting the card in her wallet, she glanced at the bank folder again. That's when it hit her—unfolding in front of her eyes like one of the flowers in Maxi's garden.

Quickly, she grabbed the phone and dialed a number she knew by heart.

"This is Kate McGuire. I need to speak with Detective Ben Abrams. It's an emergency."

After about two minutes on hold, Ben's voice came on the line.

"Kate, are you all right? Do you need a patrol car at the Cookie House?"

"No, I'm fine. And I'm really sorry to call you so early. But I think I might know what happened to Judson Cooper. And if I'm right, we don't have much time."

Chapter 50

As Kate and Ben strolled up the walkway to the door, she felt her stomach knot.

"You're clear on how we're going to play this?" he asked.

She nodded. "They're all in there?"

"Each and every one," Ben said. "Liam and Sarah didn't want to come. Flat out refused. I had to have Kyle threaten them with arrest. That seemed to do the trick. Kyle's fast-tracking that other detail. Just in case we need it. How did you come up with this theory, anyway? Don't tell me it had something to do with cookies?"

Kate shook her head. "It was something Sam said. I just remembered it this morning, and all of a sudden, I could see the whole thing. It finally made sense."

"Right-brain thinking," he said. "That plus evidence can be a detective's best friend. I think you nailed it. Given what's at stake—what we suspect is at stake—we have to move fast. But if I had a choice, I'd sure like a little more in the way of proof. Which is why we're doing it this way. If this goes sideways, it's all on me."

Ben knocked lightly on the door. Desiree opened it.

"Kate, Ben—what's going on? Have you heard from Judd?" Kate could read the stress on her friend's face.

"No ma'am, but I think we're getting close," Ben said. "Why don't you have a seat, and we'll get started."

Inside the bungalow, everyone seemed to be spread out across the living room. Liam and Sarah were stationed in a couple of well-padded chairs in one corner. With reddened eyes and a blotchy face, Sarah had clearly been crying. Liam, who was shooting daggers at Ben, looked furious.

Zoey, hunched on the far end of a long sofa, had tears streaming down her face. While Desiree, dry-eyed in a nearby chair, looked drawn and worn.

"Ms. West, thank you for letting us use your bungalow," Ben said in his reassuring baritone. "We needed a place big enough that we could all have a little chat. And I wanted us to be comfortable. Which pretty much rules out the police station."

Zoey, wiping her nose with a tissue, nodded.

"Look, Detective, my sister and I might have agreed to come over here, but we're not going to sit around all morning," Liam shouted, standing to face Ben. "We're giving you ten minutes, then we're leaving."

"Somewhere important you need to be?" Ben asked evenly.

"That's . . . none of your business!" he sputtered.

"Mr. Cooper, my business right now is finding your father. And while I do thank you both for coming out here at this hour, if you set a foot outside that door, I'm going to have you arrested."

"On what charge?" Liam demanded, his hands on his hips.

"Obstructing an ongoing police investigation," Ben said quietly, looking the man straight in the eye. "And you and I know that's exactly what you've been doing. Both of you."

Liam snapped his mouth shut and sank into his chair. Sarah Cooper started crying again, burying her face in her hands.

"Now, Ms. West, I think you have something you want to tell us," Ben declared, settling into the other end of the sofa.

Zoey shook her head, blowing her nose loudly into a handful of tissues.

"About the call Judd made Friday afternoon. To you. Telling you he'd seen Tate Ardsley at the cove—Sinus Testudinis," he finished, the Latin words rolling off his tongue.

Zoey shook her head violently. "He didn't. I don't know what you're talking about."

"Detective, this is ridiculous," Liam said, agitated. "Zoey is my father's business partner. They speak on the phone daily. You're wasting our time."

"You see, once we laid out the timeline, it just didn't make sense. Your father is committed to protecting the oceans and their wildlife. It isn't just a job, he lives it. So I couldn't understand why your father would see a lowlife like Ardsley, who he'd crossed paths with before, and not report it. I mean, we had three independent witnesses on the boat with him at the time," Ben said, holding up three fingers, "who stated that he cut the trip short to do just that. And we can account for his movements through that evening, until he left the resort at a little after ten. But he never called any of the local or federal authorities. You mean to tell me that eco-warrior Judson Cooper spotted a notorious poacher in a nature preserve—a preserve that was a known loggerhead nesting ground—and he didn't say a word to anyone?"

"Did this Ardsley take Dad?" Sarah squeaked.

"No, Ardsley's in federal custody now. Thanks to Ms. Goldsmith, who reported what your dad saw. He's out of the endangered species trade for good. Do you have anything to add, Ms. West?"

Zoey shook her head.

"OK, let's examine the situation. This is a man who's getting married the next day. And leaving on his honeymoon."

"Not this story again," Liam grumbled. "We already told you, Detective. He barely knows that woman. No way were they getting married."

"They were, actually. Applied for a marriage license and everything. Took me a while to find it, since it was never filed."

"Does that mean he changed his mind?" Sarah asked.

"It just means the wedding didn't take place," Ben explained. "You take out the license before you marry. You file it after you marry, making the whole thing official. Since your dad disappeared before the wedding, it was never filed."

"You were getting married?" Sarah said to Desiree. "For real?"

Desiree nodded. "Your dad and I love each other."

"What about Lola Montgomery?" Liam spat.

"She dated your father for a couple of weeks earlier this year," Desiree said. "They broke up before we ever met. They haven't seen each other since."

"But she said—" Liam insisted.

"She's milking the publicity," Ben interjected.

"Daddy was getting married, and he didn't even tell us?" Sarah said, sniffling

"He did," Kate said. "Or at least, he thought he did."

"What are you talking about?" Liam snapped. "And just who are you, anyway?"

"I'm a friend of Desiree's," Kate said. "Just here for a little moral support."

"Well, isn't that nice," Liam said, simultaneously crossing his arms and legs.

"Your father came off that boat Friday afternoon like a man on a mission," Ben continued. "Remember, he didn't have a lot of time. He had a few last errands to run for the wedding the next day. And he had plans to meet Ms. Goldsmith that evening for dinner. But first and foremost, he had a poacher to stop. So that was his first call. The danger to the turtles was immediate. And he didn't have a lot of time for rounds of phone tag and filing out reports in triplicate. So he didn't call the authorities himself. Instead, he phoned someone he trusted to make those calls for him. The one person whose word would carry as much weight as his own. He called Zoey West."

Zoey shook her head frantically. "No. No! That's not true."

"It is," Ben said. "He used a pay phone at the harbor. The thing's a beat-up relic, but it comes in handy. Dr. Cooper called you and he told you he'd seen Tate Ardsley at the cove. He asked you to alert the authorities. And I'm guessing he told you about all the things he had to do to get ready for the last-minute wedding. Like arrange for an officiant, and book a couple of limos to bring him and Ms. Goldsmith to the beach. You, efficient business partner that you are, offered to take those little jobs off his hands, too."

"That's why we didn't have a justice of peace?!" Desiree exclaimed. "Why? Why would you do that?"

"I didn't!" Zoey said. "Judd never called me. He's making this up. Can't you see? They just want someone to blame."

Ben lifted a cell phone from an inside jacket pocket. He tapped on the screen and held it to his ear. "Kyle Hardy, please. . . . Kyle, what did you find out. . . . Really? Excellent work. . . . Yeah, you might as well come on out here now."

"That was one of my officers," Ben said, stretching to return the phone to his breast pocket. "They dumped the records for the pay phone at Sullivan Harbor. At one thirty-five Friday afternoon someone used it to call a cell phone belonging to one Ms. Zoey West. They spoke for more than fifteen minutes."

"Zoey?" Desiree asked. "Why?"

"I understand why you didn't want to book the wedding plans," Ben said, softening his voice. "And we don't have to talk about that now. But why didn't you blow the whistle on Ardsley?"

Zoey, her arms wrapped tight around her body, clamped her mouth shut and stared at the floor.

"Zoey, we need to get Dad back now," Liam said. "If you can bring this farce to an end, just tell the man what he wants to know."

"You can't pay the ransom, you idiot!" Zoey yelled. "They'll kill him! If you had any brains, you'd know that by now!"

Desiree's eyes widened, and her mouth popped open. "What?" she breathed.

"Who has him, Zoey?" Ben prodded gently.

"Shut up, you little witch!" Liam screamed, launching from his chair.

Ben turned in his direction, but didn't bother to stand. "Mr. Cooper, don't make me put you in the back of a squad car. Because, if you do, I guarantee you won't make your little rendezvous."

"Liam, please," Sarah hissed, pulling on his arm. "Please, we have one chance to get this right."

"Who are they, Ms. West?"

She shook her head. "Just a couple of guys. They hang around one of the docks in Miami. They do odd jobs."

"Some legal, some not so legal?"

Zoey shrugged.

"Names, Zoey," Ben said. "What are their names?"

"Harry Owens and Zach Hammond. They want two hundred thousand dollars in cash."

"If we don't pay, they're going to kill our dad," Sarah pleaded.

"No, if you *pay,* they'll kill him," Zoey enunciated through clenched teeth.

"Because you know who they are," Ben said. "Because you hired them."

Zoey, staring at the floor, nodded.

"What?" Desiree and Sarah cried in unison.

"Wait a minute," Liam hissed, rising from his chair. "You? You did this? All this time it was you?"

"Zoey wanted to stop the wedding, so she hired a couple of goons to waylay the groom," Ben said.

"They weren't supposed to *hurt* him!" Zoey said, anguished. "Just keep him out of the way for a couple of days. Until she went home," she finished, thrusting her chin at Desiree.

"We'll get to the whys later," Ben said. "Where do they have him?"

"I don't know," Zoey said. "After all the tabloid stories and the news conferences, they realized Judd has serious money. And they're always droning on about buying their own boat and sailing the world. So they've kinda gone rogue."

"You lost control of them," Ben stated flatly.

Zoey nodded.

"The drop," Ben said. "Where and when?"

"This afternoon at the regatta, those two," Zoey said, pointing at Liam and Sarah, "are supposed to stuff the money into a duffle bag and bring it to them. In a go-fast boat. There's a parade of the things, so the harbor is going to be full of them. Harry or Zach will be in one, too. When Harry or Zach pulls up next to them and gives the signal, the Coopers are supposed to toss the duffle into his boat."

"One of them is staying with Dad," Sarah said. "If they see police or we don't pay, they're going to kill him."

"How do you know they still have him?" Ben asked.

Kate looked at Desiree, who went white.

"They let us talk to him Friday," Liam said. "Just for a couple of seconds, but he was OK."

Desiree's hands went to her mouth and tears rolled down her cheeks. Fear or relief, Kate couldn't tell.

"Where's Judson Cooper?" Ben asked.

"I don't know!" Zoey sobbed.

"When was the last time you did know?"

"Harry and Zach started acting all squirrelly Friday. They stopped answering my calls. Then these two"— she pointed to the Coopers—"phone and want to know about hitting their father's company for a two-hundred-thousand-dollar loan. In cash. It didn't take long for me to figure out what happened."

"She kept stalling us," Liam said.

"She said Dad didn't have that kind of money just sitting in an account," Sarah said. "Then she said that the bank would need her signature and Dad's to release any funds."

"I was trying to buy some time to find Judd," Zoey said. "If those two numbskulls pay, they've as good as killed him."

"Why?" Sarah asked.

"Because Zoey knows who they are," Ben explained quietly. "If they release Dr. Cooper, there's always the possibility she might someday tell someone. But if they kill him, Zoey can't tell anyone. Ever. Because she's now an accessory to murder. In the eyes of the law, she would be just as guilty as they were. Possibly more so, since her actions started this whole thing."

"I've been calling and calling," Zoey said. "But they won't answer. So I've been haunting the docks and marinas trying to find them."

"Give me your phone, Ms. West," Ben said. "You too, Mr. Cooper. We'll see if our tech guys can pinpoint the signal."

"I haven't talked to them since Friday," Zoey said, handing it off to him. "It's those two numbers at the top of the screen. But they're using cheap throwaways. If they still have them."

"At least it gives us a place to start. Are they on Cooper's boat?"

"They were at one point," Zoey said. "But I have no idea where they took it. Or if they still have it. They have all kinds of friends up and down the coast. So if they wanted to borrow a boat, they probably could."

"Especially if someone didn't know they borrowed it," Ben said. "Lot of the snowbirds dock around here. And if Owens and Hammond sailed out of Coral Cay, there are secret coves, inlets, and waterways all up and down the coast."

"Maybe she's still in on it," Liam said. "Maybe she just wants to get away with the money."

"How did a man as brilliant as your father end up with

a son like you?" Zoey said. "I'm the one who's trying to talk you out of paying. Remember, genius?"

"Hey, cut the snark," Ben said. "The kid's worried about his dad."

The detective pulled out his own phone and started dialing. "Patrice, I've got something for you, and this one's urgent. All hands on deck."

Ben walked into the kitchenette. Kate couldn't hear what he was saying.

Desiree stared at Zoey, who couldn't meet her eyes. "Why? Why on earth would you do such a thing?"

Studying the floor, Zoey ignored her.

Sarah rose from her seat, walked over to Desiree, and knelt by her chair. "I'm sorry for all those things we said. From the start, she told us you were a gold digger, always after Dad for money. That you were draining him dry. Then she showed us that credit-card bill. She was his business partner, so we trusted her. I'm so sorry."

Desiree reached out and put her hand on Sarah's. "Water under the bridge. I know how much you love your dad. And how much he loves you both. Let's just focus on getting him back."

Ben returned to the living room, phone still in hand.

"OK, we now have an active multi-jurisdictional effort to find the *Starfish*, find Owens and Hammond, and—most important—find Judson Cooper."

"Can we leave now, Detective?" Liam pleaded. "This thing is this afternoon, and we're still pulling together the money from friends and family. We don't have a lot of time."

"That's up to the FBI," Ben said. "Since this is now a kidnapping, they're in charge."

Chapter 51

At two o'clock that afternoon, the go-fast boat parade was in full swing. The walkways and grassy areas above the harbor were teaming with spectators and visitors out for a Sunday stroll. The bright sunlight shimmering off the water gave the scene a technicolor vibe.

To Kate, watching from over the seawall with Desiree, Maxi, and Oliver, it looked like a bathtub crowded with toy boats. There was so little space, she was amazed they weren't bouncing off of each other like bumper cars.

"I've never been so nervous in my life," Desiree said, her hands shaking as she lifted the binoculars to her eyes.

Oliver, planted at her feet, looked up, alert.

"You know they're doing everything they can," Kate said, feeling the words were hollow even as they came out of her mouth.

"I wonder how many of these folks are undercover Feds," Maxi mused. "Definitely that guy with the blue cotton candy and no kids. Adults don't eat that stuff."

"Frankly, I hope they all are," Desiree said. "Talk about the more, the merrier."

"I still can't believe Zoey did this," Maxi said. "She really had me fooled. She seemed so nice."

"Tell me about it," Desiree said.

"Was she the one who kept tipping off the photographers?" Maxi asked.

Kate nodded. "Indirectly. For her plan to work, Zoey needed a lot of people aggressively suspicious of Desiree. So she told Liam and Sarah that the police really suspected Desiree but couldn't prove anything. Then she kept checking in with Desiree and passing tidbits to Liam and Sarah."

"But what she really wanted was to make things so uncomfortable for me that I'd pack up and go home. Not likely! But I feel like such an idiot," Desiree said, shaking her head at the memory. "She was Judd's friend and business partner, and she was helping search for him. So I didn't think anything about sharing everything with her. I thought she was one of us."

"Judd's known her for a lot longer than you have, and he had no idea what she was capable of," Kate said. "How were you to know?"

"So all those things she said about Judd—how he always left a trail of broken hearts . . ." Maxi started.

"Lies," Kate said.

"Like I said, total codswallop," Desiree added. "I know my guy. He might have his head in the clouds sometimes. But a playboy, he's not."

"She's also the one who called Ben during the news conference," Kate said. "She spoofed the local crime-lab phone number and when he picked up, she said it was urgent. So he'd think they got a break in the case. Because she was smart enough to realize that he wouldn't stand back and allow Liam to slander Desiree on camera. So she had to lure him away."

"That's super sneaky," Maxi fumed. "All this because Zoey loved Judd? Why didn't she just tell him?"

"I don't know," Kate said, bracing her binoculars with one hand, as she reached down and stroked the top of Oliver's head. "But that's definitely not love."

"I saw Lola Montgomery on *Good Morning, Sunshine!* this morning," Maxi said. "She's signed a two-picture deal with a major studio."

"Hopefully, that means she'll be leaving town soon," Desiree said, scanning the horizon. "I can't believe she monetized this. She's almost as bad as the bullyboys who grabbed Judd. Girls, look!" she said, pointing. "There they are—Liam and Sarah!"

It took her a minute, but Kate finally managed to locate the boat on the water. A black go-fast boat. Liam was at the wheel, with Sarah sitting next to him. As the kidnappers demanded, they were both wearing bright yellow caps.

"What if Ben's right?" Desiree worried. "What if it is better not to pay them?"

Kate was torn. She trusted Ben. And his take on Zoey, Owens, and Hammond. But the FBI plan made sense, too. Deliver the money, pick up the kidnapper before he docks, and use him to locate his partner and Judd.

"Uh-oh, something's happening," Maxi said, focusing her binoculars.

"Oh no," Desiree shrieked. "There are two of them! In the other boat. Owens and Hammond. If they're both here, who's with Judd?"

Kate's stomach turned to lead. What if they were too late?

Out in the bright harbor, as go-fast drivers hooted,

hollered, and honked their horns with abandon, the three women clustered together, focused only the drama unfolding between two small boats.

Sarah stood frozen, clutching the duffel with both hands. Liam, still at the wheel, barked at her.

In the other boat, the man in the passenger seat frantically motioned for her to throw the bag, growing more and more agitated.

Sarah, clearly panicked, looked back at Liam then over at the other boat. One kidnapper's mouth was open so wide, Kate could practically see his tonsils. Finally, Sarah heaved the bag at him and collapsed in the back of the boat.

The other kidnapper gunned the engine, taking off into the crowd.

In a sea of similar crafts, Kate lost them almost immediately. It was like playing three-card monte with a card shark.

Which boat carried the kidnappers and the cash?

She had no idea

Chapter 52

"Let's go back to the dock," Desiree said. "Sarah's going to be devastated, and I'd like to be there for her."

Oliver, leading the way on today's leash—bright orange—wedged his way through the throng, parting the crowd as he went. Kate, Maxi, and Desiree followed in his wake.

They reached the dock just as Liam was helping Sarah out of the boat and handing off the keys. To an agent, Kate presumed.

Ben stood off to one side, in the same clothes he'd worn earlier, right down to the panama hat. In his only concession to the weather, he'd lost the blazer, rolled up his sleeves, and donned sunglasses, which he promptly removed as they approached. Like many of the people milling about, he sported a pair of binoculars around his neck.

Sarah, chilled from the spray of cool water on the bay—or from shock—was wrapped in a towel, shivering.

"Did you see that?" she babbled. "Both of them. They were both there. What does that mean? Where's Dad?"

Kate saw the agent who'd taken the boat keys exchange a serious look with Ben, who nodded ever so slightly.

"Let's get you inside and warmed up," Ben said. "Our federal friends commandeered a couple of rooms just up the path here."

Kate looked at him. Behind the professional mask, she saw pain on his face. When he finally made eye contact, he shook his head infinitesimally and looked away.

Her heart sank

As they piled into the small sitting room and spilled into chairs, Ben picked up a house phone and called for several pots of coffee.

Kate and Maxi flanked Desiree on a pale blue silk sofa. Oliver, at attention, stationed himself at her feet.

"Detective, why were Owens and Hammond both in the go-fast boat?" Liam asked. "We did what they asked. We gave them the money. They were supposed to text us his location, but they haven't. Where's our father?"

"Kidnappers aren't exactly known for keeping promises," Ben said evenly. "And the Feds will pick them up soon, I'm confident of that. That bag and your cash conceal tracking devices. But Owens and Hammond aren't going to be calling anytime soon. We've confirmed that they dumped their phones."

"But they could have other phones," Sarah insisted, teeth chattering. "They could still call, right?"

"Yeah," Liam said. "Maybe it's a test. To see if we called the cops. And if we didn't, they'll let him go. But if you guys pick them up, then they can't go back and free him."

"You have to let them get away," Sarah pleaded, trembling. "For Dad."

Ben sighed heavily. "Mr. Cooper, Ms. Cooper, Ms. Goldsmith, I'm afraid I have some very bad news. We located the wreckage of Dr. Cooper's boat. It was in a little inlet up the coast of the mainland about fifty miles. Totally hidden in the middle of nowhere. It had been blown up. The FBI is on the scene, and they'll be processing everything. And these guys are the very best at what they do."

"Dad was on the boat?" Liam asked slowly, as he wrapped a protective arm around his sister.

"We believe so," Ben said. "And I am so very sorry."

"I should never have given them the money," Sarah wailed. "When I saw they were both there, I didn't know what to do."

"It wasn't your fault," Liam said, as tears welled up in his eyes. "I forced you. I was screaming at you to throw it."

"I could have hung onto it. I should have. I wanted to. But they kept hollering. I shouldn't have listened to any of you."

Ben squatted down to meet them both at eye level. "It wouldn't have mattered. We found the boat a few hours ago, before the exchange. And from what the techs on site have discovered, the explosion happened at least twenty-four hours ago. It could have even been sometime Friday night. That's why both Hammond and Owens were in the go-fast boat."

Kate put her arm around Desiree's shoulders as her friend bent forward, sobbing silently.

On the other side of the sofa, Maxi stared straight ahead, stunned.

"Can we . . . can we see him?" Liam asked, not even trying to hide the tears streaming from his eyes.

"I don't think that will be possible," Ben said.

"But how do we know . . . I mean, maybe," Liam stumbled.

Ben stood and retrieved a brown paper bag from a side table. He opened it and carefully lifted out a plastic bag embossed with EVIDENCE in large white letters. Kate couldn't make out the weighty black object within.

"The first divers on the scene retrieved this," Ben said, holding the object in front of Liam. "They choppered it down here because they thought you might want— might need—to see it. But I have to ask you to leave it in the bag."

Sarah looked up at it, nodded, and collapsed into her brother's shoulder.

"It's Dad's," Liam confirmed, taking the object gently from Ben with both hands. "Brand new, I think. He had it on the last time we met. Before he and . . . Desiree left on their trip."

Desiree sat up and stared at the bag in Liam's hand.

Liam got to his feet, shuffled across the room, and handed it to her.

"I gave him this," she rasped. "On the back, here," she said, flipping it over and pointing. "I had it engraved."

She traced the letters through the plastic lovingly with her index finger. "It says JC + DG, with a heart around it. Like people used to carve on a tree? It was our joke, because Judd once said he'd never want to deface a perfectly good tree. So I bought him the best diving watch I could afford and had this put on the back."

"Can she keep it?" Liam asked, turning to Ben.

The detective shook his head. "Right now, it's part of a crime scene. But eventually, you and your sister will get it back. Then it's your call."

"I'm sorry," Liam said. "So sorry. About . . . about everything."

Desiree looked up at him and took his hand. "I know," she said softly. "And I know you were just being protective. Your dad knew it, too. He loved you so much. And he was so proud of both of you."

Kate glanced at Ben. The detective appeared gutted, like he'd aged five years in the last week. She knew he blamed himself. She also knew that it wasn't his fault. At every turn, people had lied, cast blame, and covered up the truth—often at cross purposes. Even when they hadn't been working together, the result was the same. They muddied the water so much that nothing was clear.

In the end, Kate realized she had had two advantages. She knew Desiree. And she'd seen Judd and Desiree together. That was love. The kind you couldn't fake. It wasn't perfect. Or something out of a rom-com script. But it was real. Durable.

So why couldn't she have just seen the truth a little sooner?

A ringing phone cut the air. Ben reached into his coat pocket. "Abrams. Yeah. OK, I'll tell them."

"They've picked up Owens and Hammond," he announced.

"What will happen to them now?" Liam asked.

"The Feds will charge them and Zoey. They'll be locked up until the trial. No bail. If they're smart, they'll plead and save us all the hassle of a trial. The Feds are going over that boat with a fine-tooth comb. So something tells me evidence isn't going to be a problem. For now, we'll have to wait and see."

"I'm sorry, Detective," Liam said. "I should have come to you as soon as they called. If I had . . ."

"You can't do that to yourself," Ben said, clapping him on the back. "From what I've heard about your father, he wouldn't want you to, either. Nothing can prepare you for something like this. You do the best you can. Those two may have acted like a couple of friendly wharf rats, but they were stone-cold. No way you could've known that."

"I think it's time for me to leave now," Desiree said quietly.

"The motel?" Maxi asked. "Why don't you stay at my house? We've got plenty of room."

"Nope, I mean Florida," Desiree said. "I promised I'd stay until we found Judd. And we have. I'm going to catch the next flight."

"Are you sure?" Kate asked.

Desiree nodded, blotting her eyes with a clump of tissues.

Ben's phone rang again. "Abrams. No, they're right here why?" He paused. "You're kidding me. Which one? OK, patch 'em through."

Ben walked over and handed the cell to Desiree. "Someone wants to say hello."

She looked at him, puzzled, and put the phone to her ear. Seconds later, her face broke as tears rolled freely down her cheeks.

"It's Judd!" she whispered. "He's alive!"

Chapter 53

Kate hurried up to Ben in the hospital waiting room. "How is he?"

"In better shape than I am, at this point," Ben said shaking his head. "Doc Patel's finishing up with him now, then you can go in."

"Where's Desiree?" she said, looking around the room.

"Are you kidding? She hasn't left his side. And I don't think she's going to anytime soon. The kids are in there, too."

"Relieved?" she asked, looking up at him.

"Oh yeah," he said, huskily. "You have no idea. Or, knowing you, maybe you do."

His dark eyes held hers for a moment.

"So, what'd I miss?" Maxi called out, as she bounced into the waiting room with Jack in tow.

Kate and Ben each took a quick step back.

Maxi held up a quart-sized mason jar overflowing

with old-fashioned roses in various shades of pink. "A little something for the patient."

"That's beautiful," Kate said.

"It's small because I'm thinking positive. If they let him out tonight it's easy to carry. If they don't, it covers up that hospital smell."

"Hospital smell?" Ben asked.

Kate nodded. "Like a combination of rubbing alcohol and tongue depressors."

"I can kind of see that," Jack said, holding a brightly wrapped package in one hand.

"You're making us look bad, Scanlon," Ben teased.

"Nah, I just stopped off at Barb's shop and picked up a little reading material in case they keep him overnight. Professor Quentin Digby's latest volume on loggerheads and their habitats."

Doctor Rakesh Patel, a founding member of the Coral Cay Irregulars, strolled down the hall in hospital scrubs with a stethoscope slung around his neck.

"Well, hello there. Fancy seeing you all here. But I'm afraid the food is not quite as good as where we usually meet."

"How is he, Doc?" Ben asked.

"Excellent. A picture of rugged good health. And a very good example of what regular exercise and a healthy diet will do for you, if you take my meaning," he said, patting Ben on the shoulder.

"Yeah, Doc, I think we all do," the detective said, ruefully.

"Can he go home today?" Kate asked.

"Many scrapes and bruises. A couple of good burns. And a very nice collection of mosquito bites. But no concussion. And no broken bones. So that is very good. All things being equal, I would like to keep him overnight. But he is very stubborn,' the doctor said, smiling. "And he wants to go home with his lady. And this, too, should be fine. Just keep an eye on him."

"No worries there, Doc," Ben said. "I don't think Desiree's going to let him go wandering for a while."

"Hey, guys, come on in," Desiree called. "It's a party."

Stretched out on the bed, Judd looked relaxed and comfortable. He sported a week's growth of beard and a large bandage on his forehead. Several smaller gauze pads dotted his neck and arms.

Desiree, on one side, held his hand. Liam and Sarah, on the other, were clearly exhilarated.

"Complete with presents for the guest of honor," Maxi said, putting the flowers on the bedside table, as Jack deposited his gift.

"We don't want to intrude," Kate said. "Just wanted to pop in and say hi."

"And we've got the getaway car warming up, when you're ready to go," Maxi added.

"Forget the Jeep," Ben said. "This man is riding home in a car with lights and sirens. He's earned the right."

"OK, that actually sounds like fun. Of course, they brought me here in a helicopter, and that wasn't bad either."

"Oh, small change in the program," Desiree said, patting his leg. "Forget the bungalow at the resort. We're now staying at the Pink Flamingo motel."

"Do they have any of those vending machines with snacks and sodas?" Judd asked. "Love those things. I spent the last week tied up in a cave, tied up on my own boat, and swimming through snake-infested waters. A kitschy motel on the beach sounds perfect."

"Unofficially, what happened?" Ben asked.

"No idea," Judd said. "One minute, I'm stepping onto the *Starfish*, the next I'm trussed up like a Thanksgiving turkey, and these two yahoos are moving my boat. The docs think they probably drugged me. Then I woke up in a cave. No idea where. But something must have happened because they moved me. And they were in some kind of hurry. But when they were marching me through the brush, I managed to move the blindfold just a little. That's when I discovered we were at Sinus Testudinis. I didn't know where we were going next, or if I was going to make it back. But I wanted to let you guys know I'd been there. So I worked the ring off my finger and dropped it in the sand. Near the fire pit."

"Oliver found it," Desiree said happily.

"I knew there was a reason I loved that dog," Judd said.

"But what about the blood?" Maxi asked. "On the fire stone."

"I faked a fall to plant the ring," Judd explained. "And my hands were tied behind my back, so my balance wasn't the greatest. Upended one of those rocks and scraped up my arm something fierce."

"You don't want to know what I was thinking when we found that," Desiree said. "Your ring—the ring you never take off. And blood."

"Thought I was going to make you a widow before I made you a bride?" he quipped, patting her knee.

"Don't you dare make fun of me," she said, swatting his leg in mock outrage.

"Your friend Tate Ardsley is the reason they hustled you out of that cave so fast," Ben said. "Apparently, Zoey wanted her guys to spirit you away from the island before anyone even knew to look for you or the *Starfish*. But Owens and Hammond were lazy, and not exactly the brightest bulbs. They'd already checked out the cave at the preserve and decided it was just about perfect. When Zoey found out they were not only still on

Coral Cay but at The Nose, she hit the roof. So later that night—"

"They moved me," Judd said, rubbing the back of his head. "I'll be darned."

"How did your watch end up in the drink?" Maxi asked.

"Friday afternoon, one of them must have realized it was valuable. He just took it. I'm guessing he dumped it in the water after the explosion—when they thought I was dead."

"It would have tied them to a murder," Ben said, nodding.

"So how did you get away from them?" Jack asked.

"Sheer, dumb luck," Judd said. "Or as good as. I'd overheard enough to realize they were ransoming me. The clincher was when they put me on the phone with you guys," he said, grinning at Liam and Sarah. "Even though I'd never dealt with those two mugs before, I recognized their type. Ruthless. I knew they wouldn't be releasing me. Even if I didn't know about Zoey's part in things. They always kept me tied up and locked in the cabin. Always blindfolded. They were around all the time, both of them. And I knew from our little excursion through the preserve that they had guns."

Kate realized that, just hearing him tell the story, she was holding her breath.

"After the phone call to the kids Friday, they locked me in the cabin again. This time, they didn't blindfold me. Somehow that was scarier. I knew I didn't have much time left. I also realized I needed a distraction. Luckily, it was my boat. I built her up from scrap. And I did it on a shoestring, 'cause back then I didn't have a lot of cash," he added, smiling.

"I managed to get myself loose and picked the lock on the cabin door. Next, I rounded up a few things in the cabin that should never be mixed together. So I mixed 'em. And when they ignited, I tossed the whole mess out the porthole onto the deck—as far as I could—and quick closed it again. I waited until I heard a commotion, then I disconnected the gas line from the stove, opened the cabin door, and slipped around the other side of the boat and into the water. I took a deep breath and swam under the surface for a good ways, so they wouldn't spot me. The fire kept 'em busy—and once they smelled the gas, they must have abandoned ship. I don't think they ever realized I'd escaped."

"They didn't," Ben confirmed. "They thought you went up with the boat."

"Anyway, the *Starfish* exploded a minute or two later. I felt the shockwaves underwater. You know, we had some really great times on that old tub," he said, patting Sarah with one hand, while playfully punching Liam with the other. "I'm really gonna miss her."

"She saved your life," Desiree said practically. "For that, I'll always love her. But just think how much fun you three will have outfitting *Starfish Two*."

Chapter 54

As the moon rose high over the cove, Kate held the night-vision binoculars up to her eyes. "There! A whole cluster of them," she said, pointing.

Down the beach, a half-dozen tiny turtles pushed up through the sand and skittered toward the moonlit water.

"Cool!" said Michael Más-Buchanan. "Wow! Look at them go!"

"They're racing," his brother Javi said, bouncing on his knees. "And they're fast!"

"They have to be fast," Desiree said softly to Kate. "They're running for their little lives."

"Like anybody else you know?" Judd said, nudging Desiree with his elbow.

"Don't remind me," she said, playfully.

"I heard Liam made things right with Brad," Kate said. "So are you guys back at Palm Isle?"

"He did, and I'm really proud of him," Desiree said, giggling. "But we decided to stay at the Pink Flamingo.

It's been a lot of fun. Less crowded and a lot more laid back."

"Plus, thanks to my buddy Jack, we got a great room," Judd said. "We just slide open the patio door and walk right out onto the beach."

Jack, stretched out on a blanket on the other side of Kate, gave a mock salute. "Happy to be of service. Hey, there are three more! Oh man."

"Come on, babies," Desiree cheered. "You can do it!"

"I'm not seeing any raccoons or other predators out here tonight," Judd said, scanning the undergrowth behind them with his binoculars. "That's a good sign."

"They know better," Sunny cackled. "Mom's been known to chase them off during the running of the turtles. I think they've learned their lesson."

"Next year, your daughter might be old enough that you can bring her too," Desiree said.

Maxi nodded. "At this stage, she'd be chasing the turtles down the beach trying to make new friends."

"They look like they're coated in cornmeal," Michael said, adjusting his binoculars. "Kinda like *abuela's tamal en cazuela*."

"OK, you're right, but I don't know how she'd feel about having one of her best recipes compared to a reptile," Maxi said. "So maybe we don't tell her that."

"They're so little," Javi said. "When do they get big?"

"They're like people," Judd said. "It will take them decades to reach their full size. But when they do, they can weigh nearly three hundred pounds."

"Is that bigger than you, *Papi*?" Javi asked.

"Yup, more than one-and-a-half of me," Peter Buchanan said.

"Whoa! That's huge," Javi said.

"You know how big they are now?" Desiree said. "About two inches."

"See, that's what happens if you eat your vegetables," Maxi said.

Behind his mother, Michael rolled his eyes.

"I saw that, Miguelito," she said.

"How?" Javi mouthed to his older brother, who shrugged.

"What's really cool is that the females from these clusters won't be ready to lay eggs for another twenty or thirty years—when you guys are grown up like your parents—but when they do, they'll come right back here to this very beach," Judd said.

Sitting cross-legged on the blanket, Kate recalled a cryptic conversation she had with Minette in the bakery the day after Judd returned.

"Did you ever find out anything about the corporation that bought Harp's place?" Kate had asked.

"You know I did," Minette said. "The name of it is Asteroidea LLC. And Asteroidea is the scientific name for 'starfish.'"

"You don't mean . . ." Kate started.

"Yup," Minette said, looking like the cat that ate the cream. "That dear, sweet man bought it himself. So whatever that rare species is, it's safe now."

"I wonder who the woman with red hair is?" Kate had mused.

"Once I found out he was trying to buy the house, that was easy. And I confirmed it by showing her photo to Carl. It was the real estate agent."

"The reason they each looked so happy was that Judson saved a sensitive piece of beachfront . . ."

"And the real estate lady was gonna make a bundle from the commission," Minette finished.

Looking at Judd and Desiree now, holding hands in the moonlight, it was hard to believe they'd ever been apart.

"Judd, Desiree told us about a rare species you found on the bluff near the big house," Kate said. "So what is it?"

Judd looked at Desiree. "Should we tell them?"

She nodded shyly.

"It's this lady right here," he said, holding up her hand with his own. "She is a very rare species. One of a kind. And I was hoping, if it pleased her, she might make that beautiful place her habitat."

Chapter 55

When the black stretch limo pulled up to the beach, the crowd cheered.

"Please notice that this time, the groom arrived first, along with the justice of the peace," Maxi said, standing at the ready with the bride's bouquet—a simple strand of white and fuchsia orchids. "That's how you're supposed to do it."

"Well, it helps that they were riding in a car with a blue light and sirens," Kate said, glancing at Ben, who was down on the beach engrossed in conversation with Judd, Jack, Peter, and Liam.

"What do you think they're talking about?" Kate asked nodding.

"This time of year? Definitely baseball," Maxi replied. "So, what was up at the hospital?"

"What? Nothing," Kate said, feeling the tinge of a blush spread across her cheeks.

"Ay, I wasn't trying to spoil the moment," her friend said lightly, as a radiant Desiree emerged from the car and the chauffeur escorted her onto the sand. "I just wanted you to know you had company."

"Are you ready?" Kate asked, as Desiree kicked off her shoes.

"Oh yeah," she said happily, as she waved at Judson. He grinned and formed a heart with his hands.

Maxi handed off the flowers and stepped back. "*Perfecto*," she declared. "And Rosie nailed it. Those earrings look *¡fabulosos!*"

"She's right," Kate said, tearing up. "You're beautiful."

A man with a telephoto lens quickly stepped in and clicked off a few frames.

"Please tell me that's the photographer they booked and not some tabloid guy," Maxi said under her breath.

"Definitely," Desiree said, laughing. "And that's the way it's going to be from here on out."

After the wedding, the party seemed to grow by the hour. As the sun sank into the water, guests bonded over cake, champagne, hors d'oeuvres, and their favorite stories about the bride and groom.

"Those aren't the same biscuits as last time," Claire said, eyeing the five-layer creation with bride and groom cookies perched jauntily on the top. "And that's definitely not the same cake."

"Time to start fresh," Kate said. "Besides, now I know that Judd's definitely not a tux-and-bowtie kind of guy. So I modeled the cookie after what he was actually wearing to the wedding."

"They're barefoot," Gabe said, smiling as he leaned in for a closer look.

Kate nodded. "That, too. Plus something told me this time around we might need a bigger cake."

"There are no strangers here, only friends you haven't yet met," Gabe replied.

"I wonder that Yeats never secretly visited Coral Cay," Claire said. "Because that's a bang-on description of this place."

"All around the bottom layer of the cake," Jack said, pointing. "Are those what I think they are?"

"Little turtles," Kate said, smiling. "Sprinkled with sugar sand."

Across the crowd, Kate spotted James chatting with Cecily, Candy, and Barb.

"How are things at Conch House?" Kate asked.

"Won-der-ful," Cecily said, greeting Kate with a hug. "After Ken Salazar shut down the show, he split the prize money between the nine of us who were left."

"The nine of us who didn't get arrested," Cecily said, holding up her champagne glass. "Almost twenty-eight grand, thank you very much. And he said we could stay at the house until Monday. It's been so cool."

"James and Howie told us how you guys helped nail Tucker," Candy said.

"Yeah," Cecily said. "None of us could believe it."

"Tucker got in trouble all on his own," Kate said, clinking glasses with Barb. "Besides, it was a group effort."

"Did you hear about Howie?" James asked.

"Yes, he stopped by on his way out of town," Kate said. "Apparently, he got a job filming one of those reality baking competitions."

James nodded, smiling. "He said it was his dream gig. He was seriously happy."

"Speaking of which, pop by the Cookie House before you leave Coral Cay," Kate said, patting James on the shoulder. "Sam and I have the check for your design fee."

"Design fee?" James said, blinking.

"For the baseball cookies. In case you hadn't noticed, they're all over the island. And that's your design. Your idea. So you get a cut. It's nowhere near twenty-eight thousand, but you earned it."

"Wow," he said, clearly surprised. "Thank you."

Kate turned to see Desiree and Judd strolling up, hand in hand.

"Oh, we finally solved the riddle of the heirloom jewelry," Desiree said, raising a bottle of champagne to refill Kate's glass. "Apparently, Judd's grandma left a lovely emerald ring. Not valuable but beautiful, with a lot of sentimental value. Anyway, one of the last times Lola was at his house, she pilfered it from his dresser."

"I thought I lost it," Judd admitted. "Turned the place upside down searching. Couldn't find it anywhere. Then a couple of weeks ago, I see Lola on the cover of some tabloid, and she's wearing it. My grandmother's ring. It's not even mine—it goes to Sarah. And I wanted to get it back for her. So when everybody was buzzing about Lola Montgomery coming to town, I figured, now's my chance."

"So you went over there Friday afternoon," Kate said.

"With food," he said. "Lola's always on a diet. And she's a bear when she's hungry."

"So what happened?" Kate asked.

"She threw a lamp, then she threw me out. I didn't even get any of that lunch. And you should have seen those chocolate cupcakes," he said to Desiree. "Anyway, I had my lawyer send her lawyer a letter. And the ring arrived this morning. Sarah's thrilled."

"I guess you heard the latest Hollywood gossip," Rosie said, as Desiree topped off her glass.

"Yes, she got a two-picture deal," Desiree said. "But at least she's out of our hair."

"No, that's old news," Rosie said, waving her hand

dismissively. "It kinda leaked out that she's been telling big ol' whoppers. Like the stuff she said about you guys. So this morning the studio fired her. Too much of a liability."

As the newlywed couple mingled with their guests, Kate found Maxi at the cake table.

"It looks like Liam and Sarah are finally patching things up with their dad," Maxi said, as she took a ladylike bite.

"It turns out that Zoey was a big part of the problem," Kate said. "One of the techs found a texting app on her phone—and on Judd's. She'd convinced him that it was more secure. In reality, it allowed her to intercept Judd's outgoing messages and send messages as him. It even let her spoof senders from his contact list. So when he thought he invited his kids to the wedding, they never received the message. While the message to Judd saying they were coming to the ceremony was actually from Zoey. She had complete control."

"But why? The guy had already decided to get hitched."

"Judd loves his kids. Zoey knew that he'd never marry someone they hated. So she worked at getting Liam and Sarah to detest Desiree. As a bonus, she figured she'd also gain a couple of unwitting allies in talking Judd out of getting married. The truly cruel part was when she convinced Judd it would be more efficient for her to handle his part of the wedding prep. So as things would come up, he'd automatically hand them off to her."

"Face it, what guy wouldn't take a deal like that?" Maxi said, taking another bite of cake. "Oh, this is sooo good."

"Well, rather than actually doing any of it, she planted nasty stories about Desiree with his friends and colleagues. That she was greedy, manipulative, and clingy. Zoey even implied that Judd was trying to dump Desiree, but she just wouldn't let go. That way, when he disappeared, it would look like he was running from Desiree and her ambush wedding. It was diabolical."

"Yeah, but she'd have to release him sooner or later," Maxi reasoned. "What then?"

"That's why she wanted to make Desiree a pariah," Kate said. "Have everyone in Judd's orbit suspect her or just distrust her. I think Zoey believed that if she could get enough people to pile on, she could shame Desiree and drive her away. Then Zoey would be right there by Judd's side to help him pick up the pieces after his kidnapping ordeal. And that would show him who really loved him. But Desiree didn't flinch. She didn't care what anyone said or thought about her. She just wanted to bring Judd home."

"I still don't understand why Zoey didn't just tell Judson how she felt," Maxi said, delicately swallowing another bite.

"Apparently she did. Quite some time ago. Before Desiree. Judd let her down gently. Lola was right about one thing: he is an old-fashioned gentleman. He didn't want to mix his business and romantic lives. Plus, he felt Zoey was much too young for him. And he said exactly that. I think she might have taken it to mean he wanted her, but didn't feel right about the age difference. What he really meant was that he wasn't attracted to her. He liked dating women closer to his own vintage—women who had things in common with him."

"Zoey heard what she wanted to hear," Maxi summarized between forkfuls of cake.

"Exactly."

"Happens all the time. Later, remind me to tell you

the latest chapter in the saga of Javi's friend, Jessica the biter."

As evening turned to balmy night, a breeze blew in from the water and the party shifted into high gear.

Ben, Liam, and Jack built a bonfire, while Amos supervised.

Nearby, Annie Kim set up her iPod. As she cranked up the music, couples took to the sand to dance.

When a sixties ballad came on, Kate saw Sam lead Effie Parker onto the makeshift dance floor.

Nearby, Gabe twirled Claire, as they gazed into each other's eyes.

"Kind of feels like this wedding might have started a trend," Maxi said, her face lighting up as she spotted Peter cutting across the sand toward her. "What do you think?"

Kate looked at Jack, chatting animatedly with Sunny and Amos in the glow of the firelight. Then glanced over at Ben, laughing at something Leonard Kim was sharing with him and Doc Patel.

Kate reached down and stroked Oliver, who stared up at her with trusting black eyes. "I think, for the first time in my life, I'm exactly where I belong."

Orange Madeleines

Full of sunny, citrusy flavor guaranteed to brighten your day . . .

INGREDIENTS

- ½ cup unsalted butter, cut into 8 tablespoon-sized pieces
- 1 cup sugar
- 4 large egg yolks
- ¼ teaspoon salt
- ¼ teaspoon baking powder
- peel of 1 orange, finely chopped
- juice of 1 orange
- 1 tablespoon vanilla extract
- 1½ cups all-purpose flour
- 4 egg whites
- ¼ teaspoon cream of tartar
- confectioners' sugar (optional)

DIRECTIONS

1. Preheat oven to 350°F. Spray the madeleine molds lightly with a vegetable oil spray or brush with 2 tablespoons melted butter.

2. In an electric mixer, at low speed, cream the butter and sugar until light and lemon-colored, about 5 minutes. Add the egg yolks one at a time, beating after each addition. Add the salt, baking powder, orange peel, orange juice, and vanilla extract. Beat until smooth.

3. Slowly add the flour, beating, and mix until the batter is even. In another bowl, beat the egg whites with the cream of tartar until stiff. Mix about 1 cup of the batter into the egg whites, then fold the remaining egg whites into the batter. Drop tablespoons of the batter into the molds. (They should be three-quarters full.) Bake about 10 minutes, until the madeleines are golden at the edges and firm in the center. Sharply tap the edge of the madeleine molds to dislodge the madeleines onto a cooling rack. Repeat for the remaining batter. After the madeleines are cool, dust them lightly, if desired, with confectioners' sugar. Serve with tea.

Makes forty-eight madeleines.

Many thanks to Nina Simonds for sharing her recipe for Orange Madeleines!

© Copyright Nina Simonds, A *Spoonful of Ginger* (Knopf, 1999). For more recipes go to Ninasimonds.com

Fat & Chewy Chocolate Chip Cookies

This one will satisfy all of those chocolate cravings . . .

INGREDIENTS

2 ¼ cups all-purpose flour
1 teaspoon baking soda
1 teaspoon kosher salt
2 sticks butter, softened
¾ cup granulated sugar
¾ cup lightly packed light brown sugar
2 large eggs
1 teaspoon pure vanilla extract
2 cups semisweet chocolate chips

METHOD

1. Preheat oven to 375°F.
2. In a medium bowl, mix together the flour, baking soda, and salt. Set aside.
3. In the bowl of a stand mixer fitted with the paddle attachment, cream the butter with both sugars until light and fluffy. Mix in the eggs and vanilla.
4. Add the flour mixture and mix until well combined. Stir in the chocolate chips.

5. Scoop the cookie dough onto an ungreased baking sheet. (Line with parchment paper for easy clean-up.)
6. Bake the cookies 8 to 12 minutes, depending on how gooey you want those centers to be.
7. Let cool 5 minutes, then transfer the cookies to a wire rack.

Makes about two dozen cookies.

Many thanks to Duff Goldman for sharing his recipe for Fat & Chewy Chocolate Chip Cookies!

—Recipe courtesy of Duff Goldman. (See more of his recipes at Duff.com.)

Acknowledgments

So many people contributed their time, talents, and wisdom to the telling of this story. I want to thank them—and also acknowledge that any mistakes in this book are most definitely my own.

A very grateful shout-out to **Dr. Ana Roca**, D.A., professor emeritus at Florida International University, for her time and patience coaching me with Maxi's Spanish dialogue. *¡Gracias!*

A few loggerhead-sized "thank yous" to **Dr. Cathi L. Campbell**, Ph.D, adjunct assistant scientist at the Archie Carr Center for Sea Turtle Research at the University of Florida, and to **Ashleigh Bandimere**, the sea turtle program coordinator at the Oceanic Society, for sharing their expertise and their joy in talking about loggerhead turtles. Poaching continues to be a problem for the nests (though packing coolers with sand was my own bit of fictional license). But the bigger threats are the use of seawalls, the erosion and development of their ancient nesting grounds, and nearby artificial light—which confuses nesting mothers and their tiny hatchlings.

So many readers have asked for Kate to share some of the recipes for her delicious creations. But my own humble baking efforts are not in her league. Luckily, two wonderful chefs generously stepped into the breach. **Nina Simonds** has allowed Kate to share her genius recipe for orange madeleines from her delectable cookbook *A Spoonful of Ginger*. And baker extraordinaire **Duff Goldman** let Kate borrow his crave-inducing chocolate chip cookie recipe. (Now all we need is a tall, cold glass of milk.)

To my team at St. Martin's Press: You guys are all the very best!

To my editor, **Alexandra Sehulster**, who worked so hard to bring the Cookie House mystery series into print and whose savvy suggestions and edits make each book so much better. Best of all, you pick up on the subtleties, laugh at the jokes, and love the characters—and their quirks. Thank you for taking as much joy in the Cookie House and Coral Cay as I do!

To assistant editor **Mara Delgado Sánchez**, who gracefully fields so many questions and keeps me on track: Please know how much I appreciate your assistance, your kindness, and your upbeat manner (especially this year)!

Also, a very grateful thank you to copyeditor **John Simko**, who catches all the errors—from the big ones (obvious to everyone but me!), to the most minute—all with patience and a wry sense of humor. You have made this book so much better.

This delicious cover (which finally brings Oliver inside the Cookie House), is the creation of two spectacularly talented artists: illustrator **Mary Ann Lasher** and designer **Danielle Christopher**. (My first thought when I saw it: Wow!) Thank you both!

And a special shout-out to my wonderful St. Martin's publicity team: **Stephen Erickson**, **Sarah Haeckel**, and **Kayla Janas.** You guys have done so much to promote this series. Thank you in advance for helping me spread the word that the Cookie House is once again open for business!

I also want to thank award-winning voice actor **Christa Lewis**, who has brought the Cookie House mysteries to life in the audiobook versions. You do Kate McGuire proud!

Finally, to my awesome agent, **Erin Niumata** of Folio Literary Management: You've been my sounding board, advisor, and friend since before there was a Kate McGuire or a Coral Cay. The phrase "thank you" just isn't big enough!